C000060639

The Welsh Marches

Book 14 in the Anarchy Series

By
Griff Hosker

i

The Welsh Marches

Published by Sword Books Ltd 2017

SWORD
BOOKS

A CIP catalogue record for this title is available from the British Library.
Thanks to Simon Walpole for the Artwork and Design for Writers for the cover and logo. Thanks to Dave, Kent and Julie, three of my New Zealand readers, for giving me such an enjoyable time in the Antipodes.

Contents

Part One

William of Aqua Bella

Prologue

October 1154 off the coast of Italy

For me the journey was necessary. I was going home. I would seek the forgiveness of my father and I would try to serve my king. I had followed the banner of Henry and his father, Geoffrey of Anjou when they had fought to regain the throne. Now it was his. I had not been there when he had succeeded. Perhaps I needed his forgiveness too. I had atoned for my carnal sins and now, with a new wife and two children, I was heading home. For my wife, Rebekah this was a journey to another world, quite literally. Her close family had all been slaughtered by an evil knight and she had chosen to come, as my wife, halfway around the world. The journey had already been fraught. We had had storms and we had had to repair our ships. With four ships, it was inevitable that one or another would require some maintenance on such a long voyage.

For my young son, Samuel and my daughter, Ruth, it was all an adventure. My four-year-old son thought that the ship in which we sailed, *'Maid of Chinon'*, was a playground for him. My men and the crew did nothing to help. They liked the lad and encouraged him. His mother could not bear to look as he careered along the pitching deck of the wooden ship. Even my heart was in my mouth but, surprisingly, he came to no harm. I should not have worried, he came to no harm. My men and the crew watched him as closely as a she-wolf watches her cubs

Although I had sent a spoken message to my father with Ralph of Bowness, I had also sent a letter to Sir Leofric. An Angevin knight had been returning home and I gave him the letter. It was a long way between the Holy Land and England. I wanted my father to know we were coming. I had left suddenly and I wanted to give him time to adjust to my return.

Once I had decided to return we had to seek ships and then pack all that we needed for a new life. My wife had many objects which were dear to her. They reminded her of her dead family. Many were precious and delicate items. It took time to gather and then safely pack all that we had needed to take for a new life in a new country. Each box we packed and each item we selected was a reminder to my wife that she was leaving the home she had known for her whole life and heading for somewhere as different as it was possible to get. Rebekah was fearful of the change.

The first part of the journey was familiar to Rebekah in that we sailed in the waters of the eastern Mediterranean. For the first week or so her land was visible off the steerboard side and then we headed through the islands of the Byzantine Empire and we lost sight of Asia. She brightened a little then for they were new sights but the land was not totally different from her home. Soon it would be. When we had stopped for a week in Constantinople it was almost like a holiday. We had not intended to visit the capital of the Byzantine Empire but one of the smaller ships needed repairs. I was not willing to split up my little fleet and so we spent a week spending money in the markets of the greatest city in the world. My name was known there and we were treated well. When we left we would sail along the coast of the Lombards and the Franks. Our captain, Michael, assured me that it was the safest route. Pirates infested the southern waters. The Empire's power had waned in recent years and the Moors terrorised all Christians who used the southern sea. For myself, I was not so certain. I had enemies there. Although we would not be landing, I felt it was a dangerous thing to do.

I was right.

Chapter 1

Masood was my scout. When his family had been slaughtered, along with that of my wife, he had chosen to come along with us. He had lived far from the sea in the high dry lands of Outremer. He had lived in a land without water and with constant heat. The further north we went the more fascinated he became with all that he saw. He marvelled and wondered at the green he saw. To the men who came from England, the land seemed almost brittle dry but Masood was keen to get ashore and see what kind of game teemed in the woods. We had to tell him that he could not leave the ship to hunt.

"Lord, will there be woods in England?"

I laughed and pointed at the trees we could see on the slopes of the mountains to the north of us. "They are woods but close by my father's estates are forests. You can travel for days through them and not see a road or a person."

"Truly?" I nodded. "Then I would like to wander that land." He pointed north. "What is that land, lord?"

"It is Lombardy. The next port we visit is Genoa. They are great sailors. Their ships fly the red cross on the white background."

"Will it take us long to get to his home?"

"Almost as long as it has taken us to get here."

"Then I will have to learn to use my legs again." He had discovered that the longer he spent on the water the more time it took him to walk on dry land. "Alciades and Remus will enjoy solid ground beneath their hooves."

"As will we all. We are coming to the end of our journey now. This will be the last stop before we sail into the deep and wild seas which border Normandy and England. This sea is a flat calm by comparison."

"I have seen wonders, lord, it is true. I thought I would miss my home but so far, I have not. There is much to see."

Samuel ran over to us. Robin Hawkeye, one of my archers, was watching over him. It was harder than fighting Seljuq Turks. Robin shook his head, "Lord, trying to watch your son is like trying to hold on to a ball of frog spawn!"

"Samuel! What have I told you about running on the ship?"

"I am sorry, father, but I will not fall."

"Come stay with me. Robin, I will watch him now. You and Masood go and check on the horses. We will be in port this evening."

"Aye, lord!" Relieved Robin led Masood off.

I took Samuel's hand. I had found it the best way to ensure he did not run. He was growing. He was four years old but Henri of Chinon, the captain of our ship and a grandfather, told me that my son was as big as a seven-year-old. I put that down to his mother's food. She insisted on preparing all the food for our children and her women. It was another reason we were stopping. She needed fresh supplies. Had it just been my men then we would have been home already. The captain did not mind as it allowed him to trade each time we landed.

I pointed astern to the other three ships. They were all smaller than the *'Maid of Chinon'*. "You see those ships astern of us?" He nodded. "They contain all of our treasure, our arms and our men. When we get to England you will need to learn to behave as the grandson of a great lord."

"Are you not a great lord, father? Mother said that even the King of Jerusalem admired you."

"The King of Jerusalem is a good man but England and Normandy are many times the size of Jerusalem and your grandfather rules a land which is far bigger than Jerusalem."

"Mother has never met him, has she, Father?"

"No, this will be her first time in England. He will like her." That much I knew was true. The Earl of Cleveland was the fairest man in Christendom. Family to him was all. He had dedicated his life to restoring Empress Matilda and her son Henry to the English throne. He had done that. Even as we were sailing homeward Henry could have been crowned.

"And will he like me?"

"Of course. You are of his blood. I am of his blood and you should always remember that Samuel. You are descended from warriors who protected England for hundreds of years. You were born in the Holy Land but your blood is English and your land is England. I forgot that for a while but I see it now."

A seaman knuckled his head, "Lord, the captain says we are ready to head in to Genoa."

"Thank you. Come, Samuel. We will find your mother. She will need to make you presentable. When we walk the streets of Genoa she would have all know that you are the son of a lord." Rebekah, for some reason, had taken it into her head that, as a Jewess, she would be somehow scorned by what she termed, the Gentiles. I did not know what she meant but she was a proud woman. Her experiences with Franks had not been good. The knight who had abused her was now the food for jackals. "How is your Greek coming along?"

"Alf is a good teacher father but I find it boring."

"The more languages you can speak the better. Knowing a man's words gives you power."

"Alf is not Greek, though is he?"

"No, he is half English but he was brought up in the Empire. He, too, has never seen England."

For more than half of my household, England was a foreign county perched on the edge of the world. The women who had chosen to come with my wife and her servants all thought that the real world centred on Jerusalem. One advantage of our long journey was that they could all now speak English and Norman. Their darker skin would mark them as foreigners but not their words.

Genoa was busy. Ships travelling to the Holy Land called there to fit out. Men who wished to join the crusades came there from all over the former Empire to seek ships. My men and I would go armed. Our surcoats, with the gryphon upon them, identified my men as the retinue of a lord. Outside of the Holy Land, it was not known but soon it would. I strapped on my sword and took a purse with me. Stepping ashore I waited for my men to come from the other ships. I had spread out my men amongst the ships. If any of the ships were attacked then my men would defend the ship. I had seven archers and six men at arms. With Sir Thomas and our two squires, I had sixteen men to command. For many knights that would not be enough but my men had been honed and hardened in the Holy Land. I would back them against three times their number.

"Brother Peter, Henri, Guy and Phillippe, go with my wife and her ladies to buy the things they need."

The priest would ensure that they were treated well and my three men were all Franks. They knew their way around a Lombard market.

"Aye lord."

"The rest of you come with me. Let us see if there are any warriors returned from the Holy Land who would like to serve a new lord."

I had come back from my atonement rich. Many men did the same. Although I had given Aqua Bella to the Hospitallers I had had many years profiting from the oil it produced. I had also been successful and taken both ransom and gold from those I had defeated. I would need good men in England. They would be worth the gold it would cost to fit them out. It was men at arms I sought. The quayside was busy. There were peddlers and hawkers who sought to sell me goods that I could buy in the markets for half the price. My squire, archers and men at arms deterred them. Alf, my squire, had also grown since he had joined me. He was now bigger than I was. That was not a surprise. His father, Morgan, had been a Varangian, and his mother, a Pecheng, was of a tribe who were known for their strength.

Once through the maelstrom of the quay, we entered the narrower streets which led to the markets and taverns. Some of my men were looking forward to those for the last drink they had had was in Amalfi and that was ten days since. I knew that Henry son of Will would be desperate for a drink. I warned him as we passed our first tavern, "First, Henry, son of Will, we find our men and then you can drink and welcome."

"Aye lord."

"And in moderation!"

"Aye lord."

John of Chester laughed at the tone. "John, I rely on you and Gurth son of Garth to make sure we get the right men."

"You can depend upon us, lord. We do not want to share a warrior hall with men we do not trust. It is bad enough suffering Henry here."

My men all laughed. Henry had a reputation for getting into trouble but when there was a battle to be fought then all of them would choose to stand with him for in battle he was steadfast and true. He reminded me of Wulfric, one of my father's most loyal knights. Both were big men who seemed out of place amongst gentle things but give them something to defend and they were both like rocks. We passed through the busy market. My wife and her ladies would be following. I saw men seated outside the taverns. Some would be heading east while others would be looking for new masters. Genoa was a crossroads. I spied a tavern close by and it was not as busy as the others. That meant it would be more expensive. It was a price worth paying for my men would all be seated and we could view the other taverns.

I ordered a pichet of wine for Sir Thomas and our squires. I asked for ale for the men. As in Amalfi, they would be disappointed in the quality. "Remember Henry, this is one drink which you nurse and coddle as though it was your last. When we have our men then you can have another couple."

"A couple, lord? A man like me has a need for ale. It feeds me."

John of Chester tapped Henry's belly, "We have not fought for some time, my friend. I think you are feeding a child in there!"

The wine was the rose coloured one they favoured in Lombardy. It was chilled. When I returned to England the only wine available would be the wine from my father's estate in Anjou. After John and Gurth had finished half of their ale I nodded and they wandered off. They would have seen the men they thought likely candidates. They were the ones with tanned skin and hardened muscles. They were the ones with heavy swords and eastern dress. It would be only when they spoke that you knew their original country.

I was enjoying the sheer pleasure of sitting out and drinking with my men when I heard a sharp intake of breath from Alf. He was frozen with his goblet halfway towards his mouth. "What is it, Alf? Have you seen a ghost?"

"No lord, but look."

I saw where he gazed. There were four men at arms and they wore a surcoat with four red stars on a yellow background. The last time we had seen that was in the Holy Land and they had been with my enemy, de Waller, but we had met them earlier in Nissa and in Constantinople. Their master, the Count of Provence had abused Alf's mother and ill-treated him. We had taken him from them. One of their knights, Guy of Èze, had sworn to have vengeance. The last meeting had not been pleasant but then we had had the protection of the King of Jerusalem. Here we would be in the land where they held the power.

"They may not recognise you but we shall be wary." In truth, they seemed not to notice us. An hour later and they had gone. They had not even glanced in our direction.

John and Gurth had done well. They had secured the services of eight men at arms. All were English and, like us, keen to return to an England free from civil war and riven by internal strife. We headed back to our ships. My three French men at arms had found us and told us that my family was safely back on the ship and that they had all that they needed. Leaving my archers and men at arms to enjoy a night in the port I went back to the ship with Sir Thomas, our squires and my new men. I would divide them between the four ships. I was pleased with the way the day had gone and I had put the red stars and yellow surcoats from my mind.

My wife was happy. She had found fresh food and she was pleased with the quality. The captain had made good trades. He had traded some of our figs, lemons and olives which might be over ripe by the time we reached England and he had split the profits with us. It was all good. We ate on the quay. The captain had tables brought from below decks. My men had often cracked their heads on the low decks. By the time my warriors returned the food was ready and the air was one of celebration. The new men were welcomed into our family. Samuel and his sister Ruth never stood on ceremony. They smiled and giggled at any new face. The warriors had been fighting for ten years and the sight of a four-year-old giggling was, somehow, exciting.

The mood was broken when I saw the approach of a number of armed men. My sword was on the ship and I had been drinking. The yellow surcoat should have warned me but the four officials wearing the Genoese livery dulled my reactions. I recognised Guy of Èze who jabbed out an accusing finger. "There, that is the slave and the ones who abducted him! I demand justice!"

His voice was high pitched and he was angry. Behind him, I recognized Robert of Nissa. He had a smirk on his face which I was desperate to remove with my sword.

One of the men in the Genoese livery spread his arms, "Lord, I am sorry to intrude but the men of the Count of Provence have made an accusation against you."

I had not had enough to drink to make me insensible. "And what is that accusation?"

"They say that you took that slave from Constantinople and he is their property."

"And to whom do I answer?"

"The mayor has a court and there is justice there. You need to present yourselves and answer the charges."

I nodded, "We will be there."

Guy of Èze became almost apoplectic with rage, "Arrest them now! They will flee the port!"

I stood and walked over to the warrior. I was taller than he was and, although he had a sword, he shrank back at my approach. "Guy of Èze, you are a rodent! I am a lord. I say that I will answer the charges in the court and that should be good enough. If it is not then

I will fetch my sword and we will settle the matter here before God!"

I could see that he was not willing to do so. He wanted more than my death. He wanted me to suffer and to be humiliated but the official settled the matter, "No, lord, that will not be necessary. Your word is good enough for us. We will see you at the court at the third bell of the morning."

I could see, in his eyes, that he was pleading with me to flee. I would not give the Count of Provence that satisfaction. "We will be there."

After they left Alf said, "I will not go back to that man! I will take my own life before I will do that!"

I turned on him, "Are you a man or something which crawled from a pond? Do you think that we will not defend you? We will settle this matter here or else it will pursue us home to England. When I reach the Tees, I want no entanglements from the past. I have suffered that before! Now tell me all!"

I sat with Sir Thomas, Brother Peter and John of Chester. We listened to Alf's full tale. Brother Thomas was unfamiliar with all of the details. When he had finished I said, "We have a case, do we not?"

Brother Peter concurred, "They have not a leg to stand on. This is a bullying tactic."

"Good, then all of you get some sleep. We will go to court and then sail home. We will not stop again!" I glanced at my wife who nodded. As I lay in my bunk I ran through the events. Had the Count of Provence wanted Alf he would have sent more men and taken him by force. His men had not been afraid to fight. There was something else going on here I did not understand.

I was awake early and I spoke with Brother Peter before we left. We went to court with swords. All men did so and we went without helmets and shields. I left my new men aboard for they did not know Alf but the rest would all come. They would be there to defend their shield brother. I also left Masood to watch my family. He had a bow and he knew how to kill. No matter what happened I wanted my family to be safe. Before we left I ensured that the captain would be ready to sail when we returned.

I saw that the men of the family of the Count of Provence were well represented. The count himself was not there but the two cousins were. They had the smug self-satisfied look of men who think they are going to win.

The magistrate was a knight, or he had been a knight when he was younger. He was a large man and he had not been astride a horse since Alf had been born. He glared at us as we entered. The Count of Provence held power here and justice would be more likely to favour him. We would not receive a fair trial. I had a plan. I had talked it through with Brother Peter and my men were all ready. Alf was worried. I could tell that. He did not want to be returned to the Count of Provence. If he did then he would die. I was not going to let that happen.

"Lord, give us your title and your credentials. Let the court hear."

I forced a smile upon my lips. "I am William of Bella Aqua in the Kingdom of Jerusalem. I am the son of Alfraed, Earl of Cleveland, the Empresses Matilda's Champion, Warlord of the North and I am here to answer for my deeds." I saw that my introduction had disturbed the magistrate. I had thrown around names that were far mightier than the Count of Provence. "I might also point out that Alf, son of Morgan is the son of a Varangian guard who died in the service of the Emperor." I smiled again.

The magistrate nodded and looked slightly less annoyed, "Who brings this case?"

Guy of Èze confidently stepped forward, "I do, on behalf of my uncle, the Count of Provence!" Had I not named Empresses and Kings he might have impressed those gathered but, I had already grabbed their attention, it fell flat. I saw that he was discomfited. He ploughed on regardless. "This so-called lord and another barbarian took this slave from my uncle in Constantinople and then fled, like felons, to the Holy Land. My uncle demands justice. He demands the return of his slave and reparation for his loss over the intervening years."

I saw now that this was nothing more or less than an attempt to extort money from me. That was why he had not taken Alf by force. He wanted the treasure that was in my ships. He was nothing better than a pirate.

The magistrate spread his hands, "My lord, what have you to say?"

I nodded, "Where are the papers of ownership?" I stared at him and saw the first flicker of doubt. They had no papers. "You say that Alf was your slave and if that is true you will have papers to prove it."

11

I could not believe that they had not concocted some forgery to prove their lie. They had thought that the count's name alone would serve.

Guy of Èze jabbed a finger in Alf's direction, "His mother was a slave!"

I turned to Alf, "Did the count pay money for your mother?"

We had been over this and, although it had been difficult for him, Alf answered truly. "The count took her as a courtesan when I was seven summers old. He used her but he did not pay coin for her."

Guy of Èze shouted, triumphantly, "There! There! He has admitted!"

The magistrate turned, "He has admitted that the count took the mother of a young boy and used her. That does not amount to ownership." I watched his face as he weighed up what he had heard. As much as he did not want to upset the count, there were fourteen warriors in his court and Guy of Èze's argument was weak. "Unless there is more evidence I cannot rule on this case. Sir William is right. There should be some documents of ownership."

It was then that Guy of Èze lost all composure. He turned on the magistrate, "You would side with a barbarian who takes a Jewess whore as his wife over the Count of Provence!"

I sensed the anger in my men but I became cold, "Apologize!"

Guy of Èze looked around for support. Apart from his own men he had none, "But it is true."

I watched the magistrate metaphorically washing his hands. He sat back. He knew that the young Lombard had gone too far.

My voice was cold and calm, "Apologize or I will meet you with sword and shield and we shall let God decide this matter."

"I will not apologize!"

The magistrate leaned forward. He looked relieved that the Lombard had given him a way out. "Then William of Aqua Bella has the right to trial by combat. I have so judged!"

Guy of Èze was no coward. He smirked, "Good! I will kill you, Englishman and then we shall see what happens. There is a field north of the city gates. I will meet you there in an hour."

Once outside I said, "Sir Thomas and Brother Peter go back to my ships and watch them and my family. I do not trust these men. It may be that they try to take the ships by force."

"But lord, this may be a trap. They do not seem like honourable men."

"Quite likely but I have my own men and we will be watched from the walls of the city. I have no doubt that many burghers will come to watch the spectacle. I cannot believe that the Count of Provence and his family are popular. Trust me. Alf, fetch my shield."

He nodded, "Aye lord and thank you."

"For what? You are my man and you are entitled to my protection. What kind of lord would I be if I abandoned you?"

He went off with Sir Thomas and Brother Peter. With the men I had left on board they would be able to defend the ships. My men took out their whetstones and began sharpening their swords and daggers as they waited for Alf to return. My archers selected their best arrows.

Henry son of Will said, "Any chance of a wet, lord? All that talk made me thirsty."

John of Chester shook his head, "Afterwards, you ale skin!"

He smiled affably, "Just so long as I get one. It will be a long voyage home to England."

Robin Hawkeye said, "And there they have decent ale."

The shield I bore had been freshly painted on the voyage from Jaffa. The gryphon was sharp and seemed to leap out. Alf had also brought my helmet. If Guy of Èze wore one then so would I. This would not be like a mêlée. There would be no unexpected blows from behind. It would be better to have a head protected by just a coif. It would allow better vision. My foe was there already. Robert of Nissa stood close by and they had brought twenty men at arms. We were outnumbered. It did not worry me. My men were better. Most of my men had lived off their wits in the Holy Land. They had existed amongst the worst of cut throats. If the Lombards tried anything they would see real warriors at work. There were also thirty or forty men and youths. They were spectators who were eager to see a fight to the death. Such events were rare. I saw money in their hands. There would be gambling on the outcome. It was ever thus. I suspected that almost a thousand years ago the same thing would have happened at the Roman gladiatorial games.

Guy of Èze did not bother with a helmet. I hefted my shield and made sure it was comfortable. Alf checked that the cross strap over my shoulder fitted well and did not snag on anything else. I drew my sword. Guy of Èze was eager for the fight. Younger than I was he bounced on the balls of his feet. From his stance, I guessed that he had learned his skills in the tourney rather than the battlefield. I had fought in both and I knew which prepared a man for a combat to the death better.

"Good luck, lord."

I smiled at Alf. "I have right on my side and skill, Alf. Luck is for those who have neither." I moved towards my opponent.

As we closed Guy of Èze said, "When you are dead then your men will die and my uncle will have his slave again!"

I was confident that my men would be watching for treachery. I held my sword by the blade and kissed it like a cross, "Let God be my judge!"

I saw a flicker of something in the eyes of the Lombard. Was it fear? If it was not fear then it was doubt and that is never a good frame of mind for combat. I had not fought since Ascalon. I had had many years of combat and as soon as I brought up my shield my body seemed to know what to do. I placed my left foot forward and held my sword behind me. It was the stance I liked to use. It invited an attack. Guy of Èze obliged. Seeing my defensive pose, he raised his sword and brought it down from on high. He was going for a quick kill. He was going for my head. He expected me to block with my shield. It would be a powerful blow and would drive me backwards. I spun around on my left foot so that the blow struck fresh air and then the ground. My men and the spectators cheered. I brought my own sword around in a sweep. He barely blocked it with his own shield. Off-balance he stumbled backwards.

I stepped forward and raised my sword. He took the offensive again and swept his sword towards my middle. It cracked into my shield and my sword darted towards his eyes. It was a feint but he reacted. He stepped back and brought his shield up. I changed the stab to a sweep. In the heartbeat it took for him to realise the blow had not connected, my sword had scythed into his mail leggings. My blade came away bloody. It was not a serious wound. If it had been my leg I would not have even worried about it but this knight had little experience. The blood seeping down his leg worried him. He sought to end the combat quickly. It was a mistake.

He roared and charged at me holding his shield before him and swinging his sword over his head. I stepped quickly back and then, as he brought his sword down, punched into the sword with my shield. I held my sword horizontally and I saw the indecision. Was this a feint or a strike? I used body sway to fool him this time. I swayed to the left as though I was going to open my body up for a wide sweep and then swayed right and spun around. He was confused and he did not move. I brought my sword around as I

14

turned quickly and it would have struck him in the back but that he managed to get his shield around in time to block the blow. It was a wild move and he tore free the strap which held his shield to his shoulder. He carried the weight now in his left hand.

It was time to end this. I moved quickly forward threatening him with a raised sword and then I smashed my shield into his chest. The blood from the wound in his leg now began to affect him and he was moving more slowly. His left arm lowered slightly and I saw my chance. I first brought my sword around in a wide sweep to smash into his shield. I used the flat of the blade so that I did not dull the edge. He reeled again and his arm dropped lower. This must have been one of the first times he had fought on foot. He was tiring. I feinted with my shield towards him. As he tried to block it with his own shield I swept my sword backhand. I hacked across his shoulders and then into his chest. Blood spurted. He reeled and both his arms dropped. I swung again at his neck. My blade went through the mail and into his throat. When the blood arced, I knew that it was a mortal wound. The contest was over. He lay prostrate on his back. Men cheered.

I had just sheathed my sword when I caught a movement out of the corner of my eye. I heard a collective, "No!" from the onlookers. His squire raced towards me with a sword held high. I began turning my shield to defend myself when three goose feathered arrows sprouted from his head. I bent down to pick up the sword of Guy of Èze. I strode over to Robert of Nissa. I did not need to look behind me to know that my men had bows and weapons levelled should the Lombards try another act of treachery. "I hope the squire acted out of loyalty. If I thought this was planned then I would slaughter all of you here!"

He shook his head. Guy had had courage, Robert of Nissa was a coward. "I swear he acted alone."

I held up the sword of Guy of Èze, "Then God has judged. I have the right!" I glared at him.

"You have the right, lord."

"And it is over now? For, know this, Robert of Nissa. If I find out that you have plotted against me or sent men to do me harm then I swear that I will return here and your whole family will suffer. Tell that to your uncle too. Do you understand me?"

He nodded, "I do, lord. I swear." His eyes kept glancing to Guy of Èze. They must have thought that his success at the tourney guaranteed him victory. They had miscalculated.

"And this sword is our reparation for the sullying of the name of Alf son of Morgan. This is weregeld for his name. Come, Alf, son of Morgan, and receive your new sword."

He came forward. The sword was, indeed a fine one. I handed it to him. "Thank you, lord."

Looking at Robert of Nissa I said, loudly so that all the onlookers could hear, "This is good?"

He nodded, "This is good, lord."

We turned and made our way back through the city towards the docks. There was a buzz as we walked for the watchers on the walls had spread the word. The Count of Provence had had his nose bloodied. I had gathered that, while he had power, he was not popular. This would encourage dissension. As soon as we reached our ships I nodded, "Now, Captain. It is time to sail home. These foreign games do not amuse me!"

Chapter 2

Alf was a changed man after that day. He was no longer looking over his shoulder. He did not fear his past and his future was now assured. More importantly, he had a sword that was the equal of any knight's. He had come to me a little rough and ready. He had not been schooled in the art of being a knight. He had natural abilities with weapons. I had no doubt he had inherited those but it had taken years to train him to be able to ride as well as Sir Thomas and we were still knocking the rough edges off him when it came to spear work. However, what he lacked in finesse, he made up in raw courage. My men treated him like a favourite little brother. Even the new men soon took to him.

As we headed west, towards the Pillars of Hercules, Sir Thomas and Henri worked with him on his sword skills. We were making the most of the clement weather and calm seas. Once we crossed into the western sea then we expected rougher weather. The pitching deck was a good training ground for you to learn how to keep your balance. It was the same as fighting from the back of a horse.

The port of Cadiz was in sight when Henri stopped to allow Sir Thomas to continue with the tuition. Phillippe and Guy appeared from below decks and the three of them presented themselves to me, "Lord, we have something to ask."

Their joint appearance did not surprise me. I had been expecting it. They, along with Robert, had been with me from the very beginning. Now Sir Robert was a lord in the Holy Land close by Jericho and I knew what they would say. For the whole voyage, the three had spent more time with each other than with the newer men. They had done their duty but something had been nagging at them and I had deduced what it was.

"We have served you since the time of the war against Normandy, lord. We have ever been your oathsworn."

I nodded, "And now you wish to leave my service." They all looked shocked and I smiled. "I have sensed this for some time. It is the right time."

They nodded. Guy spoke for them, "We are rich beyond our wildest dreams and expectations. This is down to you, lord. The war in England is almost over and you have other men at arms who can serve you well. Had we any doubts then we would not ask to be released. We would go to the Loire and become fat old warriors who breed children and tell tales of war."

I nodded, "Then go with my blessing. I will call in at Angers and trade. My father's castellan, Sir Leofric of La Flèche, may know of properties you might buy." I saw the relief on their faces. "It is good that you have returned with limbs intact. Others did not fare as well, Roger of Hauteville, Pierre of Cherbourg, Alain Azay, the list is long."

"And we will remember them. We intend to live close by each other. We have wives to find and then we can beget children. We would have them grow up together. We were not made knights but our sons will have every chance of doing so."

"And when they are old enough send them to England. We always need squires."

It seemed appropriate, as we sailed from the azure blue of the Mediterranean into the dark blue of the Atlantic, that there would be a change. Almost all the men who had first served with me were now either dead or had left my service. I was taking back, with the exception of Sir Thomas, new men who had joined in the Holy Land. It would be a new start for us all.

The last time I had been in Angers the civil war in England was in full swing but we had begun to retake the lands of Normandy. In those days Anjou had been the breadbasket for Henry and his mother, the Empress. Henry's success could be seen quite clearly. As we had passed along the Loire I had seen the extensive work being carried out on the city of Angers. Now that Henry ruled, through his wife, the Dukedom of Aquitaine, the city of Angers was even more important.

When we docked, we were something of an attraction. Most ships returning from the Holy Land had already offloaded their cargo and returning warriors. Although I had a new livery the warriors who would be leaving me were recognised. A rider galloped down from the castle as my men were having their chests, arms and treasures unloaded. The necessity of four ships became obvious as their chests and war bags piled up on the quay.

The rider dismounted and bowed, "My lord, are you William of Ouistreham, the son of the Warlord?"

I smiled at my old title, "I was and William of Ouistreham and the Earl of Cleveland is my father."

"The king's brother resides in the castle. He would have you visit with him."

"William FitzEmpress is here?"

"Aye lord."

That had me intrigued. "I have my family with me and it will take some time to prepare. We will be there when we can."

"Aye lord." He smiled, "You will not remember me, lord but I was there when you, your father and the king defeated the Franks. That was a great day."

"Aye. What is your name?"

"Richard le Breton. I am one of the Count's warriors. I will tell him."

I remembered him vaguely. He had been a squire then. It was his name that was familiar and not his face. It set me thinking of all the warriors alongside whom I had fought. How many had survived the civil war?

Before I went aboard to prepare my family I turned to Guy. "This may be a propitious meeting. The king's brother is here. It may be that I can help you to acquire land. Leave word with John of Chester where you stay."

"Aye lord but you have already done much for us."

"You cannot do enough for those who have stood shield to shield."

As I went aboard I told Sir Thomas that I would be ashore. "See if you can trade some of the cargo. It may be we get a better price here than we might further north."

He smiled, "It is good to be home, lord. I know this is not England but it feels closer to our land. I now yearn to see my father." He paused, "If he still lives."

"He will still be alive and I, too, look forward to the day when I can see my father and Stockton."

My wife was flustered when I told her of the visit. She had heard of the insults thrown at her by the Lombards and worried that her race might cause her problems.

"You take the children. I will stay aboard."

"William is a fine boy. I have known him for a long time. He is like his mother and he will not judge. Besides, when we get to

England you will have to meet his brother, the king. Regard this as a practice."

She nodded but she took more care over her appearance and that of the children than I had ever seen before. When we left, we took no warriors with us. We would not need them and that felt strange. Even in Genoa and Amalfi, we had not felt confident enough to walk abroad without armed guards. I was recognised. There were old soldiers in the town and Sir Leofric and my father were well known.

Samuel was intrigued by the whispers as we walked along. "Who is the knight of the Empress and the Warlord, father? I have heard their names as we walk along."

"They are one and the same person. They are two of the names of your grandfather. He is well known here. He fought for the Empress and was then made the Warlord of the North."

"Will we see him soon?"

"I pray to God that we do."

I did not school Samuel as we walked up to the gatehouse. It would do little good. He was Samuel and William would have to take him as he found him. I need not have worried. The youngest brother of the king had not changed. Now aged eighteen he was a man. He had not yet fully filled out but he had the same looks as his father, Geoffrey of Anjou. Henry did not take after his father. I did not know whom he took after; perhaps his mother, the Empress.

"William!" He embraced me in a warrior's hug. "You are back from your travels! It is good to see you."

"And you, lord. This is my wife, Rebekah and my children, Samuel and Ruth."

William kissed the hand of Rebekah, "And you are a beauty too, my lady. My friend is a lucky man. Come to my hall. I have food prepared and I must hear all that has happened to you."

What I liked about William was his honesty. His brother, Geoffrey, was totally unlike him. I had heard, in Constantinople, that he had even tried to abduct Henry's bride. Neither my father nor I trusted him but William was different. He felt more like a little brother. As we walked I discovered that Geoffrey was in London at Henry's coronation.

"And not you, lord?"

He had shrugged, as we sat down, "Geoffrey insisted that as the elder of us he would go and I was given the task of watching the river. The Duke of Brittany is flexing his muscles again and

Theobald, Count of Blois is also trying to enlarge his county. Last year the king had to have a castle destroyed to recover Geoffrey."

"I am thinking that he did not enjoy that."

William laughed, "When time allows Theobald will rue his actions but, until the crown is on his head, my brother stays in England. It took your father too long to regain the crown for my brother to lose it quickly."

"My father would be the first to tell you that it was not him alone."

"I know but without him? Who knows? Now tell me your tale."

While we ate I regaled him with our adventures in the Holy Land. I sanitized the deaths of Rebekah's family for Samuel and Ruth were listening but when William saw the pain in Rebekah's face he put his hand on hers and said, "I am sorry for your loss, lady. I hope that England can recompense you for the loss of your family."

I told him of our encounter with the Count of Provence and he laughed, "What kind of fools are these Lombards? Surely they know that you and your father are the two greatest living knights." I shrugged. "Now you must stay the night. I know you wish to travel home but you cannot sail until the morning tide now. Besides this will be more comfortable than the cog in which you came."

And so we stayed. It proved to be the right decision. William used his power to give manors to my three men at arms. They were small ones but they were close to Sir Leofric. It seemed right. I also learned of Henry's plans or the plans he had spoken of to his brother at any rate. The Scots still clung on to land they had stolen during the war and the Welsh were rattling their swords too. Before coming back to Anjou and Normandy the king intended to secure his borders. There would be work for me!

During the meal, the doors opened and there stood Sir Leofric. He had been my father's squire and he was the most loyal of knights. "William!" Five years older than me I had grown up with him and Sir John, another of my father's squires. There were tears in his eyes as he grasped my arm, "I received your letter and told your father. I prayed that you would survive the journey." He embraced me and then, stepping back he suddenly saw William FitzEmpress. "I am sorry, lord but…"

William laughed, "Had you done other I would have been surprised! Come and sit for you are as worthy as any to join us. Your manor is a bastion against our enemies."

The evening was perfect for I learned that my father was well and that he prospered. Even better was the fact that my family took to Sir Leofric. He was open and he was honest. He too was a father and he knew the right way to speak to my son and daughter. The next morning, as we left the river, I felt sad to be leaving William FitzEmpress and Sir Leofric. They were both part of my past and I knew that they would be part of my future. It had been good preparation for my family. They were now eager to be in England and see others like the king's brother and my father's knight.

The voyage from the mouth of the Loire north was not a pleasant one. It was bad around the Breton coast to Herosfloth. The seas were violent and the weather dire. There we traded for this was a popular port. Now that Dorestad had disappeared into the mud and silt it was a handy place to trade. We also made minor repairs to the four ships. The weather had been benign up to the Loire but now there were winter storms. I realised that it was December. The seasons did not mean the same in the Holy Land and in the Mediterranean but, here, in the northern waters, they could be an enemy! We were tossed and turned. From Herosfloth north, we encountered gales with the winds from the west and north. We lost rigging and sails had to be repaired. At one point, we were split up and woke to find ourselves alone in a grey sea. It took a whole day for us to be reunited. We could not make London or any of the eastern ports of Suffolk and Norfolk and we had to fight our way up along the Frisian and Danish coasts. When the winds changed we headed west. Eventually, I spied Whitby Abbey on top of the cliffs and knew that we were close to the mouth of our river.

My wife was on deck with our children. Since Herosfloth they had rarely dared to venture on deck. Now she stood shivering despite the furs she wore. "Is it always this cold?"

I smiled, "Believe it or not this is mild. The weather might be wild but it does get colder."

"I cannot believe that you have brought me all the way here from the warmth of my homeland. Our children will freeze."

"They will adapt and besides we both know that the Turks will retake the land. They will try to convert all to Islam. Would you have that?"

"No, but here I cannot worship my God as I might wish: with others of the same faith."

I had no answer to that and I felt guilt as we edged around the mud flats of the south bank of the Tees towards the twists and turns which would take us to Stockton. "I should warn you, Captain, that it will take half a day to sail the few miles to my home."

"At least the river is benign. Will we be able to repair our ships there, lord?"

"Aye for there is a shipyard."

The last time I had spoken with Sir Thomas he had been excited about meeting his own father again. He could not wait to tell him that he had been knighted. Oswald was a humble archer. It would have seemed an impossible dream before he had joined my father's archers. I had the same excitement about meeting my father but it was also tinged with apprehension. Would he be glad to see me?

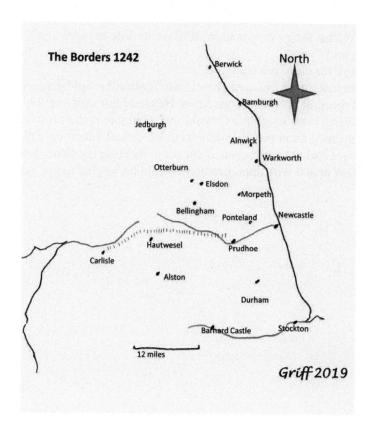

Chapter 3

The familiar towers of Stockton were a welcoming sight. The afternoon was coming to an end and the long night which accompanied winter was rapidly approaching. Had we had a delay then we would have had the most difficult task of negotiating the river at night. The journey up the Tees was not easy for any sailor, let alone one who was used to the Holy Land. I stood on the steer board side, towards the prow. I had my arm around Rebekah and held Samuel's hand. Ruth clung to her mother. Rebekah looked up at me and I saw the relief on her face. She had no idea what kind of home she was coming to. Its solid stone walls, however, looming up around the next long loop of the river reassured her.

I pointed to the northern shore. There were two seals swimming back out to sea having fed in the rich waters of the Tees. "Look Samuel, a pair of seals!"

He had never seen the like and his fingers tightened. "Are they monsters, father? What are they? Has a wizard turned a man into a beast which swims?"

I laughed, "They are not a fish and they will crawl ashore and lie in the sun when the sun shines."

Rebekah shook her head and shivered, "Does the sun ever shine here? I have seen no sign of it."

"This is winter, my love. When it is summer here there is almost no night!"

As we turned the last loop of the river Stockton was revealed. Smoke tumbled from the fires of the forges of Alf the smith and spiralled from the tanners. I saw fishermen emptying their nets and I saw the sentries on the wall. Our four ships would not be familiar to them. They would have summoned John of Craven, my father's castellan and he would have archers and men at arms standing to in case we were a threat.

As we drew nearer I saw Father Henry leave his church and head down to the quay to greet us. The fact that there was no standard flying from the tower told me that my father was not at home. I was disappointed although not entirely surprised. I turned and saw my men leaning over the side to stare at their new and unfamiliar home. Only Sir Thomas, on the next ship astern of us, knew the castle. For all of them, it was like a foreign country.

Ethelred's men were ready to catch our morning lines as they were thrown. Father Henry recognised me and I saw him shout something to the sentry. His face beamed as he shouted, "Lord, this is a wonderful day! You have returned! God be praised!"

I nodded. I did not want to engage in a shouting match for I knew there would be many questions and so I waved and led my family to the main mast where the gangplank would be lowered.

"Alf, I want you to see that my family's chests are brought ashore first. Then have the men bring them and their chests up to the castle."

"Aye lord. Is this our new home, lord?"

I hoped that it would be but I did not know. Would my father wish his prodigal son and family to share his castle? "We shall see. However, we shall certainly spend some time here."

Once the gangplank was lowered I picked up Ruth to carry her while Rebekah led Samuel. Father Henry smiled broadly. "I almost didn't recognise you, lord. Your face has been darkened by the sun. You look like a Moor!"

Before he could accidentally insult my wife, I said, "Father Henry, this is my family: my wife Rebekah, son, Samuel and daughter, Ruth." I laid Ruth down and Rebekah took her hand.

I saw his quick mind take in their names and recognise that they were not of Norman origin. "Welcome, welcome, welcome! Let us get into the warmth of the castle. I am certain that after the heat of the Holy Land the damp river will not be good for your health. I have asked Alice to prepare food."

Rebekah had recognised the priest's raiment. "Thank you, father, you are kind."

Just then I heard Brother Peter's footsteps as he came down the gangplank. He was not a small man! "And this is Brother Peter. He is a warrior priest."

"And you are welcome, brother. I can see that we will have tales to fill us with wonder."

I saw that my father's men had lined the walls to view us. I recognised many of them. That was reassuring. Sir Thomas hurried along behind me. "You too, will be eager to speak with your father, eh Thomas?"

"I will, lord, I hope he will be proud that I am a knight now."

"How could he be else?"

Father Henry stopped. He put his arm around my knight's shoulder, "Thomas, your father fell in the Warlord's last campaign. He died well."

It was a little blunt but I was not certain how else the news could have been broken. Better to know quickly. Rebekah gave Ruth's hand to me so that I held the hands of both my children. She linked Sir Thomas' arm. She spoke quietly to him, "I did not know your father, Thomas but I am certain that if he is anything like you then he will be with your god. Take comfort." I saw that he was too upset to respond. He bit his lip and nodded.

"I will go and speak with the archers. They can tell me more." He left.

Brother Peter said, "With your permission, lord, I will go to the church and pray. It has been some time since I have been in a church."

"Of course." He and Father Henry headed to the church where my mother was buried.

Some of the joy of our homecoming was gone in that instant. Thomas had looked forward to being reunited with his father just as I had and now those hopes were dashed. John of Craven and William, my father's steward greeted us at the gate, "Lord, this is a joyous day."

"Thank you, William. Is my father abroad?"

"He is in London, lord, at the coronation of the king. We know not how long he will be away."

"Did my father have word of my return from a Varangian, Ralph of Bowness?"

"No, lord. The news we had was from Sir Leofric in Anjou."

I frowned. That was worrying. What had happened to Ralph? He had left months before me. I shook the unwelcome thought away. The world was wide and dangerous. I forced a smile, "We are home and this is my family."

My father's steward nodded, "We saw them from the tower, lord. Alice is preparing quarters for you and John of Craven is making room in the warrior hall. Welcome, my lady."

I saw that Rebekah was a little overawed by the sights sounds and smells of my castle. This was not Aqua Bella. To me, it was familiar, almost comforting, but to her, it would appear dank and dirty. The wood smoke smelled different and here there was no pleasant breeze bringing the smells of lemons and oranges to waft through the air.

"Let us get inside and there we shall sit by a fire. That is a true English welcome." Alf and my men were approaching. I waved him over. "Alf, take the men and go with John of Craven. He will make sure that you are comfortable."

Alice burst into tears when she saw me. She dropped to her knees and kissed my hand. "Lord, this is a day for which I have waited these many years. Your father will be overjoyed."

I lifted her up, "Rise, Alice, you know you do not have to bow to me. This is my wife and my children."

She rose and curtsied to Rebekah, "My lord, what bonnie bairns they are!" She beamed at them, "I am Alice, the housekeeper and the cook has made some sweet cakes that I will fetch for you." She looked up at me, "Your rooms are prepared, lord. Would you drink first and eat?"

I nodded, "Aye, Alice. We need something to take the chill from our bones. The river is cold."

She walked to the fire and, taking out the poker, came over to the table where there was a jug of ale. She plunged it in and it hissed. Ruth grabbed Rebekah's arm and Samuel giggled and laughed. "I have some poshote for the bairns although we are running out of nutmeg and cinnamon."

"Fear not, Alice, we have brought great quantities."

She poured a heated ale for Rebekah and me and hurried off. Rebekah had a bemused expression on her face. "Bairns? Poshote? I know not these words, husband."

"Bairns means children and poshote is warmed milk and ale infused with a little honey, nutmeg and cinnamon. The children will enjoy it." I handed her the ale. "I know this is strange for you but it will become familiar. These are good people."

She smiled, "I know that. I hear it in their voices and see it in their eyes. All is well. It has been a long journey."

"William, have word sent to my father's lords that I am returned. I am anxious to speak with them."

"Of course. Would you have a feast for them?"

I hesitated. This was not my castle but I had returned and I was my father's son. "Of course. We have brought supplies with us. When I have finished the ale then I will see the captain who brought us and pay him off. We have chests of coin which will need to be secured."

"We have rooms for that, lord. Your father, too, has been successful. The castle has been enlarged."

"I saw not William of Kingston."

"No lord. Our ships sailed for Anjou just after your father left. We sent goods to be traded."

That explained the empty berths. I would give a letter to Michael, the captain who had brought us so that he could deliver it to Sir Leofric. "These ships will also be sailing south if you wish trade goods sent. The captains can be trusted."

"Good, lord, for it has been a mild winter. We kept extra supplies in case we needed them. They should be traded before they go off. I will deal with it."

I was heading for the river when the north gate opened and Sir Richard, my father's captain of archers, rode in. He threw himself from his horse and grabbed me, "Lord! What a joyous day!"

Dick looked older but, in his eyes, I could still see the same man I had known since a child. He had taught me the bow and the ways of the woods for he had once been an outlaw. He had never married and never changed. My father had knighted him but he had continued as he always had, serving my father. He was as close to a brother as my father had.

"Aye, Dick, and I am home. I have a wife and family now." I pointed to the warrior hall, "Thomas son of Oswald is here. I knighted him."

Dick gave a sad shake of the head, "That is both sad and a cause for celebration. I had best go and speak with him."

"Aye. He is upset and he is speaking with your archers. I have sent for my father's lords."

"That will be good."

"Where is Richard, my father's squire?"

"He has now been knighted by your father. He is at Barnard Castle. He is visiting with Sir Hugh." Dick smiled, "I think he is sweet on one of Lady Anne's sisters."

That was good. My father liked his knights to have families.

"Does he have a new squire?"

"Aye, James, the surviving son of Sir Edward. He is as dependable as his father was. He will be a sound knight."

Later that night, buried beneath blankets and furs to keep out the cold we snuggled. It had been a long day. We had dined with Dick and John of Craven as well as William son of Leofric and Father Henry. It was a meal filled with questions and answers from all sides. I learned of the war and those who had died and the others learned of our time in the Holy Land. I was pleased that Thomas looked to be coping with the news of his father's death. He had expected to bring great news to his father and, instead, had received the worst.

"Your father must be a great man for this castle is strong and the people we have met appear as strong and as loyal. Will he like me?"

"He will adore you." I was now confident of that. I had seen it in the faces of the men around the table. I had watched as Alice had doted and fussed over my children and I knew that we had made the right decision to come home. "And tomorrow you will meet the rest of my father's knights and their wives. They, too, will make you welcome."

They hastened to our castle with their families the next day. It was a feast, the like of which, I had not experienced for many years. It was truly English. My father's steward had had a bullock butchered. Aiden had hunted deer the week before, and we enjoyed that. The wine we had brought gave us a taste of my former home and Alice surpassed herself with the boiled pudding that my children devoured with relish. The talk was loud and full of laughter. Even Sir Thomas looked at ease. Alice showed her skills by ensuring that my lords, their ladies and their children, all had rooms. I know not how she managed it but she did. Sir Wulfric, Sir John, Sir Harold, Sir Tristan and Sir Gilles had all managed to get to my hall. The other knights lived further away.

Samuel was fascinated by them. He had seen knights in Outremer but he had been younger. He was more curious now. I smiled whenever he jumped at Wulfric's laugh. With his grey beard and expanding girth, he was a true force of nature. My daughter, Ruth was a little shier. She was younger but I saw her taking all of it in. She and the other girls and ladies who had come eventually sat around the fire talking with Rebekah. Her deep-set eyes and olive skin were a curiosity. She did not seem to mind and even smiled when Sir Harold's daughter, Maud, tried to rub the colour from her skin. The knights and squires questioned me long and hard about the Crusade which had ended so disastrously. I, in turn, learned more about the war. Most of the stories were of my father and I felt both proud of his actions and angry with myself for having stayed away so long.

Despite the drink, I awoke early. My father had often told me that a warrior should never ignore his feelings or his dreams. That night my sleep was interrupted by an unpleasant dream. All that I saw was a spear coming to my wife's heart. When I woke I saw that she slept, buried beneath a mountain of furs. I did not wish to return to the dream and I rose and, after dressing, walked to the hall. No one was awake and so I poked the fire and then, when it was blazing, used the poker to warm up some of last night's ale. That done I headed, wrapped in my cloak, to the walls. I had a mind to watch the sunrise.

It was Franck of Frisia who was on watch. He was now a greybeard but still an awesome man with an axe. He grinned at me as I stepped onto the fighting platform. He had lost teeth in the many battles he had fought for my father and it gave him a comical look, "Just like your father, lord. He, oft times, would come here to watch the dawn."

"Aye Franck but I had forgotten just how cold it could be here."

He shook his head, "This has been a mild winter. They say that north of the wall they have had snow since All Saints' Day. Our people in the valley have not suffered."

'Our people', my father had melded together many who came from far and wide into one band. Franck came from Frisia but he was as much a part of the land as Alf, the smith, who had been born in Stockton.

"And now that we have peace they will prosper even more."

Sometimes you utter words and it is as though some malevolent spirit, Puck perhaps, had decided to test our mettle. There was a cry from the north gate, "Men approach!"

I turned and ran. I knew not who was the captain of the night guard but, in my father's absence, I was lord. By the time I reached Ralph of Nottingham others had gathered and were pointing north to the road which led to the Oxbridge. "What is it, Ralph?"

"There lord." He pointed to the huts which were furthest from the castle. I saw two men supporting a third. The light from a hut lit them as the pig farmers who lived there, Peter the Pig and his wife, came to see what the danger was.

"Open the gate." Ralph gave me a questioning look. "Peter the Pig would not be aiding them if there was danger, Ralph. It is my command."

"Aye lord."

By the time I reached the gate, Peter the Pig and his wife had escorted the three men to the gate. "Lord, one is perilous hurt."

Thank you. Ralph, fetch Father Henry. Bring them to the guard room. Give them blankets." The man they had carried had a bloody bandage around his thigh and he was not conscious. His two companions laid him on the floor. The light from the fire showed that the two men who had carried the older wounded one were young. "I am Sir William. I am the son of the Warlord."

"Lord, we are from Fissebourne. The Scots came two nights since and raided our cattle. My father, Henry, led the men of the village to recapture them. The rest of the men were slain and we barely managed to take my father from the field. When we reached our homes, they were burned and our families had been taken. We came here for it is known that the Earl is feared by the Scots."

I nodded, "You are?"

"Henry, son of Henry and this is my brother Robert. Will my father live?"

"Father Henry is a good priest and a healer." Just then Father Henry came in with Brother Peter. "The Scots, Father, two days since..."

"You may leave him with me, lord." He looked pointedly at the two boys.

"Ralph, take Henry and Robert to the hall. Father Henry needs space."

"Come on lads, we have fine food here." Ralph was an experienced warrior and he shepherded the men out.

I hurried back to the hall. The commotion had brought my father's knights out of their chambers. Alf stood there with my sword. "The Scots have been south for a cattle raid. They have devastated Fissebourne. We ride."

"But Sir William, we have not brought our retainers."

"We have knights enough and I have my father's archers and men at arms. We will catch them. They are moving cattle and they will be moving slowly." I took my sword from Alf. "Have Aiden take Edward and Edgar. Tell him to find their trail. I want him to take Masood, my scout, with them."

"And our wives?"

I shrugged, "They can stay here. John of Craven has more than enough men to protect them." I was suddenly the knight who had led men in the Holy Land. My voice became cold and commanding. "If you do not wish to come then return home with your families."

Sir Tristan, with whom I had been a squire said, "That is unfair, William. We did not say we would not come with you."

I realised that I had been used to making decisions myself without worrying about the feelings of others. "And I meant no offence. There are women and children who are now slaves. We need to fetch them."

As I strode off Sir Wulfric put one of his huge paws around my shoulder. "These are your father's men, William. You need not ask. They will follow. Sir Tristan is just a little worried about his wife. She is with child."

I smiled at the bluff old soldier, "And you never bothered to marry?"

He laughed, "I have ploughed enough women to know that there is a harvest out there and the bastards are Wulfric's. I knew not my father and I turned out well. I like living without a woman to order me around. But you have a jewel in Rebekah. I think had I met someone like her when I was younger then I might have changed my mind about marriage."

I ran up to my room. Rebekah was there with the children. When she saw me going to my chest for my mail she frowned, "War?"

Shaking my head, I said, "Cattle raiders. They have taken slaves. Here, Samuel, you may hold my sword while I dress."

"Can I come with you?"

"When you can ride a palfrey then aye. Until then, I fear you would slow us up."

By the time I was dressed and had reached the courtyard, my knights, men at arms and archers were all gathered. I suspected we would be too large a force for cattle thieves but I wished to make a point. Alf had saddled Alciades. I wondered if it was too soon for he had sailed a long way. I would soon find out. Alf hung my shield from my cantle and asked, "Will we need spears, lord?"

"Put some on a sumpter and lead it." The two youths from Fissebourne came over. "You two remain here. We will get your cattle and your families but this is work for warriors."

Brother Peter climbed onto his horse. He had a sword strapped to his side, "I can offer aid to our men and death to our foes!" We had a healer and that was good.

We headed north. It was but thirteen miles to the small collection of houses and farms. Wulfric rode next to me. "If they have headed for Durham then we will have little chance of getting them back."

Sir Gilles of Norton shook his head, "I doubt that they would do that. Since the war ended the Bishop of Durham has suddenly found that he always supported the Empress and her son. He does not wish to back the wrong side. Your father managed to breach their walls more than once. They will be heading for the New Castle. They have rebuilt the bridge which was destroyed. We have time to catch them."

I nodded. Aiden and his two scouts could find the trail of a butterfly in summer. I turned to look behind me. I had the eleven men I had brought from the Holy Land but I also had thirteen archers under Dick and twelve men at arms from the garrison. With seven knights and squires, we would be a formidable force.

"Have they a castle on the south side of the river by the New Castle?"

Sir Harold of Hartburn shook his head, "They fortified the bridgehead. It is wooden. The castle is made of stone and they have a stone gate at the other end of the bridge."

"Cattle take some shifting and they have slaves. They will not reach the New Castle." Sir Wulfric had done this before. We passed Thorpe which now had a fortified wall around it. We had lost a family from there to the Scots. As we passed Segges Field I remembered the battle my father had fought there and bloodied the noses of the Scots.

I saw the blackened houses of Fissebourne on the valley bottom. Garmondsway Moor stretched north and west. They would not have taken that route. It was too high and the road too steep. They had even destroyed the mill, just half a mile from the main settlements. Around the hillside were the burned farms. This had been more than just a cattle raid. When we drew nearer to Fissebourne I saw Edward and Edgar moving around the burned-out huts. They had shovels.

We reined in, "Where are Masood and Aiden?"

"They followed the trail north, lord." Edward picked up a piece of cow dung. "They only left yesterday, lord." He shrugged, "Perhaps they thought they had left no survivors to give warning. Aiden told us to bury their dead." He pointed to some bodies covered with cloaks. I saw bare legs sticking out from them. "The men were butchered and had their manhoods taken but there was an old woman as well as a girl of fifteen too." He shook his head. I knew what their fate had been.

Brother Peter dismounted, "I will say words over their bodies and see they are buried in a Christian fashion."

"Thank you, Brother Peter," I turned in the saddle, "John of Chester, you and my men help Edward and Edgar. You can catch us up."

He nodded, "Aye lord. We will hurry. I would like to catch these butchers of girls and old women."

We were spurred on by the burned and devastated settlement. Wulfric said, "If they just wanted cattle and slaves they could have gone back without wasting time burning houses. They had to go out of their way to destroy the mill."

"Perhaps they wanted the flour?"

Harold shook his head, "No, Tristan, the villagers do not keep milled flour. As soon as they have wheat, barley or oats, they grind it. The grain would have been at the farms. I agree with Wulfric. This is a punishment raid. The war is over and they are trying to hurt us while the Warlord is away."

I turned, "They are that fearful of father?"

Dick nodded, "We have kept the patrols up and seen signs of scouts and spies. We should have realised. The Warlord will not be pleased at our lack of vigilance."

I saw, from the looks on their faces, that they felt responsible. What could I have done with such warriors in the Holy Land?

The road passed between woods. There were fewer farms hereabouts. Their trail was clear for they had taken many animals. My father had managed to persuade the farmers to keep more animals over winter. The farmers had been rewarded by larger herds and flocks. The Scots were reaping the benefit. They had waited until the depths of winter when the days were short and there was darkness in which to hide. Had not Robert and his brother reached us as early as they did then the Scots might have had the darkness to hide them.

"They will head for the river crossing to the east of Cuneceastra. The river can be forded there. We have had little snow melt."

"Aye Wulfric but it takes more time to ford the river. Will they not try Cuneceastra?"

"It is held by the Bishop of Durham's men and there is a hall there. If they did not head to Durham then they will not risk Cuneceastra. The New Castle is but eight miles to the north of it."

I looked at the sky. They would not make the New Castle before dark. The animals and slaves would be tired. They would have travelled almost fifteen miles. Just then Aiden appeared, almost from nowhere.

"Lord, we have found them. They have camped north of the ford. Your African watches them."

I smiled, "Masood is not an African, he is a Jew."

"He is the blackest man I have seen. I will say this for him, he is as good a scout as I have seen."

The sound of hooves behind us made me turn. It was the men who had buried the bodies. "Then take Edward and Edgar. Your horses are swifter than our war horses. We will approach quietly."

Continuing north I said, "Dick, what say we use one of my father's tricks. Take my archers and yours. Cross the bridge at Cuneceastra and get around the other side of them. I would have the captives saved."

He smiled, "They say that an apple rarely falls far from its tree. You and your father have similar minds. Come archers, Sir William's men, this will be an opportunity to see if you are the equal of my men!" They turned from our road and headed across country towards the Roman road which went like an arrow for the crossing of the river.

Without my scouts, we were almost blind. Dick and his archers had ridden before us. They were the masters at spotting an ambush. Sir Harold seemed to read my thoughts, "Do not worry, William. If Aiden said they are camped beyond the ford there will be no ambush. And I still have my ears and eyes."

I had forgotten that Harold had grown up as an outlaw and an archer. My father's first squire knew his way around the forests. The light was fading fast when Aiden appeared from the trees. I held up my hand and we stopped.

"Do they have guards?"

"They do, lord. They have lords with them. They are not attired as you are. Yet they give orders and ride horses. They have shields with emblems on them."

Wulfric asked, "How many are there?"

"There are six men on horses and they have fifty men on foot. Some have helmets and all have a weapon." His voice hardened, "We heard screams."

We had no time to waste. "Sir Wulfric, prepare the men. Alf, tighten the girth on Alciades. Come Aiden and bring the other scouts." We moved down the trail. I could smell the animal dung. Cows make a great deal and they had been moving slowly. Beyond the river, I heard the sound of the camp. The animals were making noise and there was laughter and screams intermingled. They were confident and not hiding. The smell of animals being cooked drifted towards us. Masood rose from behind a bush and held up his hand, "No closer, lord. The river hides our noise here but any nearer?" He shook his head.

Through the gap in the trees, I could see the black water. It was no more than twenty paces wide but I knew that it would be cold. "Could you four swim the river and use your knives to eliminate the sentries?"

Aiden said, "We could but your man?"

Masood gave a thin grin, "Do not worry, Englishman, I can swim as well as you and my knife has slain many of my lord's enemies already."

"Good. I will count to a thousand and then we will come. When the sentries are slain try to get to the captives. I would not have them harmed."

I walked back to my knights and my men. "Alf, break out the spears and tie the sumpter to a tree. We swim the river and charge into their camp. I hope to surprise them. They are making much noise already."

"Do we want prisoners?"

"We want the captives to be safe. A prisoner would be useful but it is not important."

I mounted Alciades. In my head, I had been counting. I still had five hundred to go. Alf handed me my spear, "Stay close behind me."

He nodded, "Will the river be cold?"

Wulfric heard him and laughed, "When you come out boy, your manhood will have hidden itself!"

I waved my hand and we walked down to the river. I did not want to make too much noise too soon. Once we reached the other bank there would be no option. I had not swum with Alciades before but, so far, he had never let me down. He stepped into the water. Once he lost the bottom I took my feet from the stirrups and laid flat along his back. Wulfric had been right. It felt as though I had been dropped into an icy bath. I kicked with my legs. Alciades was only swimming for a few paces and then his hooves found purchase. I wondered how many of the captives had survived the crossing. To their captors, any losses would be seen as ridding themselves of the weak.

As Alciades scrambled up the bank I slipped my feet back into my stirrups and saw the dead sentry. Like many of the Scots, he was heavily tattooed. I pulled up my shield and laid my spear across the cantle of my saddle. As I spurred Alciades I heard the rest of my knights and squires as they joined me. A cry from ahead told me that we had been spotted. Even as we galloped towards them I could hear orders being shouted. They would not run. Perhaps they did not know how many men they were facing.

A huge Scot wielding one of their long two-handed hammers raced at me. From his position and his gait, I deduced that he would hit my shield and hope to pulverise my arm. He did not know how agile and skilful my horse was. He was big but he had fast hooves. I whipped his head to the left and thrust with my spear as the Scotsman swung at fresh air. Even so, the hammer missed Alciades nose by a hand span. With no armour to protect him the long, sharp head of my spear tore into him. I twisted as I did so and then pulled it back. A wriggling sea of guts spilt out. I allowed my arm to trail back so that his body slipped from the spear head. Pulling Alciades head around I looked for the lords on horses.

"Lord, watch out!"

Alf's warning came just in the nick of time. The Scottish horseman was very close and I managed to pull my shield up and block the blow just as the Scottish sword swung at head height. I was too close to make an effective thrust back at him and so I swung the long spear at the Scot's head. He tried to duck but the haft of the spear rang against his head, making him unsteady. I dropped the spear and, continuing my turn, drew my sword. He had lost sight of me for his helmet had fallen slightly forward. He had donned it in a hurry. He had quick reflexes and his shield, smaller than mine, came up just as I swung at him. Alciades now came into his own. He was a war horse. The Scot was riding a palfrey. Instinctively Alciades tried to bite the smaller horse of the Scot. Naturally, it jerked away and I was able to swing my sword backhand as he tried to control his horse. My blade bit through his back and I felt it grate on his backbone. His back arced and he fell from his saddle.

Four Scots ran towards me shouting curses. I suspect I had killed their mormaer. Two of them suddenly pitched forward with arrows in their backs. A warrior darted alongside me and Alf thrust his spear into the screaming mouth of one of them. The other tripped over his companion's body. There was a sickening crunch as Alciades hoof smashed into his skull.

Suddenly the survivors threw their weapons down and held up their arms. I saw why. There was a ring of archers behind them. Their chance to flee had gone. With their four lords dead, there was little point in fighting on. I turned and shouted, "Thank you, Alf. Did we suffer wounds?"

He shook his head, "Not that I could see." He picked up the banner which lay by the side of the dead lord and handed it to me.

"Then God has smiled on us. Let us pray that the captives have survived their ordeal."

Chapter 4

There were just six Scots left without wounds. I saw my men at arms going around the wounded with Brother Peter. When he shook his head, they gave the wounded man a warrior's death. Others he tended to. I dismounted and took a handful of grain from my saddlebag. It was from the alehouse and was the remains of the brew. Alciades loved it. He nodded his head as he ate. "You deserve this, my friend."

I saw Dick and his archers. They were gathered around the captives. I saw that there were four old men, fifteen women of varying ages and ten children. That seemed a lot for such a small place as Fissebourne. I took off my helmet, "I am Sir William of Stockton, the son of the Warlord. Henry and his sons found us. I am sorry that you had to suffer this ordeal. We will make the Scots pay for this."

One woman, she looked to be twenty or so summers said, "Aye lord, and we thank you but that will not bring back our husbands, will it? Who will look after us?"

I saw Wulfric giving me a sideways look. He was comparing me with my father. This was an easy decision. I had heard my father utter these words more times than enough. "You will come to Stockton. None will have to return to Fissebourne who do not wish to. You are young enough to start new families and we have men who seek wives. We will camp here tonight and head back to Stockton in the morning."

An old man said, "I am not certain that I will survive another dousing, lord."

"Fear not, we go back along the road."

Wulfric came next to me, "You will do, William. I can see that you grew up while in that heathen land."

"Meaning I was a pretty poor wretch before then?"

Wulfric was honest and many a man would have lied but not him, "If I am to speak true then I would say that you were. Whoring and carousing are not the acts of a married man. You have atoned and are the better for it." He leaned in close to me, "But if you hurt that wife of yours, young William, you will have me to answer to."

"You need not fear. My eyes became clear in the desert."

We discovered that most of the animals had survived. That meant a long slow journey back home. Part of me wanted to head further north and make a reprisal raid on the Scots. Then I realised that would be the old William. I saw that the prisoners, wounded and fit alike, were being guarded by Ralph of Nottingham and my father's men at arms. Six of the wounded had survived. They varied in age from boys of eleven summers to two greybeards. Brother Peter was just applying a bandage to one of the greybeards when I approached. "Where are you from?" The one with a bandage nodded north. "I know that. Answer me civilly or the others will watch me undo Brother Peter's work. You raided English families. You killed them and abused their women. Will they go to heaven, Brother Peter?"

"Not until they have confessed their sins to me and received absolution."

"As you see, your souls are in my hands." I saw hands going to wooden crucifixes.

"Berwick."

Berwick on Tweed was close to Norham. That had once been the northernmost bastion of England. They had come a long way. "Why raid down here?"

He shrugged, "We have had a bad winter. A man grows tired of fish. This was the closest we could get to England." He smiled and I saw that he had lost teeth in the battle, "All the rest is now Scotland."

Ralph of Nottingham drew his dagger, "Not for long! Now that King Henry is back we will retake it."

I put my hand on Ralph's arm. "There will be time for that later. And the lords we slew? Was one your mormaer?"

"Aye, his father will be angry that you have killed his two sons. He will seek revenge."

"Then he knows where to come. Or perhaps we will visit him."

The old man pointed north. "The land to the north is filling up with Scots. We are taking it back and cleansing it of you English."

Sir Wulfric had wandered over, "Kill the old bastard. He is more trouble than he is worth."

"It may come to that but we will take them home and let my father decide. This land is subject to his justice."

The next morning, we rose early and headed south. We made the Scots drive the animals behind us. Dick and his archers rode behind them. When we reached Cuneceastra we halted to rest the captives and to speak with the commander of the Bishop's garrison. He was a sergeant at arms. The garrison had but ten men and I suspect they were there to guard the valuables in the church rather than the tiny collection of huts, houses and farms.

He bowed when he saw my banner. He could do little else for we outnumbered his men many times over. "What is your name?"

"Richard of Elsdon, lord."

"Who is the Bishop these days?"

"That would-be Hugh de Puiset, lord."

The name seemed familiar, "Thomas, de Puiset do we know him?"

My knight nodded, "There was a family of that name related to Stephen of Blois."

Of course. He was the nephew of King Stephen and, more importantly, Henry of Blois, Bishop of Winchester. This made sense and explained why the Scots had not tried to use the Durham Road. The Bishop was in a parlous position.

"I am Sir William of Stockton, the son of the Warlord and I am recently returned from the Holy Land. I would have you send one of your men and tell him that we have tracked Scottish cattle thieves and murderers who entered the Palatinate. I would remind him of his duty. He is here to guard the northern borders of my father's land. I would hate to have to come to Durham to remind him."

"Of course, my lord." He looked around nervously. "May I speak in private with you?"

I was intrigued. I had met assassins before but this rather portly man did not seem to pose a threat. We walked away from the others and I sat on the wall which ran alongside the graveyard. "You have my attention."

"Lord, did you live at Aqua Bella?"

The hairs on the back of my neck stuck up. How did he know that name? I had not mentioned it. "I did. Where did you hear it?"

"Seven days since, I was collecting some holy relics for the Bishop at Jaruum. A ship landed there and a monster of a Viking got off. He asked how he could get to Stockton. He said he had a message for the Warlord from William of Aqua Bella."

That was Ralph of Bowness. "What happened to him?"

"Well, my lord, I told him where Stockton was but then a Scot, Mormaer Alexander Keith, visiting from the north, brought his soldiers and had him taken away. He must have overheard him ask for you. He had a loud voice."

"He went peacefully with them?"

"No lord. He laid out four with his fists until he was hit on the head with a hammer."

"Tell me, how did you escape?"

"We were under the protection of the Bishop, lord. The Scots do not like us but they fear the church."

"And do you know where this Mormaer lives?"

"He has been given the manor of Warkworth, lord. It is said he is building a castle there."

I took a gold piece and gave it to the man. "This is for the information and for your silence."

"Silence, lord?"

"Tell no one else of this."

"Of course, lord."

When I returned to my men I saw that they were intrigued. I waved Wulfric and my knights over. "I have just discovered that Ralph of Bowness has been taken prisoner and is being held north of the Tyne."

Wulfric frowned, "Ralph of Bowness?"

"Let us say that I sent him on the errand which had him captured. I am honour bound to rescue him."

"North of the wall?"

"Aye Tristan. I ask no man to follow me save my own men and those of Sir Thomas. We owe much to Ralph of Bowness."

Wulfric said, "We will all come."

"That you cannot and for two good reasons: firstly, we need to get these people home and secondly, you have to protect the valley until my father returns. You have families."

"As do you!"

"And you, Wulfric, will protect my family."

Dick said, "We will come with you. We know the land there. Sir Thomas is the son of one of our own. If he goes then we go." I looked at him. He laughed, "William, there will be no argument! I swore an oath to protect you when you were a child. I will do so again. Wulfric does not need us to watch the captives and drive the animals."

And so it was decided. We took the spare horses and supplies and we turned around and recrossed the bridge to cross the Wear. My wife would understand, or so I prayed.

Masood did not know the land but he had good senses. I conferred with Dick and we decided to send him ahead with Aelric. Aelric was the most experienced of Dick's archers. After we had crossed the river we headed north and west. "We should cross the Tyne by the old Roman bridge to the west of Hexham. Sir Hugh had a fort there and the Scots will have made sure that they keep a good watch over the bridge."

I shook my head, "No, Dick, for that would take us further west and add half a day at least to our journey and, besides, we would have to cross the Tyne twice."

"The second crossing is easy. There is an abandoned Roman fort on the north branch and as for the time," he shook his head, "use your head, William. He was taken a week since. He is either dead or, more likely a prisoner. This Scot heard your father's name. He will seek information."

I glowered at Dick. He spoke to me as though I was a child and yet, to him, I was a child. He had been with my father for many years. Was he right?

"I say this for your own good. You may be a target for this Mormaer. He might see an opportunity to catch you and use you against your father. It is how we lost King Stephen after Lincoln. He was exchanged for the Empress' brother. We must avoid contact with them until then. There is a small ford on the Wansbeck north of the Tyne and that will bring us to the Coquet Valley. Between here and the Tyne there is nothing."

I could see that he was right and I nodded, "You offer good advice. I can see that I have much to learn."

"I am still unsure how we will recapture your friend and, more importantly, get him back. It seems to me that every Scot north of the Tyne will seek us."

"And that is why I wished to bring only my men. I did not want to endanger my father. You and the others are his walls of steel. I am honour bound to fetch him if I can."

"And your wife and family? What if you perish in the attempt?"

"Then my father will have a grandson and granddaughter to bring up."

"Leaving your wife alone in a strange land. You have much to learn. I can see that God has sent this as a trial for me to see if I still have my skills when my beard sprouts white."

I laughed, "You will never grow old. Your eyes and mind are as sharp as ever."

"We shall see. We will camp to the south of the Wansbeck. If we ride hard we can make forty miles this day. That will give us the opportunity to approach this castle cautiously."

"Do you know the place?"

"There was no castle there when we campaigned around Norham but there is a harbour. If he builds a castle then I know where he will build it. The river bends around a knoll. It would not require much work to throw up a castle. As your father discovered, it takes years to build a castle in stone. He has been building Stockton for the last thirty years and it is still not finished. It is more likely to be in wood."

That gave me hope. When we had spoken with the captives we had discovered that the Scots had been systematically destroying farms and settlements. This raid was the first south of the Palatinate. As we headed north we saw the devastation of their raids. We passed burned-out farms and fields full of tares. Hugh de Puiset had been too busy consolidating his position as Bishop. He should have been leading his knights against the Scots and their privations.

Masood and Aelric stopped every five miles or so. They chose a spot where we were safe. We would catch them up and they would then continue. We would rest and water our horses and allow them to graze. This was the best way to cover a long distance without killing horses.

Alf shook his head at the second stop, "Lord, this is such a cold country. Why do you choose to live here?"

"It is my home and it was the home of your father too."

Sir Thomas laughed, "And besides, Alf, this is not even cold. For winter, this is mild." He pointed to the west. "See how there is snow atop those hills. The further north we get the colder it will become. The ground will be harder."

"And, Alf, remember that we go to the aid of Ralph. We owe him much."

"You are right, lord. I am learning but it is taking time."

We saw few people. The ones we did see took cover but they were always in the distance. I guessed that they were the survivors of the English who had lived here. They were eking out an existence in the remote parts of the land. The civil war had been very expensive. King Stephen had spent the treasury which King Henry had accumulated and the Scots and the Welsh had taken the opportunity of robbing England of land and people. Instead of wasting my time in the Holy Land, I should have been at home by my father's side.

The abandoned Roman fort was really just an oblong ditch with a mound within. A few of the wooden palisades remained. It would do. The Romans always built as close to a road and water as they could. We would be able to defend it and give our horses the grazing and water they needed. While the archers cut down old brambles to make a hedge the squires and men at arms watered the horses. The movement of our feet revealed the grass beneath the hardened ground. With the grain, we had brought we would have enough food.

I stood with Dick, Brother Peter and Thomas while our men went about their business. Night would fall soon and Masood and Aelric had not yet returned. Dick was not worried, "Aelric can outwit any Scotsmen and from what Aiden said to me, Masood is his equal."

With a fire going we cooked the food we had brought. Oats and salted meat was hardly an appetising meal but it would keep us warm and fill empty bellies. The advantage was that we could share the grain with our animals. We relied on them as much as they needed us. Masood and Aelric slipped silently across the river. They looked exhausted and they were leading a spare horse.

Aelric said, "We found a Scot. He was riding north. Before we cut his throat, we questioned him." He jerked a thumb at Masood. "He is a real terror. The Scotsman was eager to spill all that he knew. I think he was relieved when we gave him a warrior's death."

"What did he say?"

"He had been sent from Warkworth by the Scottish lord. He was to go to Hartness and ask the mormaer there to keep watch for you and to detain you."

Dick nodded, as though satisfied, "As I thought. It is you they seek. Is this Ralph worth risking not only your life but the future of the valley?"

I nodded, "And you know that my father would do the same as I."

He laughed, "Oh yes. Then tomorrow, Aelric, I would have you and Masood scout out Warkworth. I need to know the number of men in the garrison."

"Our horses are tired." It was not a complaint. My father's men did not complain. It was an observation. If they had to then they would run. If they could not run they would walk and if that failed they would crawl. They were tough men.

"I know."

We kept a good watch but there was no danger. We were in a remote spot and there had been no sign of any horsemen. I had asked Aelric if the Scottish scout had spoken of men being sent south but he said the scout had not mentioned it and that was all that he knew. I wondered about that. If they planned to take me when I arrived back then they would need more than the men who were at Hartness. There was no castle there and the wall could be easily breached. What the Scots would have there were ships.

Masood and Aelric moved out while it was still dark. With such short days, we needed every moment of daylight that we could find. We left before dawn had broken too. We crossed the stream which barely came to our horses' bellies. There was a village to the west of us called Hartburn and, to the east, Morpeth. Ralph of Morpeth had held that for us in my father's time. He was now dead and that was a strongly held stone-built castle. Perhaps the lord there was not as eager to beard the Warlord as the Mormaer of Warkworth. We forded the icy Wansbeck river and headed towards Longhorsley. We needed to cross the Coquet at the small, rickety bridge at Wheldon. Dick remembered it from the campaigns in the north. There was a castle further east at Felton. I was still annoyed at having to take such a long route east but I understood the reasons.

It was just before we crossed the Coquet that we were almost discovered. Masood and Aelric were close by Warkworth. We had told them to watch the castle. We had Long Tom and Rafe scouting ahead of us. The road we were on was not Roman. It was a greenway. Trees arched overhead. It was not well used and we had to bend our heads beneath the trees. The galloping hooves made us stop and draw our swords. Rafe said not a word. He swept his hand to the side as did Long Tom. Danger was heading our way. He held up his right hand five times with his fingers spread. There were at least twenty-five men heading our way. Although the trees arched over us and formed a canopy there was space between them. Every warrior headed into them.

Dick and his archers were able to use their bows from the backs of their horses at the close range that we would be. I did not bother with my shield. If there was danger and we had to fight then it would be fast and furious. A shield was handy when facing a spear but the back of a mailed mitten could be just as effective. We waited. I turned and saw that Alf flanked me on one side and John of Chester on the other. My wild man, Henry son of Will was on the other side of Alf. That gave me comfort. When Henry drank he was

46

unpredictable but in combat, he was a rock. None would get close to Alf's right!

I heard hooves. It was tempting to head back to the greenway and see where they were and how they were armed. That would be a mistake. In the murk and gloom of a January day, we were safer hidden, motionless in the trees and undergrowth. We were ten paces from the greenway. With our ventails and cloaks were as close to hidden as we would get. I had time to speculate that these men might actually be from Felton. The question was, what were they doing on such a quiet greenway? The answer to that question would have to come after the skirmish for I knew that there would be one. It was one thing to remain hidden for a short time but their horses would detect us. Dick and his archers were at the southern end of the road while I was at the north. I would attack when the last of the men passed us. Of course, if we were discovered then we would attack as soon as the alarm was given.

I heard their voices as they approached. There were three knights and squires who passed us. They were walking rather than trotting. As with many Scots, they wore armour and bore shields much as had been worn at Hastings. Their helmets hung from their saddles. I had donned my full-face helmet. I preferred the open one but I had worked out that it hid my darkened skin. I wished to remain anonymous. My gryphon shield and standard were unknown in England. After the squires came men at arms. Unlike ours, the ten who followed wore only metal-studded leather jerkins and round helmets. I saw why they were walking for twelve men on foot trotted behind. These wore no armour at all and carried long spears with their shields around their backs. Their helmets hung from their spears.

One of the knight's horses, closer to Dick than us gave a neigh of alarm and reared. I yelled, "For the Warlord!" I spurred Alciades and we leapt from hiding. I swung the sword sideways at the spearman who tried to swipe his spear around at the same time as he swung his shield from his back. Hampered by the helmet hanging from the end of his spear he managed neither. My sword hacked across his chest. As he fell back the next man was knocked to the ground and trampled by Alciades. I heard Henry son of Will give his war cry as he lay about him. Henry loved nothing better than a battle. Alf had used his spear and I saw that he had skewered one Scot so hard that his spear had struck a second in the thigh. Our ambush had been almost perfect. We had weapons drawn and they did not. With archers ready to grab riderless horses I wanted our attack to be hidden from all.

The men on foot were slaughtered without striking a blow. My archer, Jack, however, was unlucky. He had released two arrows to hit two mounted men at arms when a third appeared from nowhere and speared him. Brother Peter was the closest to Jack and he, giving a roar, fell ferociously upon the Scot with his sword. The death of one of my men spurred my men and John of Chester and Henry son of Will fell upon the men at arms with such ferocity that they were all butchered. One knight and two squires surrendered. Before sheathing my sword, I glanced up and down the greenway to make sure that there were no more Scots and that we had lost no more men.

I saw Brother Peter speaking over Jack's body. This would hit my men hard. It had been a long time since we had lost a man in combat. I heard Dick ordering his men to capture the horses. "And put their shields on their horses with the weapons. They may come in handy."

"Do not slay the prisoners!"

Sir Thomas said, "There are only five, lord, and one of those looks as though he needs Brother Peter."

Brother Peter heard him and, after laying a cloak over Jack he stood and went to the wounded men. I dismounted and handed my reins to Alf. I took off my helmet and walked to the knight and two squires. The knight looked stunned. He was younger than Sir Thomas and he stared at a body of his squire, a boy who looked to be just eleven or so summers old.

He pointed a finger at me, "This was unprovoked and broke the peace!"

"I did not sign a peace with your king. I have broken no treaty!" That was not true of Dick but the young knight did not need to know that. "You surrendered your sword?" He looked at the blade which was stuck in the ground. I saw thoughts racing across his face. Could he grab it and slay me? I still had my sword unsheathed. I said, quietly, "If you have not surrendered then fight me. Otherwise, give me your word that you will not try to escape."

I saw conflict in his eyes and then he nodded, "I surrender. Padraig and Angus, surrender too. These are butchers." They both nodded.

I heard Henry son of Will say, "I would slit their throats, my lord! They seem a little insolent to me!"

John of Chester laughed, "I can see England is good for you, Henry. You are learning new words."

"No one will have their throats cut. Who are you and who is your lord?"

"I am Sir Malcolm of Dunblane and I serve the mormaer, Sir Alexander of Warkworth."

One of the squires could not contain himself, "And when he and the rest of our men find you I will laugh as he slays you!"

"Padraig!"

"Sorry, lord."

They were hiding something. I had no time to find out what it was but, when we stopped I would try to discover whatever it was. I turned to Brother Peter. He had just finished tending to the one surviving man at arms. He said, "When we stop I will have to take his hand and burn it with the fire. The tendons have been severed. I have stemmed the bleeding."

"Then you, Henry son of Will and John of Chester can watch the knight, squires and wounded man at arms. They should give you no trouble but if they do then you have my permission to kill them, Henry."

"With pleasure, lord."

Dick rode up to me, "It could have turned out worse."

"I still lost a man. You take your archers and meet with Aelric and Masood. We will bury Jack then follow."

He nodded, "Do not berate yourself so much. We will lose more before we have rescued this one man. I hope that he is worth it."

As Brother Peter spoke over Jack's grave I pondered Dick's words. Was Ralph of Bowness more important than Jack? When we headed north Robin Hawkeye who acted as my leader of archers for he was the best nudged his horse behind me. He had been close to Jack. "Lord Jack was unlucky. Any of us could die. We serve you and we fight for you. Jack is in heaven now, is that not right, Brother Peter?"

There was a slight hesitation and then my warrior monk said, "He is with God, that is for certain."

"There, lord. You have it from a priest."

As Robin headed beyond us to act as a scout I said to Brother Peter, "You cannot fool me so easily. He did not confess."

"He was a good man with no sins that I knew of. He will be in a better place."

That brought back memories of another priest who had tried to console me. It had not worked then either. "And that is what I was told when my wife and children died from the plague."

I spurred Alciades and found a space ahead of my men. I needed to think. We headed towards the ford which crossed the Coquet again. From what Dick remembered that would be the best approach to the newly built castle.

Chapter 5

By the time we reached Dick and my two scouts my mind had been cleared. I decided I had two choices: turn around and leave Ralph of Bowness to his fate or carry on and accept that more of my men would die. I chose the latter for to do the former would waste Jack's sacrifice.

"Good news, lord."

Aelric's voice brought me hope, "And we are desperate for such news."

"Two columns of men left the castle. One headed down the Felton road."

Dick said, "I think that was the one we met. We can ask our prisoners. It should be easy to confirm."

"And the other?"

"It headed for Morpeth. It was led by a knight with a banner. The same banner which flies from the castle. There were thirty men in the conroi."

It was dark and I could not see the castle. It was hidden by the trees "How many men are left inside?"

Aelric shrugged, "I would not know, lord. I know how many left but as I do not know how many remain I cannot answer."

I smiled. My father's men were nothing if not honest. "Fetch one of the squires. Keep the others apart." Turning to Brother Peter I said, "If you need a fire to heal the man's hand take some of my men and go back about a mile so that you are hidden by the woods."

"Aye lord, you are a Christian."

"Aelric, see if there are any houses in that direction. We passed none but I know the main road south to Amble and Hauxley lie in that direction."

"There were some, lord, but they are burned out. There are fishermen in Amble and a couple of huts at the harbour but none where the priest goes."

"Good." They had brought the one called Angus. He had seemed the least belligerent of the three and I knew that Brother Peter would frown on interrogating a wounded man. I smiled at the boy. "This is your castle?"

He nodded. "I come from Hauxley, lord, my father was given a farm there by the mormaer for services against..." his voice faltered.

I smiled, "The Warlord?"

"Yes lord."

"Good. And you left earlier today to head south while the mormaer took other men towards Morpeth." By saying what the boy knew to be true I was making it easier for him to give me the answers to my questions. He nodded, eager to please. "And you have a prisoner in the dungeon. A large man whose head has a wound."

He nodded, "Aye, lord, a Varangian they say. How did you know?"

"I know many things, Angus. I am just testing you to see how truthful you are. If you answer me truly then I will let you return to your father." His face beamed. "How many men are left in the castle? Now answer me truly for I shall know if you are lying."

I had held out a ray of hope and he grasped it. "The seneschal, Robert fitz Comyn, has twenty men there, lord."

I nodded, "Good, that is what I thought. You are a good boy. Alf, keep him close and away from the others. Take him to Brother Peter. You may be able to aid him."

I stared through the trees at the castle which was hidden there. I had an idea how we could take the castle without loss. An escape might be harder to achieve but the task now seemed easier. Dick said, with a smile in his voice, "You have a plan, William?"

"Is there but one gate?"

Aelric nodded, "One gate into the outer bailey and a climb to the palisade and the second gate to the inner bailey."

"Dick, if we were in that castle and some of our men galloped towards us followed by Englishmen, then what would we do?"

"We would not open our gate to admit them but I can see your plan. The Scots would let you enter and then slam the gates shut behind."

"Then here is my plan. I take my men and archers. We use the shields we captured and the standard we took when we retook the slaves. You will chase us. When we enter the gates, I will ride with Sir Thomas and my men at arms. My archers will feign exhaustion.

When we are through the second gate, my archers will secure the walls and open the gates."

"A bold plan but risky. You have less than fourteen men."

"And they are my men. I trust you and your archers to follow up swiftly. We only need to hold the ones at the inner bailey for the time it takes for you to cross it. Aelric, is the castle a large one?"

"No, lord. It is but a hall perched precariously on a motte! It might work."

"Then we will try that on the morrow."

I gathered my men around me. I could see the eagerness on their faces. They were keen to have some vengeance for Jack. We hunted the same men who had raided England; these had abducted Ralph and he was a friend. "Robin Hawkeye, when we ride through the gates, if they let us through, then I want you to pretend that your horses are lame or you are tired. You remain at the gate until we gain entry to the main hall. I will be shouting and attracting their attention. Whether we gain entry or no I want you and your men to clear the gate of our enemies and then open the gate for Dick. When Dick and his men enter then join us for we shall be outnumbered."

"We will not let you down, lord, and we shall do this for Jack. Fear not, lord. God is with us in this enterprise."

I turned to Masood, "I want you with me. You will need to wear the cloak and helmet of one of the men we captured. If we have any trouble at the gate then I want you to go over the wall."

He smiled, "Do not worry, lord. I will be there. I am getting used to the cold and this land. I like the men who fight for your father."

"Alf, you must carry the banner until we are within the second gate and then discard it and reveal who we are. I would not fight under false colours. All of you will have the shields we captured. Keep your cloaks tied tightly around you so that they cannot identify us."

After we had eaten our cold rations I lay down to try to get some rest. I was throwing the bones and I hoped that they would fall the right way. If they did not then my father could be raising my son. Brother Peter joined me, "I cut off the man at arms' arm, lord. I had to cut it below the elbow. He can never fight again."

I nodded, "Then tomorrow, he and Angus can go home no matter what happens."

"And where would you have me, lord?"

"Safe. Stay with the captives. They gave me their word but a warrior monk should ensure they behave."

"If not, then my fist will have to do."

That night I prayed to God that our journey would not be in vain. I hoped that Ralph of Bowness would be alive and that we would be able to rescue him. Of course, I had no idea how we would get home. That was out of my hands. If God willed it then we would succeed. If not…

That night I dreamed and it was not a dream of England. It was a dream of mountains and bogs. It was a nightmare of half-naked warriors throwing themselves at me and trying to hack my body to pieces. What I did not know was that this was not a dream but a foretaste of what was to come.

The next morning, I left Long Tom with Brother Peter. He had not mentioned it to anyone but he had been cut about the leg by one of the men at arms during the attack in the woods. I would not risk him and it meant that Brother Peter did not need eyes in the back of his head. We congregated inside the eaves of the wood. I went with Dick and Sir Thomas to survey the castle. Aelric had been correct, it was a small castle but it was well-positioned. The river ran around in a great loop so that there was but one entrance. It was over a moat that ran to the river. The bridge could be raised. The outer bailey was large and there were buildings there. I guessed that at least two had to be warrior halls for they were large. The mound on which they had built the lord's hall was high but small.

We had five hundred paces to ride to reach the bridge. The ground fell away on both sides and I could see, on the other side of the eastern arm of the river, the sea. This was a good site for a castle. Had it been made of stone then I would not have been able to even contemplate my plan. I checked, again, that my surcoat was covered by my cloak. I held the unfamiliar shield. If I needed it then we would have lost already. Turning I saw that my men were well disguised. We watched as the light from the east brightened the grassy mound. The frost of night evaporated and then they opened the gate. Two guards stood on the side nearest us. Two more stood by the gate. On the gatehouse, I saw six men. That was eight of the garrison accounted for. As the light improved I saw that there were sentries every forty paces around the outer palisade. That meant fourteen of the twenty-one men were on the outer palisade. We would only have seven to deal with. I spied hope and it encouraged me.

I waited until I saw the first cart head towards the gate before I made my move. "Ready, Dick?"

He laughed, "Aye lord, for it is like being with your father when he was a young buck. Go and we shall be behind you."

I turned and said, "Remember you are Scotsmen!"

Henry, son of Will said, "Does that mean I get to show my arse?"

I laughed, "If it gets us in then aye! Ride as though the devil was behind you!"

I spurred Alciades and we burst from the trees. I kept turning around in my saddle and I began shouting. I saw the men with the carts begin to hurry. They were being pulled by oxen and they did not move quickly. The guards on the wall pointed at us and shouted to someone I could not see inside the walls. I hoped they would see the shields we carried and the banner carried by Alf. I looked over my shoulder and saw Dick and his men burst from the woods some hundred paces behind us. Aelric launched an arrow. He was a good archer but when it whizzed over my shoulder to land thirty paces from me I wondered. I think that was what decided the men on the gates. The two men on our side of the bridge tried to hurry the ox-cart over. The other two left their post to go inside the gatehouse. They would, no doubt, raise the bridge once we were through.

I could see the faces of the guards at the bridge. They were not watching us but Dick and his archers. My father's archers had a reputation that was well deserved. The ox cart was in the middle of the bridge as I clattered over. I shouted, "The Warlord is coming!"

The sentries began beating the oxen to get them inside as we galloped through the gate. I turned in the saddle and shouted something deliberately incomprehensible while continuing to race towards the second gate which remained open. I saw that two of the sentries were standing by the bridge over the second ditch. I kept looking behind me as though I feared death at any moment. My archers had dismounted and were racing to the fighting platform. They had barely managed to get the oxen in before they started to shut the gates. I saw three of the sentries pitch from the fighting platform as Dick's archers struck them. The others cowered down.

Masood was on a small horse and he was racing ahead of me. He had no armour. The cloak and helmet, along with the borrowed shield were his disguise. The two sentries allowed him to gallop through. As I approached them they shouted, "Who are you?" In that instant, I saw that they saw the ploy. The guard turned and shouted, "Close the gate!"

It was too late. Masood was inside and I saw him leap from his horse and gut one of the two men on the windlass. He turned quickly with his razor-sharp blade, eviscerating the second one. I drew and swung my sword in one smooth motion and one of the guards lost his head. Alf rammed the borrowed standard into the second sentry before discarding it and raising my gryphon. It was not known until then but it soon became known as a harbinger of doom! I saw the other men rushing from the fighting platform and down the steps to the inner bailey. A huge warrior, in full armour, stepped from the hall. He had one man with him. My men at arms galloped after me and, as the men descended from the walls, they were slain. When my archers rode in the four men who were left, including the huge warrior, threw down their arms. Unbelievably we had succeeded.

"I am Robert fitz Comyn! You have dared to attack the hall of my lord!"

I stepped from my horse and strode up to him. "And I am William of Stockton, son of the Warlord. I am here for my friend, Ralph of Bowness. If you have harmed him you shall die!"

I saw him pale and he seemed to shrink.

I turned, "Alf, Masood, go and find him. John of Chester, secure these men. Sir Thomas, have our men find food and close the gates. We will rest before we return home!"

To my huge surprise, my men began banging their shields. Dick's joined in as they chanted, "Son of the Warlord! Son of the Warlord! Son of the Warlord!" I felt humbled. It was through their efforts that we had succeeded. If we had succeeded.

John of Chester forced our prisoners to their knees. Robert fitz Comyn glared at me. He had failed his lord and he knew it. He would be dangerous. He would slay me if he had the opportunity. I would not allow him such a chance. Dick rode up behind me and dismounted, "I have sent for Brother Peter and our prisoners. I have my men on the walls." He shook his head, "Wulfric will be more than annoyed to have missed this. A castle taken without a single man lost. Even your father could not have done what you did."

"I think he could but it is kind of you to say so."

Just then Ralph of Bowness appeared. He had to be supported by Masood and Alf. Where his right eye should have been, was a bloody mess. His legs and arms were scored with wounds. I ran to him, "Ralph, what happened?"

"This bastard tried to make me talk. I did not. I did not tell them when you sailed nor where you would sail to. Even when they took my eye I did not speak. Had you not come they were going to take my balls and then my dick."

I drew my sword and whirled around, "I told you what would happen if you hurt my friend!"

Robert fitz Comyn actually whimpered and then cowered. My men all drew their weapons. Ralph was our friend. He was our shield brother and we would avenge his hurts.

"No, William. I beg you to give me your sword and give this Scot one. I will face him man to man and I will kill him myself."

"But you are injured!"

He laughed, "I am like your grandfather and the great Aelfraed. I am a Varangian. If I am to die then let me face my enemy and do so with a sword in my hand."

I nodded and handed him my sword. I picked up the sword from the dead sentry and threw it to Robert fitz Comyn. "But his sword is better than mine!"

"Think yourself lucky that I gave you a sword. Defend yourself."

Ralph turned to me, "If I lose then let him go."

"But…"

He smiled, "For the honour of the Varangians."

I nodded. I knew why he did it. He wanted a fair fight. If the Scot thought he was doomed he would not fight well. I saw Robert fitz Comyn grin. He saw before him a weak and broken man. He saw a man without mail. Ralph was half-starved and in pain. What he did not see was the Emperor's Guard. It was his one mistake.

I waved my arm and my men made a circle of shields in which the two men would fight. I did not want Robert fitz Comyn to escape. I nodded to John and then the other prisoners. He would watch them. I did not know how Ralph could fight him. He barely had the strength to lift his sword. Robert fitz Comyn, on the other hand, swung the blade easily. He raised it and, with a roar, rushed in to hack at Ralph's head. Ralph barely had time to block the blow but he did so and as the Scot's sword bent a little I saw him grin. Ralph turned his head to me and winked.

As Robert fitz Comyn looked at his sword Ralph rammed his hand up under the mail shirt and he grabbed Robert fitz Comyn's testicles. He ripped his hand away and held up a bloody and gory trophy. As the Scot screamed in pain, Ralph took his sword in two hands and hacked into the hamstrings of both legs. The Scot could not support himself and he tumbled to the ground. He began whimpering.

Ralph handed me my sword, "Thank you, William. I knew the sword of a true warrior would defeat anything this animal held. He will not die from these wounds. At least not for a while. I would have him suffer as I did. He has no honour. I will not give him the warrior's death."

He walked up to the Scot who was lying face down and he drew the man's dagger.

"He will die slowly. As I thought I was going to die until my friends came for me." He reached down and slashed both Achilles tendons. The Scot screamed. "He will beg soon as I begged for a warrior's death." He turned over Robert fitz Comyn, grabbed his tongue and cut it off. Blood poured. "I cannot hear him!"

"Stop this, lord! It is not seemly!"

I turned and saw Brother Peter. "Stay out of this priest."

"Next he will try to pray as I prayed." He slashed down, first on the right hand and then on the left. The fingers were severed. "No prayers then." He stood. I knew that he had more punishment he wished to inflict. I had seen enough and was about to intervene when Brother Peter raised his sword and, in one blow, took the Scot's head.

Ralph whirled and roared, "You have deprived me of my pleasure!"

Brother Peter made the sign of the cross and then, after sheathing his sword put his arm around Ralph, "Come, my son. Let me heal these wounds and then we can repair your soul."

As I looked at the bloody and butchered corpse of Robert fitz Comyn I wondered what we had begun.

Dick broke me from my reverie by shouting, "See to the animals and get some food. I do not think we will stay here o'er long."

I turned to Alf, "Have the weapons taken from their dead and make sure that our captives are safe." I saw that the warrior who had lost his arm and Angus were standing where Brother Peter had left them. I walked over to them. "Do you give your word that, if I let you go, you will go home?"

I saw both of their eyes flicker towards the dead. They nodded. Angus said, "My lord is dead. I will return to my father."

The one-armed soldier said, "I too have a father. Perhaps a one-armed man might be of some aid to him. I can fight no more."

"Then go." I pointed to the gates and shouted, "These two may leave!"

I watched Gurth son of Garth wave acknowledgement. I headed into the hall. I saw now that it was very small. This had been thrown up in a hurry. It was really a large wooden tower. As I opened the door I saw that the horses were stabled in the bottom and a ladder led to the first floor. I heard Brother Peter's voice as I ascended. The first floor was where his warriors ate and slept. There were many hay-filled sacks littering the floor and spare clothes and personal items. As there was another floor above I guessed that was where the lord ate and slept.

I saw Brother Peter cleaning Ralph's eye. "I am sorry it took us so long to reach you, Ralph."

A thin smile formed on his lips, "It was my own fault. Instead of doing as you asked me and going to either Anjou or Stockton, I travelled across the Empire." He sighed. "I did not think you would be heading home quite so soon and I wished to see the lands of the Frank before I died. Eventually, I found a ship in the Low Countries and travelled to London. I thought to speak with your father. There were no lodgings to be had for the king was about to be crowned. My ship had sailed and I took the first vessel I could find. It took me to the Tyne. I believed that if the war was over it would be safe. I was wrong."

"I am sorry you were mistreated. It is my fault."

"No, my young friend, it is the weird sisters. Just as they brought young Alf here to us so I was fated to lose an eye. I will live." His one eye glanced at Brother Peter. "I will live, won't I?"

"You are a strong warrior. You will live. I will make a patch until your eye socket has healed. I have applied a salve to speed the process. As for your other wounds… time is all that you need."

"And we need to leave this night. I have the horses and men resting. I have no doubt that the knight of this castle will seek us. We will have to move and move quickly. We are fortunate that we captured so many horses. We will be able to ride faster. With luck, we can be south of the Wear by dawn."

Brother Peter asked, "And the ones who survived?"

"You want to know if they shall live?" He nodded. "They will but I will ensure that they will not fight us again."

"How, lord, I am curious?"

"They can swear to me or they will lose their right thumbs so that they cannot wield a sword against me."

The body of fitz Comyn was left on display as the survivors were gathered. I had Brother Peter hold a Bible. "You have a choice: swear on this Bible never to take arms against England or lose your right thumb."

I saw their eyes flicker to fitz Comyn's body and their answer was obvious. They all swore. One, bolder than the rest, said, "Lord, I should warn you that this warrior is related to the Comyn family who seek to rule Scotland. He will not take the death of his brother kindly."

"Thank you for that. I have heard of the Comyns."

Chapter 6

We left while it was still dark. The dead had been thrown into the ditches. We had no time to bury them. Dick had set slow fires in the buildings: smouldering coals which would burn through and eventually ignite the walls of the hall. The coals, suspended in a chest would take time to burn through the wood and then they would drop onto oil-soaked kindling to spread the fires. With a trail of straw and kindling, it would spread to the walls but not until we had left the area. Dick was a master with fire. With a chest on each floor, the burning hall and walls would draw every warrior and man from miles around and would allow us to escape.

Ralph of Bowness rode with Brother Peter and our prisoners. Masood and Aelric rode ahead as we left the castle to head south and retrace our steps. My men led either one or two horses. The captured horses had not been the best and we would ride those first. I rode a grey palfrey. Alciades was on a tether. If we had to flee then we would release the Scottish horses. They were not valuable. Our own horses were.

Having ridden along the greenway north we travelled boldly, even in the dark. With Masood and Aelric sniffing out danger I was confident that we would be alerted to our enemies. We had ridden ten miles when Alf drew my attention to the glow in the sky to the north of us. The fire had taken hold of the castle. Lord Alexander Keith would have to rebuild his home. It was then that I thought of my new foe. He had headed to Morpeth. It was now clear to me that he had used two columns to disguise his numbers. Would he know that his second conroi was lost? Had he headed south from Morpeth towards the New Castle? Both contained men he could use. Our lack of numbers meant that I dared not risk the more direct route. I would have to stick to my more circuitous route south and west. I knew that there would be few men that we would meet and, more importantly, we would outnumber any that we did.

We stopped to change horses at the Roman camp we had used. Masood and Aelric were both there waiting for us. We were close to Morpeth but the roads were not good ones and it was night. I counted on the acute senses of the archers to sniff out danger.

I used the time to speak with Sir Malcolm. "Tell me where you were headed."

"I will not offer you any more assistance. I gave my word not to escape. I will not become a traitor to my lord too."

I could have threatened him. I could have used torture but he was young. I did neither. I walked off to speak with Sir Thomas and Dick. "If this Lord Alexander headed for Morpeth and New Castle why did he send young Malcolm on the Felton road?"

Dick closed his eyes. I knew what he was doing. He was visualizing the road. He opened them. "Hexham. There is a garrison there. They were the ones who slew Sir Hugh Manningham. It is a good castle. There is nothing bigger for miles around. We still hold Barnard Castle. The only other strong garrison is at Carlisle and that is too far away then we must assume that the column was heading west. He was making for Hexham."

"And we have to cross the river west of there. That is too much of a risk."

"Then we must use a bridge and the only one that I know of is the one at the Roman fort, Corebricg. If it is not guarded it will shorten our journey home."

"How far away is it?"

He stroked his horse. We were changing to our own horses. "We will reach there not long after dawn."

"Then you and your archers shall be the vanguard. If you spy danger then I will use my men at arms and Sir Thomas to clear the enemy." We had found a great number of spears and Scottish lances. They were on sumpters. If the enemy formed ahead of us then we would use their own weapons against them.

Dick went to speak with our two scouts. We would now be travelling on a different path. In one way, it would be easier for there was a Roman Road which led south to Corebricg. On the other hand, we were more likely to meet enemy forces. The road south, whilst straight, rose and fell over small valleys and streams. It would be easier travelling along them at night. During the day, you risked reaching a crest and finding an enemy. As dawn broke we saw the thickly wooded hillsides. They were without either farms or animals. This area had still not recovered from the border wars.

King Henry and my father had much work to do in order to make it safer for people. It was a desolate and debatable land.

Masood and Aelric galloped back towards us. Dick stopped to speak with them and, as the archers slipped their bows from their backs, I knew that we had enemies ahead. I nudged Alciades forward. "What is it, Dick?"

"The bridge is a mile away, just over the crest of the hill. The Scots have men there. They have a temporary camp. I think it must be more men sent by Lord Alexander."

Aelric added, "I spied two banners, lord but most of the men were poorly armed."

"How many?"

"Thirty or forty. Masood here crept close," he smiled, "he told me their numbers by using his fingers."

We had made our decision and we now had to bear the consequences. I turned in the saddle. "I want the poorest of the Scottish horses unsaddling. Alf and Stephen, you need to tether the rest to your saddles. You will be at the rear. Break out the spears for the men at arms and Sir Thomas and me. Aelric, rejoin the archers. Dick, you take your archers and outflank them."

"What is your plan?"

"I intend to drive the spare horses towards them. If you can keep their flanks occupied then the horses will disrupt them and my handful of men at arms should be able to deal with them. You will follow afterwards."

He nodded approvingly, "Clever. I would not have thought of using the horses. Who knows, we may be able to recapture some on the other side."

"It matters not. They are a weapon and we shall use whatever we have to. Brother Peter, you and Ralph of Bowness will ride with the prisoners. Remember Sir Malcolm, you gave your word."

He nodded but I could see that he was regretting making that decision. Alf had sorted the horses out. We had twenty we would stampede. That left our two squires with five decent horses each. They would probably have the hardest job. Riding with a string of horses was never easy and if Scots were trying to kill you then it would be even harder.

"Jean de les Monts and Gurth son of Garth, I want you to drive the horses before you. You will not need spears. Follow the horses and you should break through. Secure the south side of the bridge."

"Aye lord."

That left four of us with spears. It was not a great number but we would fill the bridge and plough through any who remained. If we were lucky then the knights Aelric had seen would fall and, without leaders, the rest might panic. "Sir Thomas, John and Henry, our job is to make sure that the prisoners and our squires get through. We make a hole through which they can escape. Listen for my command to fall back across the bridge."

"Aye, lord!" Their voices were confident. I hoped that confidence was justified.

Dick waved and he led one column of archers east while Aelric led the rest, my archers, west. My two men at arms began to herd the horses forward. One rode on each side while the four of us held our spears before us to discourage the animals from returning north. I spurred Alciades and he gave a snort. It was a message to the lesser horses before him to move. Once they began to trot it became easier. Jean and Gurth used the flat of their swords to encourage them to run faster. Once they crested the top I saw the bridge and men ahead. The horses galloped faster for they were on the downhill section. It was a short gradient and then it flattened out. I saw that the men at the bridge had heard and seen our approach. There was activity as they sought arms and mail. It meant they were not looking east and west to their flanks. The danger lay along the road and that had their attention. I could not see my archers but I knew they would have one of their number holding their horses while they approached on foot.

I knew the archers were in position when men began to fall. They had been struck by arrows. They had found decent cover. The drumming of the horses' hooves on the cobbled Roman Road meant I could not hear what was being shouted some three hundred paces from us but it became obvious what it was when the Scots turned their shields to the new threat. As our stampeding herd closed with them I saw those on the bridge take evasive action and move from the obvious path of the animals. It caused disruption to the walls of shields and more men fell to Dick's arrows.

I pulled up my shield as the first of the horses thundered across the bridge. Two men hurled themselves into the river to avoid the deadly hooves. I saw Gurth son of Garth raise his sword and strike. When it rose above his head again I saw that it was bloody. I slowed down Alciades. Pulling back my arm I thrust my spear at the knight who came at me. He blocked it with his shield but it was a powerful blow and he was on a slope. He could not keep his balance and tumbled backwards into the river. I pulled back my arm and thrust into the gap he had left. My spear went into the side of a man at arms. As he fell his shield pulled a second man at arms into the river.

I turned as Brother Peter and the Scottish squire galloped across the bridge. Just then Sir Malcolm jerked his horse to a halt and shouted, "This is the son of..."

He got no further for Ralph of Bowness struck him across the side of his head with his fist and knocked the knight from his saddle. There was a sickening crunch as his head hit the parapet of the bridge. Even Brother Peter would not be able to save him. The Varangian galloped over the bridge followed by my squires. I thrust my spear at the man at arms who came at me with his spear. As mine struck him in the thigh his tore through the mitten on my right hand. I felt warm blood seeping.

"Back over the bridge!"

The other three all thrust at their opponents and then wheeled around to gallop across the bridge. I was the last one to cross. I turned on the other side and saw Dick, and all of our archers, gallop towards the enemy. They had their swords out. They vastly outnumbered the handful of men who remained standing and they thundered across unharmed. As I watched I saw that more than half of the Scots were in the river and were trying to extricate themselves. I knew that Dick and the archers could have forded the river for it was both wide and shallow. This was better. His last charge had disrupted the Scots even more. It would take them some time to reorganize. When they did they would send for help. Even more fortuitous was that six of their horses had joined the stampede. Jean and Gurth were calming them.

Ralph of Bowness rode to me, "I am sorry, lord. I had to silence him."

"I know. God has punished him for breaking his word. Still, we can now head to Barnard Castle and Sir Hugh. The Scots will not expect that!" I turned to Padraig. "Dismount."

He looked up at me, "You would kill me?"

I smiled, "No, but I am going to teach you a lesson. You will run. Move!" He started to run. "Masood, Henry and Jean follow him. Head south and west. Take the right fork. We will catch you up."

"Aye lord.

Dick and his archers arrived. "That went well, lord." He saw the torn mail. "You are wounded."

"It is nothing. Come, we head south and west."

"West?"

I smiled, "Trust me, Dick, I have not lost my senses. The Scots are watching. I want to fool them."

The archers each took a horse. They would not be fit for riding for a while but if we could give our own horses ten miles respite from carrying an armoured man it would help. We reached the fork in the road. One went south and east and the other south and west. Soon we were hidden in the woods which spread on both sides of the road. I galloped forward and found Padraig. He had not run far but the prodding spears of Henry and John had made him run faster than he expected. He was panting. He was a squire and more used to riding than running.

"Bind his hands behind his back and cover his eyes." If Henry was surprised by my words he said nothing. I dismounted and Alf held my horse. "Scot, I am going to let you go. You and Sir Malcolm have been too much trouble."

He could not speak for he was out of breath. He nodded his thanks. When he was bound and his eyes covered I pushed him before me and led him into the woods. When we were forty paces from the road I spun him around ten times and then slipped away, quietly. I remounted and we continued on the western road. After half a mile, we joined a small road that ran due east. Dick had told me of it. I held up my hand and led my men east. We walked. We were now heading in the direction of the valley. Hidden from the Scots on the bridge, Padraig would still be wandering around in the woods. He would eventually free himself and make his way back to the bridge. He would tell the men there that we were heading for Barnard Castle and, hopefully, the Scots would try to catch us. I was buying us time to get further south. This was our most dangerous time. We were less than four miles from the castle at Hexham.

When we rejoined the road south I waved Masood and Aelric forward and we increased our speed. In a perfect world, we would make it to Stockton in one march. We had spare horses and we could change but it was an unlikely outcome as we had almost fifty miles to cover and more than forty of those miles were in the hands of the Scots. Added to that were the thick black clouds which rolled in from the east. It was some years since I had lived in this part of the world but I knew that meant bad weather and, perhaps, even snow. We had to move south as fast as we could.

In the end, we just made Wolsingham and the hall of the Bishop of Durham before we had to halt. The blizzard had begun at the huddle of huts that lay five miles from the Bishop's estate. Durham was a few miles away but I still did not know if the Bishop could be trusted. I thought we could force our way through the blizzard but the snow was too deep for us and we barely made the welcoming light of the Bishop's hall.

The bishop had armed men there but they were no threat. There were but eight of them. The canon who was responsible for the estate welcomed us. It was a reserved welcome and he stressed that he was doing it for weary travellers. Clearly, he was not risking the ire of the Scots by giving us sanctuary. My father's name and the shields of Dick's archers had told him exactly who we were. Our horses needed the rest and, if I was to be honest with myself, my men needed it too. They had had little sleep and running battles since we had set out on our quest.

That night, as I ate with Ralph, my knights, squires and Brother Peter we talked of the events of the last few days. Ralph and Brother Peter argued, "I care not what you say, priest, the events were as a result of the Norns, the Weird Sisters!"

"Nonsense! It is God's hand I see in this."

Dick laughed, "It was Ralph's hand which struck the young knight and the Norns who decided to smack his head against the parapet or did your God intend him to die?"

Brother Peter was silenced briefly but he began again with robust arguments. Leaving them to it I said, "You know the weather better than I do. Will this affect our chances of making it home before the Scots catch us?" I was no fool. They would realise that we were heading for Stockton and not Barnard Castle. I hoped that the snow would delay the pursuit.

"I fear we will be stuck here for at least a day. The roads are not good around here and we would be foolish to leave the safety of the Bishop's hall and risk freezing to death on the road."

Sir Thomas frowned, "But will this not slow up the Scots too?"

Dick shook his head, "They will have this snow, even further east, but there the roads are better and the snow will be less thick. Lord Alexander is at the New Castle. He will be ahead of us soon enough and a delay of a day means we will have to fight him to return home."

Sir Thomas' face fell, "And we have just two knights, two squires and four men at arms."

I saw Dick's face darken. I said quickly, "Are you forgetting your father's comrades, Thomas? Our archers are more than the equal of a man at arms. They can use a bow and a sword." Ralph of Bowness and Brother Peter had stopped arguing to listen to us,

66

"Perhaps we should trust to God and not the Norns. Ralph's Weird Sisters have placed us in this predicament. Let us hope that God wishes us to be saved."

Chapter 7

We were stuck there the next day while the blizzard raged. It would have been foolish to move. The hall was warm and we had food. Even if the canon wished us to leave we could not. Our horses benefitted. There were feed and shelter. My men were able to recover. Brother Peter saw to our wounds. He applied salve to my hand. Ralph's eye looked angry when Brother Peter tended to it but, as he wore a patch, it was normally hidden. The food also helped the Varangian to recover. We had found his axe, mail and helmet at the castle of Warkworth. He had insisted upon wearing them despite the fact that I knew the helmet was uncomfortable. He had been struck on the head with a hammer. He was a hard man. We had recovered some of his goods too. He had arrived in England with the coin he had collected while serving the Emperor but Lord Alexander had taken a good half of it. The theft rankled. I had asked him what were his plans.

He looked a little discomfited at first and then smiled. He had lost a couple of teeth in his beating and his smile was somewhat lopsided. "You have always been honest with me and I will be the same. I would serve you or your father. I am no horseman but if you wish a wall defended or for someone to stand shield to shield then I am your man. I feel I owe these Scots something. I thought I had enough of fighting but since landing in England I have reconsidered. I am not yet ready to hang up my shield or take up the cross." He had flashed a grin at Brother Peter who was not put out in the least. "I think I can still fight." He shrugged, "You asked me…"

"And I will answer you. I will take you as my bondsman and welcome." If he gave me an oath then he would fight to the death for me. A warrior like Ralph would make a welcome addition to any conroi.

As we rode south and east on a cold, clear day, Ralph of
Bowness sang as we rode down the snow-covered road. The fact
that he had a new task made him happy. The song was a Varangian
marching song. I recognised some of the words. The snow had
stopped a frost had made the road hard if a little slippery. We took it
steadily.

Rather than being put off by the snow, Masood actually
welcomed it. He kept shaking his head as he grabbed handfuls of it,
"A man will never be thirsty in the country. There is always cool
water to drink. In my land, there is never enough water."

Henry son of Will laughed, "Now if it rained or snowed beer,
that would be something!"

John of Chester jibed, "You would never be sober!"

Henry sniffed, "And drunk or sober have I ever failed to do my
duty?"

John had to concede that he always did his duty, "But I could
live without the snoring and farting when you sleep drunk!"

"That is just nature's way of showing that I am content!"

Sir Thomas nudged his horse next to Dick and me, "I wish my
father could see what I have done, lord. I think that he would be
proud."

Dick smiled at my young knight, "I knew your father and I can
tell you that he would. You have achieved much. When we reach
Stockton, find yourself a wife and make a son. Call him Oswald and
it will be as though your father has never died."

He laughed, "Aye, Dick, I will!"

We had thirty miles or so to go but Dick and I had decided to
travel as far south as we could before turning east. We would be
further away from pursuit. I wondered if Lord Alexander would
dare to cross the Palatinate. It would risk angering the Bishop of
Durham. I hoped that King Henry would show the Bishop that he
was not like King Stephen had been. We needed a strong king to
make our borders strong. We had warriors like my father to defend
those borders but our enemies needed to know that the king himself
was willing to take action.

We had had to move at a steady and sedate pace. There was little
point in hurting our warhorses. We had already asked them to do
more than they ought. The clear skies and the fact that we were
moving along a Roman road made us easier to see. We had passed
the bishop's hall at Auckland and just emerged from the valley
heading for the Rushy Ford over the Woodham stream when Aelric
came racing back.

"Lord, there are banners ahead. You will see them soon enough."

I knew who they were but I needed confirmation. "Scots?"

"That would be my guess, lord. Sir Harold's home is many miles to the east and Sir Phillip far to the south. It is a small garrison at Gainford for Sir Hugh is still at Barnard Castle. It is a mighty host, with many banners."

"And they have seen us?"

"Against the white snow, you stand out, lord. "

"Go and fetch Masood. He can do nothing where he is." As Aelric galloped off I looked around. There was a slight incline before us and I had seen, as the archer trotted off, that his horse found it difficult to gain purchase. "Dick, what say we make a stand here?"

"It is likely to be a last stand for they will outnumber us."

I turned. There were trees forty paces behind us and the slope was steeper there. "If my men at arms, knights and squires block the road, our archers could use the trees for cover. I will not surrender and, who knows, Brother Peter's God might save us."

Ralph of Bowness said, "And the weird sisters might still have a hand in this."

Snorting the Bishop shook his head, "And you call yourself a Christian!"

"I have seen many strange things, Brother and they cannot all be explained away easily. I think it is a good plan. If we are to die then let us make them bleed eh?" Ralph would be able to fight with the good earth beneath his feet. That was the way of the housecarl.

Dick nodded, as did Sir Thomas, "Then let us go back but we will walk. I would not have us hurt our horses."

Once we reached the trees the horses were taken into the woods and tethered. Ralph chose some of the spare spears and made a barrier to our flank. He rammed the hafts into the earth. The snow meant it was not rock hard. It would deter an enemy. Masood and Aelric rode back, "There are sixty of them, lord. I recognised the banner. It is Lord Alexander. They have ten knights with banners."

"Archers?"

He grinned, "No lord."

"Then you two join the other archers." I turned to Alf, "Find a prominent place and plant my banner. Let the Scots see the gryphon. They will learn to fear it as they fear my father's sign!"

"Aye, lord!" There was a drift of snow and, after piling more there, Alf jammed the banner in so that it fluttered above our heads. He packed more snow around it to make it firm.

The road was wide enough for four men. Sir Thomas, Ralph, Brother Peter and myself stood in the first rank. Stephen and Alf were in the second with spare spears. Next to them were John and Henry. The other two, Jean and Gurth, were in the third rank. They would replace the ones who fell. Brother Peter hefted the borrowed shield. He stood on the left next to Ralph. I had Sir Thomas next to me and I planted my sword in the ground. If I needed to draw it then it would be quicker. I raised my spear, "This is for the Earl of Cleveland, the Warlord of the North! If we stand firm then no one can defeat us!"

Amazingly, my men banged their spears against the shields and their swords against the trees. I had never fought such great odds but, with these men with me, we could not fail. I donned my helmet and we faced our foes.

The Scots had seen us and our numbers. Even though the trees hid my archers they would have seen them riding up the road. Even so, Lord Alexander came along confidently. He had seen but three banners. He had three times the number of knights. He had his knights arrayed in a line ten wide. All of his knights were in the front rank. Behind them came the squires. A few horsemen were behind but there did not appear to be many. Not many were mailed. Half their number were on foot.

Masood was in a tree, perched like some monkey or bird and he shouted, "Lord, there is another banner and more men coming behind them. I counted forty!"

Just as I had begun to believe that we had a chance my hopes had been dashed. Sixty men we might have held, but a hundred? It would be hard. Lord Alexander made his second mistake when he was three hundred paces from us. He spurred his horse and the twenty odd horsemen began to ride faster. The ground was icy and some horses slipped and slithered. His line became ragged. A line of horses worked best when they attacked together. The speed was not important, it was the cohesion that counted. The ragged line drew within bow range.

We had only twenty-one archers but they were the finest in any land. I heard Dick roar, "Draw!"

His next command was a death sentence. "Release!"

Twenty-one arrows flew and, in the time it took to draw breath, another twenty-one flew closely followed by a third. Even while the third flight was in the air they were drawing again. The weather affected the flights but, even so, it was devastating. All twenty-one arrows hit something. Some struck shields. Others hit the rumps and

71

flanks of horses. Some hit mail. It was only those which hit shields that did no damage. My men had arrows that were not barbed. They were intended to penetrate mail and they did so. Two knights and three squires along with two men at arms were plucked from their saddles. Six more arrows hit the men on foot who laboured up the slippery slope. The next flight was even more devastating as knights, squires and men at arms fell and failed to protect their neighbours. They had lost their cohesion and the protection of a neighbour's shield.

Ralph snorted, "This man is a fool! I knew it when I spoke to him!"

As if to confirm his words Lord Alexander stood in his saddle and exhorted his men to ride faster. The next flights of arrows struck more men. The horses slipped and slid on the ice. Had they gone slower they might have made more progress. Lord Alexander bore a charmed life. Arrows struck his shield but did him no harm.

Our archers continued to rain death. Their rate of arrows would slow but each arrow brought death or a wound to someone and that gave us hope.

Then Masood's voice came like a crack of thunder, "Lord, more men are coming along the road from the south. I count ten banners!"

There was no point in speaking. Ten banners meant another fifty or so men at least. We had to hold on. There was no other choice. The riders had been thinned. There were now five knights and six squires labouring up the road towards us. They were not in one line. I could leave the archers to deal with the men following. We had to kill as many of these knights, squires and men at arms as we could.

"Brace and lock!" With a round shield amongst our long heart-shaped shields, that would be difficult but with spears rammed against our feet and shields touching we were ready. My squires and men at arms had their spears level with ours. They lay over our shoulders to protect us from the enemy. We would have more power but it would present a barrier which horses would not like. It was not Lord Alexander who reached us first. A young lord, eager for glory, slithered and slipped towards us. Brother Peter's spear took the horse in the throat and Ralph rammed his spear at the knight. It penetrated his chest. Horse and rider reared and fell. For the Scots, it was a disaster. The horse slipped down the slope and took out two squires and their horses as they tumbled down the slick and slippery road. Unable to protect themselves my archers' arrows ended their lives. I thrust my spear at a second knight. I was lucky. The horse's neck and the cantle guided the spear into the gut of the knight. He did not die immediately but, as I withdrew the intestine wrapped spear head, I knew that he was dead.

I saw Lord Alexander throw his spear at Ralph of Bowness who contemptuously batted it aside. Then stopping, the Scottish lord raised his shield and shouted, "For the glory of Scotland! On!" He was willing to let his men bleed on our spears so long as they held us and then his next two waves would finish us off.

As Sir Thomas slew another knight I began to hope that, despite the odds, we might win. From behind me, I heard Dick shout, "Rear archers turn! We are attacked!"

"Jean, Henry and Gurth, turn and face the foe!" We were being attacked from two sides. It was all over.

The Scots facing us only had two knights left and six squires in their front rank. We had already killed more than I might have hoped. The ones on foot had little armour. Only one man at arms remained on a horse. However, there were reinforcements coming, even I could see the knight bringing the next wave of Scots to assail us and the banners of the third wave were a blur in the distance. We would have to endure another two bands of warriors. Could we survive? Every bone in my body thought that we were going to die.

Sir Thomas struck his spear at a knight who was eager to get to me. His spear penetrated the Scot's thigh and his horse's side. Even as the horse fell sideways the last knight on that flank rammed his spear towards Sir Thomas. I saw it hit his shoulder. At the same moment, one of the squires reared his horse. Just as Stephen, Sir Thomas' squire, speared the horse, the Scot's spear struck my knight in the face. The spear head went into his eye and then his skull. Watching his body fall I knew that he was dead. His squire, Stephen, was beside himself. He extracted his spear and then rammed it into the belly of the squire who had killed his master. As the spear was torn from his grasp he drew his sword and, disobeying all orders, hurled himself at the Scots. He ran at them flailing his sword like a berserker of old.

"Alf!"

We had a hole in our front rank and it needed filling. My squire stepped into the gap left by my knight and his squire. I watched Stephen as he hacked through the leg of the last man at arms. He raged like a man possessed, screaming curses, and then the men on foot fell upon poor Stephen. A spear took him in the chest and then he was butchered before our eyes. The Scots hacked and chopped at a body already dead.

The enemy warriors were still falling to my archers' arrows but there were fewer of their deadly missiles and they were falling more slowly. Before us was a wall of dead horses, knights and squires. The enemy would struggle to force through them. "Lord! We need help!"

Jean de les Monts did not ask for help unnecessarily. "Henry, go to their aid!"

"Aye, lord!" We now had a perilously thin line to face the next attack. We would not hold against fresh warriors.

Lord Alexander seemed to bear a charmed life. His shield appeared to be covered in arrows yet he and his horse were unharmed. He was directing his men forward. He urged them to get to me! His reinforcements had reached us. I saw the next knight and his men were now pressing against the men on foot who laboured up the slope. I rammed my spear into the face of the first Scotsman on foot. It hit his unarmoured chest and, even as he died, he pulled the spear from my grasp. Alf was no longer there to pass me another and I drew my sword. I saw that only Alf still had his spear. Ralph of Bowness was swinging his axe before him and men were afraid to face him. Brother Peter was besmirched with blood and he held his sword before him. Sheer weight of numbers meant that it was only a matter of time.

One Scot, eager to take the head of a knight swung his two-handed sword wildly at me. I dropped to one knee and, as the sword slid over my head, rammed my blade into his middle. He had a surprised expression. As I rose I punched his dying body and he fell against the men ascending the slope. The blood had made the slope even slicker. I took advantage of the fact that they could not approach rapidly and I swung my sword sideways in a long sweep. I was lucky or perhaps Ralph's Norns intervened. My sword hacked into the side of one warrior and his dying fall allowed my blade to tear across the unguarded throat of a second. Alf, Ralph and Brother Peter seemed to bear charmed lives. Perhaps it was because they were so much better than the men they faced. Whatever the reason all who came close to the four of us died. The ground before us was a sea of blood and guts. The greatest danger would be in weapons blunted by so much fighting. Each time we used a sword it became less sharp. Eventually, we would be wielding iron bars. I had two daggers in my belt and right boot. If my sword would not cut then I would use a dagger. I watched as Ralph hooked his axe head around the edge of a Scot's shield and, pulling it forward, smashed the boss of his shield into the warrior's face. The man was rendered unconscious. As he fell to the floor, Ralph swung his axe before him and then stamped on the man's windpipe.

Any hopes that we had a reprieve were dashed when I felt pressure on my back. It was John of Chester. "Lord, Jean de les Monts is dead and Gurth son of Garth wounded. We are hard-pressed."

"Then, this day we die, but we die with honour! No surrender!" I lifted my sword and raised it so that all men could see that it was bloody and it was notched. I was my father's son and I would not be taken as a trophy to be paraded before the King of Scotland. They would have to hack my bloody sword from my dead hand. I would yield it to no man.

Beside me, Alf renewed his attack. His mighty strength slew two even as I brought my own blade down to smite a Scot and split his head in twain. My men all cheered and roared. I prepared to meet my maker. My father would care for my family and I had redeemed myself. It was wyrd!

The Welsh Marches

Part Two

Alfraed

Chapter 8

I had thought the coronation had gone well. Henry and Eleanor had looked magnificent and there had been cheers aplenty. All of the lords present swore an oath of fealty to the King. Henry had ensured that all of the Earls, Counts and Dukes were present. He wanted no dissenting voices to mar his new reign. I was looking forward to going home and, having received word that my son, William was coming home, I was desperate to head north and to greet him.

Had I been an ordinary knight I might never have overheard the treason. I had been trained well and I had a useful ability, I could move silently. After the coronation, we had returned to the White Tower where I had been afforded accommodation. I was alone. I had not brought my squire, James and so I was heading to my chambers. I wished to change from the mail I had worn to the coronation. As I climbed the stairs I heard voices at the landing ahead and, recognising the king's brother, Geoffrey, speaking, I stopped. Geoffrey had attempted to abduct Eleanor when she had been travelling to meet with Henry. I had thwarted the attempt but, although he and Henry were reconciled, I did not trust him. I paused on the stairs and I listened. Many would have said that was not honourable. Where Henry was concerned I would do anything I could to keep him safe. After all, he was my son. I recognised Geoffrey's voice. He had a sulky tone and, to my mind, whined. He had not got that from his mother and I suspected he was more like his father and grandfather. The other voice I did not recognise. It was a Norman one. The accent was clear.

"Lord, the time is right. There are many in Anjou who would support your claim. It is right that we have a Count of Anjou. Why should that not be you?"

"Do not underestimate my brother, Charles. He has the support of that devil, the Earl of Cleveland. Many men have thought that they could neutralise him but all have failed."

"He will return home to his northern lands soon and if not then a knife in the night might end his threat. If we take a ship in the next day or so then we will steal a march on everyone. We could be in Anjou. The lords there have not sworn an oath."

"They are already bound to my brother as Count of Anjou."

"Yet your father told you that you were to be Count. You are merely taking your birth right which was stolen from you."

"You talk treason."

"No, lord, for the County of Anjou is your due. I do not speak for myself alone. Theobald of Blois would also support your claim!"

"Even though he held me, hostage, last year?"

"A mistake, lord. He would be a powerful ally. The County first and then... who knows. There are others who wish to see you rule in Anjou. Trust me, lord, to guide your path."

There was silence and I wondered if I should move. I wondered what else I might hear.

"I will think on this. I will speak with you after the feast this night. I commit to nothing. I wish to keep my head upon my shoulders."

I heard footsteps and they receded. They were not coming down my corridor. I turned around the top of the stairs and headed for my room. I would speak with Henry when I could get him alone. The only person around him whom I truly trusted was his wife Eleanor. His brother William was also trustworthy but he had been left in Anjou. I wondered if his life was also in danger.

The feast that night was a relatively small affair. Henry had invited only those who would support him. The Church was heavily represented. The Archbishop of Canterbury, the Bishop of London and the young priest who was highly thought of, Thomas Becket were there. They held power. It had been the church who had thwarted his mother's attempts to have the throne. I suppose I was the most powerful lord who was present. After all, I had been the one who had never lost a battle against Stephen and his supporters. I was the bane of the Scots too. Sadly, most of the other lords who had supported the Empress were now dead or retired to priories. The war had gone on for longer than many lifetimes. My position as the king's key advisor was shown by my place at his table and close by his wife, Eleanor. I had brought her from France to marry the future king and Henry trusted me with her.

As we ate I saw the resentment on Geoffrey's face. It had been hidden during the coronation. Having heard his words, I now watched like a hawk. Although he had been forgiven by his brother I saw that Geoffrey was not satisfied with the arrangement. I wondered why he had come to the coronation. I answered myself as soon as the thought entered my head. He wished to allay any suspicions from his brother and he was looking for whatever he could get. Looking around the tables I could not see a Norman called Charles. I had looked around the hall when the knights had entered but I saw none I did not recognise. The fact that I did not know this, Charles, was not a surprise. I had spent most of the war in England. My son, William, might know him.

I saw Geoffrey leave towards the end of the feast and before the entertainment. He spoke briefly with Henry and then left. He did not speak with me. He just flashed me an irritated glance.

"You are quiet tonight, my lord."

Eleanor of Aquitaine was an astute woman. She had been married to the King of France and had survived many intrigues at that court. She knew how to read people. She was the best woman Henry could have married. Older than him, she was able to control some of his wilder tendencies. She was a thoughtful woman.

I smiled, "I am anxious to get home, your majesty. Despite the peace the king made with them I do not trust the Scots. They still have large swathes of English land and many English women and children are still Scottish slaves. Now that I am no longer needed here I would defend the north again."

She lowered her voice, "There is still danger here, my lord. I do not trust some of those who now smile at my husband. I am always more comfortable when you are by his side."

"I am an old man now, my lady. It is time for the younger knights to stand by the king."

"Men like your son perhaps?"

"I have had a message that he returns from the Holy Land. He got on well with Henry's father. But I am selfish. He has been away for some years. I would spend time with him. But I agree with you, your majesty, there is danger here. I will speak with you and the king when time allows."

She raised her eyebrows but our conversation ended for there was entertainment. A troubadour sang a dreary song in praise of Henry. It was flattering and was composed by someone who did not know him. The acrobats who were followed were more entertaining for at least they had talent. When the evening finished I waited until the king and the queen were ready to head to their chamber. Henry smiled, "Good night, old friend. I am glad you stayed for the entertainment."

Before I could reply Eleanor said, quietly, "I think the Earl has something he wishes to say to you in private, husband."

Henry was quick. "Then come to our chamber. That is as private as anywhere."

There were two of Henry's bodyguards on the door. Phillip and William knew me well. I had stood in a shield wall with both of them. Once inside I told Henry of what I had overheard.

My words made Eleanor frown. I saw Henry considering what I had said. "Of course, you did not see my brother. He would deny it if I confronted him." I nodded. "This Charles, it maybe he is Charles of Alençon. The people there have always hated my family ever since my great grandfather had the hands cut off those who opposed him. He was not at the feast tonight. I wonder where he was?" He nodded and then slapped his right hand against his left palm. "I will keep Geoffrey close by me. William is watching Anjou for me. I trust my little brother. And he has men such as your Sir Leofric to aid him." He smiled. "I take it you do not relish going to Anjou for me?"

"No, your majesty. My son is on his way home and I would see him."

"I think I will have Charles of Alençon brought to me. I will question him."

"It may not be him."

I saw, that night, coldness in Henry's eyes. He had grown since he had served as my squire. He now showed that he could be ruthless. "I did not invite him to the coronation. I will ask him why he travelled from Normandy. It is not unreasonable. If he has nothing to hide then I will find out. If on the other hand, he has treason in his heart…"

I slept a little easier having told the king of my suspicions. However, when I met Eleanor the next morning she had a worried look upon her face. "Where is the king, your majesty?"

"He has taken men to seek Charles of Alençon. He rose early and went to seek him. Somehow the knight must have heard he was being sought and he fled." She paused.

"He should have woken me. Hunting men is something I have done before."

There was little point in following now. They could have gone anywhere. There were many ways out of England. He might have had a ship at Dover, Southampton or even London itself. He might not even have fled the country. There were still many of Stephen's supporters who would hide the Norman.

The king returned at noon and was in a foul mood. "He had a ship waiting for him east of the city. He has fled. His flight is evidence of his guilt."

"Will you follow, your majesty?"

He shook his head. "We have too much to do in England. I know, lord, that you wish to see your son but I need you with me when we go to deal with Welsh. They have encroached on my lands."

"And the Scots too, majesty."

"And that is why I propose that we ride to your castle. It will be a royal progress and I can display my standard at Oxford, Lincoln, York and then the borders. I would have the Scots know I am coming. You know this new King Malcolm do you not?"

"Aye, your majesty. Not as well as his father, Prince Henry but I know him. He is young: perhaps no more than fourteen. He studied warfare. Prisoners I took told me that he was very studious. His father had skills in strategy. At the Battle of the Standard, he almost took the day. He is, however, inexperienced. This would be a good time to meet with him."

His brother Geoffrey begged to be allowed to stay in London. The king agreed and put him in charge of the White Tower. I know why he did it. He was giving Geoffrey some power to see if he could handle it and to prove his loyalty. It was a mistake. I did not trust him and I did not like the idea but, equally, I was keen to return home to be there when my son finally arrived. I did not press the matter and that proved to be a mistake. They say that when you look back you have perfect vision. Perhaps that is so. I did not know that Geoffrey would take me away from my son, again.

The journey north began in the heartland of the Empress's supporters, the Thames Valley. When we headed up to Lincoln it was nostalgic for me. Lincoln had seen our greatest victory over Stephen. But for the Empress's brother making a misjudgement at

Winchester the war could have ended then and the Empress been crowned queen. The castle was now back in the king's hands and I was delighted to find the widow of the Earl of Chester there. Maud was the Empress' niece and as valiant and doughty an ally as any warrior. She had held Lincoln for us. Ill served by her husband who had been murdered she had shown her resilience by keeping Lincoln safe for her cousin.

"I am pleased to see you here, my lady but wonder why you are not in your Castle at Chester?"

"I am on my way there. I came to London with my son for the coronation. We did not stay for the feast." There might have been a criticism that the king had not invited her but Henry's cousin was the most loyal of subjects. She understood the politics of the land.

She and Eleanor got on well and we stayed there longer than I would have liked. I was anxious to get home but the king and his wife enjoyed the company and the stories the countess told. In many ways, it proved propitious for a messenger caught up with us there and told us that Geoffrey had taken ship for Anjou. He had waited a day and then fled. Perhaps it had all been planned that way and Charles had been arranging passage. Henry was angry. Like me, he felt that his brother had now made the decision to begin the road to treason.

"I thank God that my little brother holds the fortress of Angers for me. We have time to deal with Malcolm and then go to Anjou."

My heart sank, "And the Welsh?"

"They can wait. We need to quash this rebellion in the bud. I have sent word to William to detain Geoffrey but I think Geoffrey is too clever to risk incarceration. He and William have never got on. However, I must continue through my land for I want all to see their new king."

The message proved the spur for us to move speedily. As we passed each major town and castle, Nottingham, Sheffield and the like, peasant and noble cheered the king. For the peasants, they were just pleased to be without war. They could plant their crops and rear their animals. When we reached York, we stopped a little longer than at the other towns. York was a bastion against the Scots. Since they had been given Carlisle by Stephen they no longer had to cross the Tees. They had learned to avoid me.

We left the city in a buoyant mood for both church and noble, peasant and freeman had welcomed us. We were heading north past the sites of the many battles I had fought against Stephen when we were ambushed. King Henry had brought ten of his household knights and twenty men at arms. It should have been enough but he had no archers and no scouts out. It was I who spotted the ambush. I was riding next to William of Le Havre, one of Henry's bodyguards and we were approaching the village of Craythorne, not far from Yarm. The road through the forest was not particularly straight. It followed the contours of the land and the village lay just off the York road. It was but a handful of huts and the families who lived there were charcoal burners and foresters. When you have fought as long as I have then you develop senses you do not even know you have. We had passed the village of Appleton not long since and I had been greeted by the villagers who had recognised my surcoat. They had cleared and now farmed the land on either side of the road. It was an open area but, a mile or two ahead was the forest which lay to the south of Yarm. I glanced back and saw that the queen's women and the servants were dallying. We had watered our horses but they had dismounted and, unlike the men at arms who watched them, were slow to mount.

William and I had drawn perhaps thirty paces ahead when I felt the hairs on the back of my neck prickle. You learned to trust such warnings. I peered ahead to the forest. There was no smoke coming from the charcoal burners. Of course, only I would have known that there were charcoal burners there. But they kept their fires going all the time. If this had been my men then Dick and his archers would have already been in the woods. They would have sought out the charcoal burners.

I slowed up.

"Lord?"

"Something is not right."

William of le Havre peered ahead, "It seems quiet, lord. We are close to the castle of Sir Tristan."

"There are no fires burning and there should be. See there are no birds ahead. I fear a trap. If it is one then let us see if you and I can set it off."

We urged our horses on. A good scout was always well ahead of the main group. I saw the road bend and climb ahead. If I was right and there was danger then that would be the perfect place. Our horses would be going slower and they could have prepared any number of traps. I said, quietly, to William of Le Havre. "Have your weapon ready. I suspect danger."

He knew me well enough to trust me. I turned and donned my helmet. Henry was busy talking to Eleanor but Phillip of Aix attracted his attention and pointed to me. When I lifted my shield, the king nodded. Phillip of Aix moved to flank the queen so that she had two shields to protect her. The horse I rode was not one of my horses. He was one of the king's. I preferred my own for they were clever beasts who could almost read my mind. My helmet was open-faced. It was not my war helmet with the mask but it would do.

I turned to William. "Let us ride and see if this is an ambush." "Aye Warlord."

I drew my sword as I spurred the chestnut up the road. As we turned and the trees seemed to reach above us and make a canopy I saw the logs which had been hewn and laid across the road. "Ambush!" Turning to William I shouted, "Follow me!"

The ambushers expected us to turn and run back to the main column some fifty paces behind us. I glanced ahead and saw metal that indicated helmets, spears and swords. They thought we would be afraid. I would not oblige them. I dug in my spurs and headed right. Our shields protected us and the arrows that suddenly flew from the woods hit our shields. This was a hunting forest. The foresters had kept the undergrowth cleared. Tristan of Yarm enjoyed his hunting. It meant we could ride faster that way. As arrows thudded into my shield I whipped my horse's head around and rode at the archers who were busy drawing another arrow. They were not as good as my archers and were too slow. I swept my sword sideways and it bit deep into the neck of one archer. William of Le Havre brought his sword down on the head of another.

I counted six more archers and, closer to the road, the metal of helmets and men at arms or knights. Henry's household knights and men at arms, forewarned were now galloping up both sides of the forest. Henry and Phillip of Aix would be guarding the queen. Although there were just two of us the archers were terrified. They were not locals. If they had been they would have known the forest better. They would have prepared hides for themselves. A horse can run down a man on foot easily. A knight with a good sword can strike with impunity. One archer lost his arm as he raised it to protect his head. Another fell beneath the hooves of my horse and the others were hacked and slashed by William and me.

When we looked up I saw men at arms led by a knight riding towards us. They wore a dark green surcoat and their shields were painted black. There was no way to identify their lord.

Behind us, a voice shouted, "We are coming, Warlord!" The forest was not the place for battles between knights. There is not enough space. You need fast reactions and even faster hands. You

84

cannot gallop and you must watch the ground. The first man at arms who galloped towards me had a spear. It was the wrong weapon. In his eagerness to get at me he lunged and found the tip of his spear caught up in a branch. Instead of coming towards me, it rose in the air as his horse continued galloping. I held my sword horizontally and my blade almost cut him in two.

The ambush had failed but that did not mean that we were out of danger. I had no idea how many men were in the forest. I realised that there was a danger that the king and queen could be attacked as they were isolated. Henry's knights and men at arms were bent on killing as many enemies as they could. I reined in my horse and turned left. It was fortuitous that I did so. A knight's spear suddenly appeared and thrust into the space I would have occupied had I not turned. I hacked down with my sword and chopped through the ash shaft. I pulled back on the reins and my horse reared. The movement made my enemy's horse flinch and it turned from me. I swung my sword hard into his back. He was moving away and I did not manage to inflict as much force as I might have wished. Even so, off-balance and hurt by my strike he fell from his horse.

"William, with me. The king needs us!"

"Aye lord."

I spurred my horse back to the road. The sounds of combat filled the woods. The road, however, was empty. I cantered down the road. I saw, just beyond the pile of logs that Phillip and Henry were having to fight off a knight and five men at arms. They were hampered as they had to protect the queen. I spurred my horse and galloped. I could not afford the time to go around the logs and so I trusted the horse and made him jump. It was a risk for I did not know how good he was at jumping. I was lucky for his rear hooves caught the top of the logs but he did not fall.

Our momentum crashed us into the back of two horses. I swung my sword and punched with my shield. I used my knees to guide the horse. My sword cut through the mail of one man at arms and, coming away bloody, I raised it to finish him. I had no need for he slid from his horse. The other man at arms struggled to hold on to his reins and I was able to slide my sword under his arm. It rose through his neck. I tore it out and was sprayed with his blood. The King and Philip of Aix were doing their best but, had we not arrived then things might have gone ill. As it was disaster almost struck when one of the men at arms took advantage of the King and Philip moving apart. The man at arms darted in and grabbed Eleanor's reins. The two horses of the men we had just slain blocked my path.

As the queen's horse was jerked to the side I saw her reach into her belt, pull out a long dagger and plunge it into the neck of the man at arms. He put his hand to the wound and turned in surprise that a queen would have had a knife. Then he tumbled from his horse.

"Philip, William, guard the King and Queen." The immediate danger to King Henry and his bride was gone but our knights and men at arms were now chasing the assassins through the woods. I saw that the women and servants had stopped. Their guards had joined the chase. I cupped my hands and shouted, "Fetch the women and the baggage here! You will be safer."

"Who are they, Warlord?"

I shook my head. "I know not." I dismounted and picked up one of the black shields. "They are trying to hide their identity. I do not recognise the surcoats. They were chosen to help them hide in the woods. It was a sizeable ambush."

"Then they are not bandits or brigands?"

"Bandits and brigands do not wear mail and they would not be foolish enough to attack the King and the Warlord this close to his home.

"Scots perhaps?"

"Perhaps. We need a prisoner."

Just then the first of the knights and men at arms began to canter back towards us. They came in ones and twos from both sides of the road. Some led their horses. Other horses stood forlornly in the eaves. Some were the enemy horses but some were ours. We had lost men in the attack. That was not a surprise.

"If we ride to the logs we can remove them. We are not far from Yarm. I would hasten there with all speed."

The women were weeping and wailing, Eleanor turned, "You are not hurt, not even close to being harmed. Compose yourselves."

Henry said, "The dagger was propitious, my love."

"After your brother tried to abduct us I thought it a handy weapon to bring."

Henry suddenly turned to me, "Could this be the handiwork of Geoffrey?"

"If so, lord, it is a bold move and a dangerous one." I shrugged. There was nothing to be gained by wondering. A prisoner would tell us more. "There is little point in idle speculation."

When we reached the logs and as the men at arms collected the loose horses, I had the wooden barrier removed by the servants. I remembered the young knight I had knocked from his horse. I waved forward Sir Richard Osbourne. He had served Henry a long time and was a reliable knight, "Come with me, Richard, there is a prisoner we can question."

"Aye lord. They were tough men. We lost four men at arms in the chase."

"How many were there, do you think?"

"I counted at least eight archers and twenty men at arms. I did not see many knights. I was in the western side of the woods." He pointed to the archers I had slain. If we add these then the number rises. They had no livery and are not men of honour."

The knight's horse had not strayed far from the fallen knight and its movement guided me to it. The knight still lay on the ground. I thought him dead but, as we dismounted, he opened his eyes. He did not try to move.

"Who are you? Who sent you to ambush us?"

He closed his eyes and I was not certain he had heard me, "I had heard that the Warlord was old. I saw the chance for glory. I would be the knight who slew King Henry's Champion. I would end the life of King Stephen's bane."

"Who sent you?"

"You have killed me, lord. My back is broken. I cannot feel my legs and already I see death on my shoulder. I will tell you nothing. If you are the honourable knight all men speak of you will put my dagger to my lips so that I may kiss the cross before I die."

"It is a mortal sin to kill a king." I dismounted.

He gave a thin laugh, "Thanks to you, lord, we did not commit that sin and we did not try to murder. I will go to heaven for I am no traitor."

I slid his dagger from his scabbard and placed it on his lips. "I could tell your family where you are buried."

"I have lost my family, lord. My name dies with me and my lips are…" His eyes glazed over. He died and he retained his honour. But his death left us with a question. Who had sent him?

"He was brave, lord."

"He was and we know one thing. He is neither Scots nor English. He is Angevin. I think I know who was behind this."

Chapter 9

Sir Tristan was not in his castle. It was dark when we arrived. Although we were not far from my castle I did not want to risk running into the survivors of the ambush. His seneschal, Ralph of Wiske was pleased to see us as his wife hurried to clear chambers for the King and Queen. "Your son is returned, lord. He, and his family, recently arrived back in England. He visited all of your knights to tell them and he invited them to a feast, some days since."

"Good." My voice was calm but inside my heart was beating quickly. I would see my son. He had a family! All that I wanted to do was to ride through the dark to my home. I could not do so for I had a duty to the King. We had lost men.

"Ralph, we were ambushed. In the woods close by Craythorne there are dead men. Tomorrow, have the mail collected and their bodies buried. You had best check to see if the charcoal burners were slain or merely hid."

"Aye lord. Had Sir Tristan not been away he might have ridden a patrol. I have failed in my duty."

"You were not to know and besides you might have lost more men that way for this was a sizeable force."

That evening the King and Queen dined with me on plain fare. The small castle was overcrowded but we had managed to find a corner where we could eat alone. I told them what I had worked out. "He was Angevin, lord. I think that your brother and his friend Charles have a hand in this. They were not Scots and I do not think that they were Stephen's warriors. Besides he gifted the crown to you. Your enemies lie closer to your home. They knew where we were going. Your brother had to have told them that for Charles could not have known."

Henry still did not like to believe his brother was a traitor. "We travelled slowly. Our enemies would know where we were heading by our progress."

I saw Henry was worried. Eleanor looked to me, "You are my husband's most senior knight. What do you suggest, lord?"

I was torn. There was an answer I ought to give and one I wanted to give. "You need to go to Anjou and end the threat. You could take a ship from Stockton and be in Anjou within the week. Word will take longer to reach those who ordered this. The survivors will be hunted down. I will set Sir Tristan and Sir Richard to find them."

"And the Scots?"

I sighed, "My son is returned. He can be trusted, I think."

"You have not seen him for some years, Warlord."

I looked at Henry, "I know my son. He has my blood in his veins. He came home and that means he has atoned. Why else would he return to England?"

Eleanor put her hand on mine, "And we will be taking you away from him before you can spend time with him. You are making sacrifices even when we have the crown."

I forced a smile, "I swore an oath, my lady. I keep my word. Besides, I do not think that these would-be rebels will give us too many problems. Your husband is a skilful general. Geoffrey and his friend have spent more time plotting than fighting. They are not his equal. There will be time."

I felt safer when we left the tiny wooden walls of Yarm to head along the south bank of the Tees to the ferry. We could have risked the river at Yarm. However, Eleanor's ladies had proved already that they were not as hardy as the queen. The greenway along the river was not pleasant at this time of year. The frosts and snows had not come and made the ground hard for it was wet and without frosts. With the warmth had come rain and, in places, the track was a muddy morass. Our horses were besmirched and bespattered. I had tired of travelling long ago. The journey home had taken far longer than I would have liked. I yearned for the familiarity of my castle and my people.

I could have gone to Thornaby Castle to speak with Sir Wulfric but as soon as I saw the standard flying over my castle I knew that I would cross the river first. I was becoming selfish as I grew older. Sir Wulfric would have understood. As we waited for the ferry I realised that there were no ships tied up at the quay. We had a couple of ships we used. Where were they, I wondered?

It was Harry who brought the ferry. He was the youngest of Ethelred's sons. He would have to make two journeys. The King, Queen and her ladies boarded first along with me. As we were pulled across the chilly Tees I said, "Is my son at home? I am anxious to see him."

"No, lord. Scots raided Fissebourne. He took your knights and half of the garrison to recapture the animals and slaves the Scots took."

I looked at Henry, "I told you, your majesty, that the Scots are still a threat."

Henry frowned, "So it seems. And there are no ships to take us to Anjou. It looks as though we will have an enforced stay here then, Alfraed."

Eleanor said, quietly, "It is not the earl's fault, husband. This looks like a comfortable castle. What difference can a few days make? Your people have been taken. The earl's son has acted well." He nodded but I could see that he was distracted by the events which had occurred since his coronation.

My steward greeted us as we stepped ashore, "You have heard, lord, of the raid?"

I nodded, "William, have my chambers made ready for the King and Queen. We need room for the Queen's ladies."

"Lord, we have the wives of some of your knights. The castle is crowded."

Eleanor put her hand on Henry's, "Then we shall have a convivial time, will we not?"

William said, before turning and scurrying up to the castle, "I will tell Alice and the Lady Rebekah."

Eleanor linked Henry as we walked towards the river gate. I saw Henry casting a military eye over the walls, "This is a stoutly built castle, Alfraed. You have improved it since I was last here."

"As this last raid has proven we need stout defences against the Scots. They still hold much English land."

We entered the gate, "And yet I have a rebellion in Anjou to quash. I had thought that the crown upon my head secured all."

"Keeping the crown and the throne are never easy. Your mother thought she had both after Lincoln."

"You are right. A lesson for us all. Until we have strong borders and more knights like you guarding them we cannot rest easy."

We stepped into my hall and I saw William's wife and his children for the first time. His first wife had been a beauty but that was eclipsed by Rebekah. She was exotic. Her deep-set eyes exuded calmness. The two children were both hale and hearty. I saw the boy staring at me. I had not had much to do with William's first children. I would make sure I got to know these two grandchildren.

She bowed, "Your majesty, my lord, I am Lady Rebekah, the wife of Sir William. This is your grandson, lord, Samuel and your granddaughter, Ruth." She put a hand behind each one to move them forward.

The girl, Ruth, spun around and hid behind her mother. Samuel, however, boldly stepped forward. He stared at me, "Are you the Warlord? Can I see the scars from your battles?"

I laughed and swept him up into my arms. I felt joy then such as I had not known for many years, "Aye, I am the Warlord and your grandfather! As for the wounds, we shall see." I held him close and just took in the realisation that I had a family again. I closed my eyes for I felt them filling and that was not seemly.

I heard Eleanor say, "Come husband, let us leave the earl to greet his family."

I opened my eyes and saw Alice bowing, "If you come with me, your majesties, I will take you to your chambers. I have some mulled, spiced wine to take the chill from your bones."

"You are kind." Eleanor turned and smiled, "Enjoy your family, Alfraed."

Still holding Samuel, I held out my hand for Rebekah, "Come, I shall show you my secret place where we can be alone and talk for I have much to ask and you have much to tell me."

Samuel gasped, "You have a secret place?"

"I have. Only I go there but I shall let you, your sister and your mother share it with me."

Rebekah squeezed my fingers and said quietly, "You are just as your son said you would be. I can see now why he wishes to be just like you."

I led them up the stairs to my solar. I closed the door behind us. I knew that Alice would know where I was and that she would bring refreshments for us. It was cold for there was no fire there. I sat in my chair and put my cloak around Samuel. Ruth sat on her mother's knee.

"Now tell me all."

Rebekah began with her first meeting with my son. We were briefly interrupted by Alice and the servants who brought mulled wine and lit the fire. Alice had brought a fur for Rebekah and it was cosy. I sat silently as Rebekah, often interrupted by Samuel, told me of my son. There were some things I was not told. I could hear that

in her voice and in the silences in the story. Her eyes begged no
questions when she glossed over some of the events in their life.
That was to be expected. She did not want to upset her children. I
would not pry. Either she or William would tell me in due course.
They had questions for me. Samuel was fascinated by the fact that I
had been at the coronation. He wanted to know everything about the
knights and lords there.

There was a knock on the door and Alice peered in, "Lord, I
have prepared food for the King and the Queen."

I smiled, "And I have indulged myself long enough, thank you,
Alice. Where would I be without you? Let us join our liege, eh
Samuel?"

The meal was a merry one but tinged with unanswered
questions. The ladies of my knights knew not the fate of their
husbands. I saw the worry on Rebekah's face as Henry questioned
William and the ladies about the raid. It was Eleanor who reined in
her younger husband, "Your majesty, it is better to ask these
questions of your knights when they return. For myself, I would
know more about these delightful children." I knew why she asked.
Her eldest child, William, had died the previous year and she had
left her young son, Henry, in London. She had not wished to risk
losing a second child in infancy. I suspected that she was with child
again for she had been putting on more weight but not eating more.
I had not asked for that was a private matter. The look on her face
as she spoke with each child told me that she had children and
babies in her thoughts.

As she spoke with them I took the opportunity of asking
Rebekah about my son. I did not wish to know about his martial
accomplishments; she had told me that already. I wished to know
how life in the Holy Land had changed him.

She looked thoughtful. "I did not see much of a change. The man
I married was the man I first met when he brought me from my
aunt's. But after the renegade de Waller slew my family he
hardened a little. He did not change when in the company of his
people or his family but he became more ruthless on the battlefield.
His men told me that. They were not criticising him for he did what
he had to. If I was to answer you honestly, lord, it would be to say
that he has become stronger. He will be a good leader." She stared
into my eyes, "That is what you are really asking me, is it not? Has
he changed from the wild youth who caroused and, what is the
word? Wenched."

"He told you?"

She had a beautiful smile, "Lord, there are no secrets between us. I tell him all and he does the same."

My son had changed and become the man I always wanted him to be. I nodded, "You are an intelligent woman and my son has chosen well. I could not have chosen better for him. Thank you." I did not say but I thought that both my sons had chosen well. If I had had to choose a bride for them then it would have been Eleanor and Rebekah who would have been my choices.

I slept in my solar. The castle was crowded and I did not mind. I had been on enough campaigns to be able to sleep anywhere. Besides, it meant that, when I awoke, I was able to see my river. This was my valley. I had not been born here but it was now in my blood. I awoke before dawn and went up to the river gate. I met with John of Craven.

"You are up early, lord. Was the bed not comfortable?"

"It is this raid which concerns me. Why are they not back? Fissebourne is not far away."

"You did not question the survivors did you, lord?" I shook my head. "They said that the Scots took a great number of captives and animals. I would not have expected them back yet. They will return soon."

"Thank you, John. You have comforted me." I saw a pained expression on his face. "Something ails you?"

He smiled, "Just old age. I have seen sixty summers, lord."

I realised that I had seen fifty-three. I did not think of my age much. John looked old. Did I? "You would like to have an easier life?"

There was the slightest hesitation that told me that his answer was not entirely the truth. "It is just the winter, lord. When the new grass comes then I will have less ague and aches!"

Although we both smiled I determined to find another seneschal for my castle. John deserved to enjoy a quiet end to his life. My father's followers had not had that luxury. They had been slain by the Scots. That would not happen to John or any of my other retainers.

It was in the early afternoon that the sentry on the north wall shouted that our men were returning. Henry, also eager to speak with them, joined me at the gatehouse. My knights led. Even at a distance of a mile, Sir Wulfric could be identified. As they drew closer I identified the others. I realised that two were missing, Dick and my son. What had happened. I wondered why they had not sent Aiden, Edgar or Edward back with news. Then it came to me, my son and Wulfric had taken all the knights. He had not known that we would be there. They would now for my banner and that of the King fluttered from our battlements.

Henry pointed at the captives and the animals, "It seems your knights have reclaimed what was ours but I cannot see your son."

King Henry had been my squire and knew my men as well as I did. I nodded, "He and Dick may well have another errand. Wulfric will tell all."

We descended. The animals would be taken to the pens we had close by the town walls. The nearby well of St. John would supply them with water and there was grazing there for there was no frost. The captives would have to be housed in the town. William, my Steward, was at the bottom of the steps, "William go and ask Alf to have the captives housed with the townsfolk until we can make better arrangements."

He smiled, "I have already done so, see lord." I looked and saw Alf waiting with the women of the town to greet and care for the captives. We had done this before. I knew that some would return to Fissebourne but many would stay in the town. Some would marry single men at arms and archers. Others would marry the young men of the town. Alf and Ethelred were successful and had many sons. The women might have lost husbands and fathers but life would go on and they would be cared for. That was what my people did.

As soon as my knights saw the King they leapt from their horses and bowed. Henry smiled, "Rise Wulfric. I may wear a crown and sit upon a throne but I am still the young warrior who suffered the sharp edge of your tongue and the flat of your hand."

Wulfric shifted uneasily, "I am sorry, your majesty. I…"

The king waved his hand, "Tell us the tale swiftly unless your words are not for all to hear." King Henry had grown. Eleanor had been good for him. She had shown him how to be more sensitive. If my son was dead then the King would have us hear that privately.

He shook his head, "No, your majesty. All are safe. We encountered the Scots and defeated them. We recaptured the animals and captives. All would have returned but," he lowered his voice, "when we reached Cuneceastra Sir William discovered that the messenger he had sent to tell his father of his return had been taken by the Scots to their castle at Warkworth."

King Henry frowned, "We have no castle at Warkworth."

Wulfric said, bluntly, "They have built one. We saw evidence that they are improving their defences all along the border."

"And the Bishop of Durham, de Puiset?"

Wulfric was nothing if not blunt, "He squats, like a toad, behind his walls and does nothing, your majesty."

"I will have words with the Bishop. Carry on with your tale."

"Sir William said that he was honour bound to rescue his friend for he was a Varangian." He looked at me, "He knew your father, lord. Dick went with him. He would not take more of us for he said that the valley needed protection and it was his quest alone." He smiled, "Dick was forceful!"

Henry nodded, "You have a noble son. He takes after you, Alfraed. I can see that I was meant to come here. What will you do?"

"I will ask my knights to fetch their men at arms. I will send to Piercebridge and Normanby for their men. It would take William some days to reach Warkworth and it is now deep into the land the Scots have stolen. Tomorrow I will send Aiden and his men north to the New Castle and beyond. I would have them find either the Scots or my son." I turned to King Henry and said, quietly, "I know that we have an uneasy peace with Scotland, your majesty, but if they have hurt my son then I will have vengeance."

He held up his hand, "You have no argument from me. However, I will ride tomorrow to Durham. I will take my knights and leave the Queen here. It is time that I reminded Hugh de Puiset of his duties. I only ask that you await my return. It will take some days to gather your men in any case. You must not leave your castle unguarded. The Queen's ladies are here."

"That I will not. Thank you, your majesty."

"I owe my crown and throne to you. William served my father well and was a valiant warrior. He deserves our support no matter how foolish his quest." He clasped my arm as his grandfather had once done, "And when I return here your knights can swear their allegiance to me." He held up his hand, "I know that they do not need to for they are as loyal as any but I asked those who attended the coronation to do so and I must be seen to be fair."

I shook my head, "Your brother Geoffrey swore. It seems an oath means little to some men. Do not fear, majesty, my knights and their squires will be more than happy to take an oath."

My knights had little time to rest. I sent them home to return with men and archers. I despatched riders to ask Sir Phillip and Sir Gilles of Normanby to bring their men too. It was only then that I thought of Rebekah. I hurried to her quarters. I saw that she had been weeping. She had heard the news. Samuel looked confused and Ruth clung to her mother.

"He will be safe. He has my archers with him and they are the finest in England."

"But he is not in England is he, lord? He is deep inside Scotland. I know why he goes. Ralph of Bowness was of great help to him but my husband has too much honour. He has children now and a wife."

I sat on the bed and put my arm around her. "And he will return. I feel it in my bones but I will not sit idly by and just wait. I have summoned my men and we will ride to find him. I cannot go blindly for there are many ways he could return but I will not rest until my son is back here in the bosom of his family. You must trust me in this, Rebekah. I have only recently met you and yet I see steel beneath that fragile frame of yours."

She turned and, burying her head in my chest, wept. I said nothing for there was nothing to say. She had to let out those tears. She would be stronger for it and be able to face her children.

Her tears did not last long, "Thank you, lord. Your son is right. Your enemies may fear you but I can see why your friends love you. My father and brothers would have enjoyed meeting you. You are unlike the Normans we saw in our land."

"Perhaps that is because I grew up in the east or, more likely because I was raised by men who came from this land before the Normans came. Ralph of Bowness sounds like such a man and it is why my son risks all."

We heard squeals from the corridor as Samuel and Ruth raced along pursued by Alice who was playing a game. For my housekeeper, the arrival of the two children had been the greatest gift she could be given. Denied children herself, she was as protective of them as a she-wolf.

Rebekah smiled, "One cannot be sad for long with those two around."

"They have brought light to this castle and joy to an old man's heart. Come let us go to them."

As I passed the window, I saw the flakes of snow falling. The fine weather was ending. What did this portend? Would it aid or hurt my son?

Chapter 10

The snow fell all night and lay like a white blanket over the valley. It added urgency to my plans for my travels. There was a great deal to be done before we could leave. I sent Aiden and his two scouts to find my son and they left before dawn. This time they took spare horses. "I promise, my lord, that I will find these Scots and, hopefully, your son."

"But you are less confident about William."

He smiled, "That is because I know how good he is at hiding. The Scots? A man deaf, dumb and blind could find them, but William? He is clever. Fear not. I would bet money on his survival." He pointed to the snow-laden skies. "This snow is lying deep. It will slow down the Scots."

Then we had to prepare our weapons and animals. I chose the oldest men to stay behind at the castle. I did not need a large garrison. The King and his household knights would remain. There was no need for him to risk himself. My steward was an expert in preparing supplies. I did not think we would be away for long, perhaps two or three days at the most, but we needed tents and servants. The snow had dictated that. By the end of the day, we were ready and the first of my knights had arrived.

The ones who came earliest were the ones who lived closest: Hartburn, Elton, Norton and Thornaby. Normanby and Piercebridge took more time. Richard and James were kept busy. They had to make sure that all of my knights had accommodation and that I would have all that I needed. Richard had been knighted but he had yet to take a squire and he helped James. They had both been my squires and were close. Only Wulfric and Dick, of my knights, had not been my squires. James would carry my banner. It had been some time since we had ridden against the Scots. The battle for England had taken precedence. Now they would feel my wrath. They knew the wolf standard and they feared it.

It was disappointing when neither the King nor my scouts returned during daylight. The gates were closed and a watch was kept but I knew that they would not return after dark. The King was obviously impressing himself upon the Bishop and my scouts must have had to ride further than they thought to find the Scots.

The next morning passed and there was still no sign of either the King or my scouts. Sir Philip and Sir Gilles arrived with their men. We would have eight knights along with over a hundred men at arms and a hundred archers. With such a force, I could take the New Castle!

King Henry arrived after noon. He looked contented. Eleanor excused herself to go to her room, "I had forgotten that the north could have snow! I hope there is a fire in my room. I will need it to drive the chills from my bones."

Alice appeared, "Fear not majesty, I have hot drinks to warm you."

King Henry smiled as my housekeeper led his wife away. "Is there somewhere we can talk in private?"

"My solar."

When we were alone he said, "You were right about the Bishop. He was fence sitting. I think de Puiset was waiting to see if I wanted the north back! Once he realised that I did then his attitude changed. He told me that his men had found Scottish scouts on the borders of the Palatinate. When I asked him why he had not taken action he spoke of the agreement I had made with the King of Scotland!" He shook his head, "Churchmen! I told him that the agreement had only been reached to buy me time to defeat Stephen. He did tell me that one of his men at Cuneceastra had met with your son but he had heard nothing since. There were, however, rumours of battles and skirmishes to the north of his lands. I think William is still alive."

"Thank you, majesty. Now I wait for my scouts."

"And I will gather your knights and take their oath." We descended to my hall where my knights were gathered already.

It was a solemn occasion and my knights and squires all took it seriously. They had sworn oaths to me before but this was different. They were swearing an oath to a king. Only Wulfric and Harold had done that before when the king's grandfather had ruled.

Perhaps it was the swearing of the oaths that changed events; I know not but, no sooner had we left the hall when Edgar galloped in, "Lord, your majesty! We have found the Scots!"

I ran over to him. There was no need for a dignified walk. If he had found the Scots then I would soon find my son.

Edgar pointed to the north. "There are two columns of them. Aiden and my brother are watching them. One came from the north. They are heading for Auckland. The other was waiting north of Fissebourne," he paused. "They have your son trapped between them. He is outnumbered."

I nodded, "Mount! We ride. Edgar, lead us." As I mounted Badger, I saw Rebekah standing at the doorway to my hall. She looked so small and vulnerable. She held her children tightly. I nodded and, as I slid my sword from its scabbard and raised it shouted, "Death to the Scots! Long live King Henry!"

My men echoed my cry and the sentries banged their shields. It was a cacophony of noise but it was also a message. The Warlord of the North was going to war and his enemies should fear him. I spurred Badger, he was getting old but there were still battles in him. Scout may have died but his spirit lived on in my other horses. With my banner fluttering behind me we rode from the north gate. The townsfolk stood and cheered as we galloped by.

We headed west. We would go through Redmarshall and Aycliffe. It was a good road, my men kept it well maintained. We would be at my son's side within a few hours. No one had ridden down the road. It was virgin snow. That made it easier for us although I suspected that those at the rear would be riding through slush and mud when all the hooves had passed over it. The passage would not be so easy for them. The skies had cleared and visibility was good. It meant that we would see the Scots, and hopefully, my son when we were some distance away. I prayed that would give him hope. Often in a battle, it is the thought of defeat that defeats you. So long as you have hope then anything is possible. I took comfort from the fact that he had Dick and his archers with him. It was not just their arrows that were deadly. They were the masters of the short sword and buckler. Woe betide a knight or man at arms who thought he had an easy prey. We kept up a steady pace but we were not thrashing our horses. We would have a battle to fight at the end of our journey. Outnumbered, my son would have found himself a good defensive position. With a handful of mounted men, he would dismount and use his archers to thin out the enemy. This was my land and I had ridden over every part of it. Edgar's description had told me where William would be. It was as we climbed a gradient and Badger's hooves slipped that I knew where my son would be. He would be on the slope which led to the Bishop's estates. I almost shouted for joy. My son had a chance.

My hopes were almost dashed as we neared the battle. The clear air had carried the sounds of cries and the clash of steel on steel towards us. We heard the battle before we saw it. When we drew near I saw that my son had, indeed, chosen the best position. I knew, from Edgar's report, that my son was surrounded. There was a mass of men before him. It seemed impossible that they could survive. There were, however, open fields to the left and right of us. I shouted, "Form a long double line. Knights in the centre, squires behind. Sir Philip take your men ahead and try to thin them out."

"Aye lord."

Sir Philip's men at arms joined my men while he led his twenty-four archers to gallop ahead of us. It would be little that they could do but even if they just distracted the Scots then it might buy me the time I needed. Many of my knights carried spears. Wulfric and I did not. I carried my sword and Wulfric a double-handed axe which he wielded with one hand. He was to my right and Sir Harold to my left.

We were four hundred paces from them and I could see a banner I did not recognise, it was a gryphon. That had to be my son! I spied the Scottish banner of the Keith family. My son's men were being pressed hard. I spurred Badger and he opened his legs. While we were on the flat we had the chance to build up speed. When we reached the slope, it would be a different matter. I saw Sir Philip's men. They had dismounted and were releasing arrow after arrow at the enemy. As men began to fall to the deadly missiles the Scots, at the rear, turned around. They spied my double line of horsemen and my banner. I saw them physically recoil. The Warlord was back!

Numbers were impossible to estimate. It was a whirling mass of men who were hacking and slashing at each other. Wulfric and I were slightly ahead of the rest and we were the ones to strike first. The men at the rear had neither mail nor spears. They had pot helmets, curved swords and small round shields a little bigger than a buckler. We tore into them. I had my sword by Badger's rump and I swung it in an arc from behind me. It ripped up the middle of a Scottish warrior as Wulfric's axe split the skull and chest of a second. We were at the slope but going so fast that we were through their first men before we slowed up.

My sword was raised and I brought it down to hit the next Scot between his shoulder and his neck. My sword hacked deep into his body and it slid, dead, from my bloodied blade. I now saw my son and a giant of a warrior wearing mail and besmirched in blood. Next to them was a wild man with a black patch over his eye who appeared to be dressed in red. He was hacking and swinging with his sword as though he was invincible. I saw arrows flying from the woods. Dick still had archers. I took a second look as I saw a priest laying about him with a sword. I had never seen the like. It made me even more determined to reach them.

As I had slowed I used that to my advantage. As the rest of my knights and men at arms caught up with me I stood in my stirrups and pulled back on my reins. Badger responded magnificently. He reared. His great hooves clattered down and flattened two Scots. As I landed I lunged forward at the knight who had charged at me with a spear held before him. The spear was aimed at my right shoulder and, as I lunged I lay flat along my saddle. The spear scraped along my surcoat, tearing it and rasping off the mail. His impetus cost him his life. My sword slid along his cantle, through his mail and into his guts. Lord Alexander Keith died with a surprised look on his face. He had thought that he had killed Scotland's greatest enemy. He must have believed that such an act would bring victory and he would be hailed a hero. He fell, unceremoniously, from his saddle and his body was mashed to a pulp by the horses of my men.

The battle was not over but the moment had swung it in our favour. All of my men at arms and knights were engaged. Our two lines had become one. We were hitting men on foot. Our horses were a deadly weapon. Our numbers were doubled by our well-trained horses. Sir Dick and Sir Philip had their men raining arrows down on the enemy. We had turned the enemy's ambush into a trap of our own. It was a slaughter.

The Scots had courage. They fought beyond all reason for they were the ones now surrounded. I saw that, as they turned to face us, my son led his men back into the woods to fight the enemy there. We had to destroy the will of the men before us and go to my son's aid. If he fell now it would be a tragedy with which I could not live.

"On, for England! King Henry and the Warlord! On my heroes!"

It worked for my men fought with renewed vigour. Badger was now tiring and so I used him judiciously. I wheeled him around to allow me to use my height and long sword to slash and strike at unprotected necks and chests. The Scottish spears lay shattered for they had broken them in the first charge. Their curved swords were wickedly sharp but they were shorter than ours. Soon I had a wall of bodies around me. I saw that Wulfric's horse had been injured and he had dismounted. With his shield strapped to his back he and his dismounted squire hacked and slashed their way through the Scots. Swinging his double-handed axe, none could stand in his way. With their leader dead, it was inevitable that they would all be slaughtered. I did not mind that, they were the interlopers but as I saw two of Wulfric's men at arms slain I decided I could not live with more of my men dying.

Standing in my stirrups I shouted, "Surrender or die! If you lay down your weapons I swear that you shall live!"

Amazingly all fighting stopped. To be fair men were weary and any excuse to have a rest was welcome.

A single Scottish voice shouted, "And be slaves?"

I shook my head, "No! We will keep you and let your king bargain for you. I cannot offer any better terms than that. You will live!"

A blood besmirched Wulfric spat out a tooth and said, "Let's just kill the bastards!"

He said it loudly enough to be heard and it was the final act that decided the Scots. A grey beard knight threw down his sword and said, "We surrender but I hold you to your word."

I took off my helmet, "You know that I am the Warlord and I am never foresworn!"

"Aye, you are a bastard but an honourable one!"

I dismounted and, sheathing my sword, pushed my way through the many Scotsmen who were throwing down their weapons. I was anxious to get to my son. I saw him descending to greet me. He too had taken off his helmet. Like me, he was covered in the blood of friend and foe alike. He seemed bigger than when last I had seen him and was burned almost black by the sun. But he was still William. He threw his arms around me and he hugged me. I said nothing for the words would not come. I squeezed him as I had when had been born. He said nothing but I heard him almost sobbing. Perhaps it was the exhaustion I know not. I opened my eyes and saw that my knights and squires had formed a circle around us. Their backs were to us. They were giving us privacy in this charnel house of a battle.

Eventually, he relaxed his grip and I held him at arm's length. Before I could say a word, he dropped to his knees, "Forgive me, father. I have seen the error of my ways. You were right. I should never have doubted you."

I raised him up and smiled. "This is as it was meant to be. Had you not left you would not have met Rebekah and two bonnier bairns I have yet to see. The hand of God is upon your return. You are alive. Henry is king and all is well with the world." I shouted,

"Come, we need to bury our dead and get back to my castle. We need a real celebration."

My men all turned and cheered. That loud cheer that would have echoed to Durham and back was the final blow that defeated the Scots. Even had they harboured any ideas of resuming the fight, that single resonating cheer sucked all the fight out of them.

William held his hand out and said, "This is Ralph of Bowness. He would serve you at the castle."

I saw before me the one-eyed giant who had fought so ferociously. I smiled and clasped his arm. "Then you shall serve me and welcome."

"This is Alf, my squire. Like you, he was named after grandfather's friend, Aelfraed."

I saw a younger version of my father, "*Wyrd*!" His squire, Alf, was the giant I had seen fighting at my son's side.

Ralph of Bowness laughed, "Aye you would be Ridley's son!"

I saw a bloody Dick and his archers returning from the forest. He was alive. I grasped his arm, "Once again, old friend, I am indebted to you for saving my son."

"Lord, I swore an oath to protect you and your family. How could I have done other."

"Then this is a glorious day!"

William shook his head, "It would be father were it not for the fact that Thomas, son of Oswald the archer and knighted by me, now lies dead as does his squire, Stephen. They fought bravely and both were young. All their hopes lay before them. Their harvest is now a field of weeds and I cannot rejoice."

I put my arm around his shoulder. "I understand, believe me, I do," I shouted. "Put our dead on their horses. We shall bury them at Stockton." I looked at the Scottish knight, "We will help you bury your dead unless you wish to burn them?"

"The ground is hard and there are animals who would despoil them. If we had a priest then we could burn them."

My son said, "Brother Peter will speak over their ashes."

The knight nodded, "Aye then we shall burn them. Away lads, let's find kindling so that our brave brothers may have a seemly end."

The sun was beginning to set as we headed back to Stockton. The fire behind us burned brightly and our column was silent and sombre. There were neither songs nor rejoicing. Both Scot and English were silent. We had each fought a good battle but we had lost friends. We trudged through the icy fog-filled night and headed for my castle and the King. We had a victory! It was the first since England was reunited and was a sign of hope for the future.

Chapter 11

I sent my scouts back to warn the castle of our arrival. The animal pens would be used to house the prisoners. We had over one hundred of them. Another sixty Scots, including most of their knights, lay burned in the fields to the south of the battlefield. We had lost men. My son grieved for both his knights and his men at arms. Dick had lost archers. Had we not arrived when we had then all would lie dead. It was obvious to me that none would have surrendered.

My son and I rode together. Once again, our knights and men at arms protected us. Dick and Wulfric were at the van. They left a gap before and behind us. William and I spoke. He told me of the rescue and his promise to Ralph. He asked if the Varangian could serve me. I nodded, "Then once again this is ordained, my son, for John of Craven has told me that he wishes to have an easier life. From what I saw at the battle he is a rock and will be a good leader of our men. He reminds me of Erre."

William smiled, "Aye, I had not thought of that but you are right he does.

"But I fear I will have to leave soon."

"Leave?"

I lowered my voice, "There is dissension in Anjou. Geoffrey fitz Empress is trying to take power."

"The King's youngest brother is there. I met him. He is loyal and Leofric is there too. They will fight Geoffrey."

"The French are stirring the pot. They have ever been thus. They did the same with Stephen and Eustace of Blois. Unwilling or unable to defeat us they undermine us with allies. I will have to go with the king and deal with the problem."

"But, father, you have done much already. Is it not time for you to sit before the fire and enjoy your grandchildren?"

"I do not think that is my fate. When I met old King Henry in the woods in Maine, it changed my life. Since that time, I have been bound to this family whether I will or not."

"And after Geoffrey is brought to book?"

I sighed, "The Welsh have been doing as the Scots have done and encroached into England. The difference there is that there is none to oppose them. Here, even without me, there are my knights," I patted my son's arm, "and now my son."

"Me? How can I take your place?"

"You have been preparing all of your life for such a task. I will be honest with you, William, when you chose to stay in Anjou and serve Geoffrey I wondered if I had lost you. Now I see that it was meant to be. You were learning to lead and to be a knight without the shadow of your father. Just as your time in the Crusades was decided by others. You have a wife and children you would not have had if you had not gone there. You learned how to lead in the Holy Land. I have spoken with Rebekah and learned much. The King of Jerusalem had you as a trusted leader. You have been prepared for this task."

My son suddenly turned in his saddle, "There is something you should know about Rebekah."

I shook my head, "There is a secret she bears. Something scarred her, almost killed her and you were her salvation."

"You know?"

"No, but with age comes the ability to see into a person's eyes and read beneath their words. I do not need to know the details. I saw the pain in her eyes. Had I been meant to know then she would have told me. I know all I need to know about the mother of my grandchildren. You are a lucky man. If I had been able to choose your bride I could not have chosen better. This is well." I had a sudden thought, "If you wish to live elsewhere…"

"Do not fear, father!" He laughed, "I am home and home I shall stay."

There was still sadness at the deaths of Sir Thomas and the others but my son and I had healed our rift. All was well. Lights from my castle guided us through the last foggy steps. William and Alice were there to greet us as was Rebekah.

"The children are asleep, lord. One of the servants is watching them."

"Thank you, Alice." Rebekah and William embraced. "Is there food for the men and the prisoners?"

My steward nodded, "There is, lord, and John of Craven has assigned guards. We have rigged shelters."

Wulfric reined in next to me, "With your permission, lord, we will head back to Thornaby. The castle will be crowded enough as it is."

I nodded, "Thank you, Wulfric, once again you were my rock."

"Perhaps lord but time is taking its toll of me. My horse would not have been hurt once upon a time. I am slowing up. One day I will not terrify my enemies and Wulfric will be no more."

"That is true of us all. Take care, my friend."

Rebekah came up to me and kissed me on my cheek, "Thank you, lord, you said you would bring him home and you did."

I nodded and William led his wife into the castle. I ensured that all was well and that every knight was accounted for. I walked amongst the Scottish prisoners before I entered my castle, "You will be given food and shelter. Your wounds will be healed but if you try to escape you will be hunted down and slain."

The old knight nodded, "We understand. The men will not try to run. We are many miles from home and it is winter. The change in the weather is a sign from God."

I understood what he meant. Alexander of Warkworth had led his men south when it was clement weather. The sudden snowstorm and the harsh conditions had contributed to their defeat. Most warriors were superstitious. They understood omens and signs. It had helped us win the battle.

As the gate slammed behind me Alice put her hand on my back, "Lord, you must look after yourself. There are others who can do this! I have laid out food and drink in your solar." She pulled away her hand, "This is soaked through." She turned to James who had followed me, obediently on my tour, "Master James, go and fetch your master a clean tunic!"

James might be a fearless warrior on the battlefield but he would not argue with the force of nature that was Alice, "Aye Mistress Alice."

She was right, of course. Once my mail and wet surcoat and cloak were removed and I had changed into a dry tunic, I felt much better. There was a fire in my solar and the spiced mulled wine was just what I needed. "James, get yourself to bed. I will eat and sit here before my fire."

"Aye lord." He turned, "It is good that your son is back, lord."

I nodded.

Alice said, "If there is aught you need then just send Egbert for me." Egbert was the armed servant who stood at my solar door.

"I will and you take some rest. The castle has strong defences, Alice, but without you, it would crumble into dust."

She shook her head, "Lord, the things you say."

I did not go to bed. I had much to think about. The arrival of the Varangian and the return of my son seemed to me to be significant events. I had thought that, with the war over, I could enjoy my life. My journey north with the king had shown me that this was not true. Geoffrey needed to be curbed and King Henry had never fought the Welsh. I had, with his grandfather and his uncle. I knew that they would be harder to defeat than the Scots. Their knights and men at arms were not worth worrying about but their archers were the equal of ours and they had many of them. They had a land that helped them too. The castles which old King Henry had built were now in Welsh hands and they would be hard to take. Stephen's short tenure had cost the country dear.

I had a small chest in the solar and I took out the maps I had of our kingdom. The ones at the bottom had lain untouched for many years. They were the ones I needed. I was still studying them as the first light of grey appeared in the sky. It would take time for the sun to burn off the fog but daylight would not be too far away.

I ate some of the bread, ham and cheese which Alice had laid out for me. If I did not then she would fret and worry. These days I did not need as much food. I looked wistfully at the empty flagon of wine. It had been delicious and I yearned for another. When I heard the sounds of movement and the noise of children I put my maps away and descended. Samuel and Ruth were up and were with their parents at the table laden with bread, honey, porridge, ham, cheese and pickled fish. Samuel saw me as I entered the Great Hall, "Warlord! You are up! Let us play!"

Rebekah admonished her son, "You call him lord! Be respectful to him!"

I shook my head, "Samuel may call me anything he wishes. What game shall we play?"

"I have a wooden sword. I would play knights and the Scots. Ruth can be the Scots!"

"That does not seem fair. She would be alone. What say I teach you a game which is like knights and the Scots but is less dangerous."

"A game?"

"Chess." I looked at William, "Have you taught him yet? I taught you when you had only just learned to walk."

He shook his head, "Chess... I have not played this game for many years." He looked directly at me. "I should have for you taught me that all you need to know about battle is on that black and white board."

"Then the three of us will enjoy it together."

Thus it was that King Henry and Queen Eleanor discovered us together playing chess before a roaring fire. Alice continually refilled the table with food as it was consumed by my guests. As we ate William and I told the King of the battle and the victory.

"Good. We can use those prisoners to our advantage." He nodded to his queen who was sitting with Rebekah and playing a game with the children. "My queen and I have spoken. As soon as your ships return I would return to London. Queen Eleanor misses our son. When they are safely ensconced in London I will go with you, Alfraed, to Anjou and we will bring my errant brother to heel."

I nodded, "As you wish, your majesty."

He smiled, "When your knights have risen I will tell them."

My knights and their wives arrived in ones and twos. Half were there when Ralph of Nottingham entered, "Lord, the '*Adela*' is approaching."

"Your ship?"

"Aye lord."

"Good." The last of my knights, Sir Gilles of Normanby arrived. King Henry said, "Good, then I can make my announcement and we can pack. I am anxious to sail!" He picked up a metal cover from the warmed ham and, taking out his dagger began to beat upon it to gather attention. I smiled as Alice winced. He was denting her best dishes. "Lords, I pray silence, I have an announcement."

They all turned to look at the king. He laid down the dagger and the cover. Queen Eleanor came to his side.

"Know you that I offered the Earl of Cleveland the title of Duke of Cleveland. Modest as he is, he declined. I now appoint Alfraed of Stockton to be Earl Marshal of the Horse of England. He will be the most senior knight of the realm. Only I will rank above him. When I return to London I will make the proclamation so that all may know."

I nodded, "I do not deserve the honour, your majesty, but I accept the title for I know that it means I will serve you still and work towards the enlargement of England!"

My men all cheered until Henry raised his arms, "I have not yet finished. The northern borders are still filled with danger and we need a strong hand here to control it. I hereby appoint William of Stockton to be Earl of Cleveland and I charge him with the protection of the border."

I saw the look of surprise on my son's face. I gave the subtlest of nods. He said, "I too am honoured and flattered and I accept."

We were both surrounded by my men and squires who were as pleased as if they had been awarded the honour. James asked, "Lord, what is a Marshal?"

"It is the title given to the senior knight of the realm and the one who advises the king. The Earl of Gloucester was one and Stephen had a marshal too. It is a great honour."

"But you will not have land, lord."

I smiled, "Stockton will ever be my home and I do not think that my son will deny me shelter."

King Henry took William's arm and mine, "Come we have much to do. Alfraed, tell your captain that we sail on the next tide."

"James, go and inform William of Kingston of the king's command."

"Aye lord."

Once in my solar King Henry said, "William, I will be taking your father with me and we shall be away for some time. I leave you in command of the north." He took out a parchment. "Alfraed, I had your steward write this document for me. It gives William the power to speak for me." Handing it to my son he said, "I want you to make contact with King Malcolm. You will offer the prisoners we took in exchange for the return of the land south of the Tyne and the Eden."

"He will not agree to that, lord!"

"Perhaps not but he will make some concessions. We do not need the prisoners and the return of them will spread the word that you are as formidable a foe as your father. When Geoffrey and the Welsh are contained then I will turn my attention back to the north. The Bishop of Durham will aid you. Between you I want you to put pressure on the Scots. Do not let them build castles and do not let them get comfortable. I will instruct my tax collectors that Cleveland pays no taxes. That way you can use your money to build up your armies. I cannot afford to bring men from Wales to retake the north. You will have to build up the army. I am certain that you can do it."

William nodded, "I will need more knights."

"Then knight them. You are the new Warlord of the North. I know, from speaking with your wife, what you did in the Holy Land. There you served a king and served him well. I would have you do the same for me. King Malcolm is young. Use that to your advantage. Do whatever you must to regain our lands. If you do it manor by manor then so be it. From what your father said you have performed miracles with a handful of men at arms and a couple of dozen archers. The fyrd owe you thirty days a year. Use them!"

"Then I will do as you suggest."

"Alfraed, you will only be able to bring your squire and a servant. The ship will not accommodate more, you know that."

"I need no servant and besides, Leofric has servants for us in Anjou. I am content."

"Then I leave you two to say your goodbyes. I will send most of my knights home over land. They can reach London in ten days. It will take me time to organize the ships I need. Earl William, you will have the castle to yourself. I know that we have put you and your father to great inconvenience. It is appreciated."

After he had gone William asked, "Am I ready for this? Can I lead Wulfric and Dick?"

"You know you can. I am not worried. Trust to your blood. This is your castle now. When I return, I will be as your guest."

"But…"

"No, arguments. William knows where my treasure is kept. I will take some with me for who knows what expense I might have. The rest is yours. It is your inheritance. Use it."

"You will not need coin for you will have the king to pay for whatever you need."

I laughed, "Then you do not know kings. Fear not. Before I go I will speak with John of Craven and William my steward. I am sorry that we have not had more time together. When we have pushed the Welsh back…"

"There will be a room for you here."

"Care for my horses. I would not inflict a long voyage on them. Badger has fought enough. He should now sire young horses. Aiden will see to it."

He nodded, "I cannot believe that I travelled so far to see you so briefly. We have had but one night!"

"I know." I put the palm of my hand on his heart. "Know that I am always here and so is your mother. I will return."

"I know and I will go and visit my mother's grave with my family. They should know her."

I gathered John of Craven, Alice, William my Steward and Ralph of Bowness. I met them in the room Alice had used to sew with the ladies. "This castle is now my son's. William, he has access to all of my treasure. All!"

"Aye lord."

"Alice, I need no words for you. You are the heart of the castle and there is now young life once more."

I saw that she was welling up and she merely nodded.

"John of Craven, you have served me well." I handed him a bag of golden coins. "Here is your pension. You are welcome to stay in this land."

"Aye lord and I will. I know there is a fine piece of land north of the Ox Bridge. I will seek Sir Harold's permission to build there. There is a stream and a wood. I will be content."

"I am certain that Sir Harold will acquiesce to your request. And Ralph of Bowness, I said last night that there was a place for you here. That place is as constable of my son's castle. What say you?"

He grinned a gap-toothed look of pleasure, "I am beholden to you, lord. This is a fine castle and I will defend it with my life!"

"I hope it will not come to that. I go now, my friends, old and new. I know not when I will return but I know that when I do I will be coming home."

My last visit was to the church and my wife's grave, "Our son has come home, Adela. He has a fine family and I know that your spirit will watch over them. My life is full once more and I am content. Forgive me for all that I did to wrong you."

I knelt in prayer. I am certain that I heard a whispered voice say farewell. Perhaps it was my age and I was now hearing voices.

Chapter 12

I watched the mouth of the Loire estuary as it grew larger. I stood at the prow with James my squire. It was two months since we had left Stockton. The King and Queen had much to do. I had hired four servants in London. There were many old soldiers from the civil war. Maimed and handicapped there was little for them to do save beg. I chose four who all impressed me with their demeanour in the face of adversity. One, who would look after the horses I would buy in Anjou, and the other three to cater to James and me. All were old soldiers. All had suffered a wound. They knew me and had, at one time or another followed my banner.

Tom had been hamstrung in his right leg but he knew horses like no one save Aiden. Wilfred had taken a spear to the chest and suffered shortness of breath. Brian had been disfigured by an axe that had taken his eye and gouged a hole in his cheek. Osbert had lost three fingers on his left hand at the battle of Lincoln. All had been living in dire circumstances when I had found them. They were more than grateful to be serving as my servants. I would hire men at arms in Anjou. Archers were a different matter. I would have to rely upon Sir Leofric. He had some of my old archers and they had been training young archers for many years as well as finding English archers who had lost their way in Normandy, Anjou and France.

The King had commandeered eight ships to take him and his household knights to Anjou. His youngest brother, William was trying to contain Geoffrey. He and Sir Leofric had limited success. Some Angevin lords saw it as a family squabble and did not involve themselves. Henry would punish those at a later date. I had been impatient to leave. The longer Geoffrey was on the loose the more mischief he would cause. In addition, the news from the Welsh border was not good. Their kings, for they had three of them, had stolen more land. Geoffrey's rebellion was more than unwelcome.

Now that we were close to Anjou I was happier. I would see Sir Leofric once more. He had ever been a faithful knight. We had prospered because of his skilful management of my Angevin estate.

I turned to James, "You will need to learn the local words quickly while we are here, James."

"I know, lord. The servants are also worried."

"They need not be. I intend to ask Sir Leofric for one of his archers. That will make it easier for us."

"It is a shame that the King has to fight his brother."

"I am afraid that where thrones are concerned there is no love lost between brothers. The king's grandfather kept one brother imprisoned to make sure he was not threatened. King Henry will have to be as ruthless. He has inherited a far larger realm thanks to his mother."

Just mentioning Matilda made me look north. It was some time since I had seen her and now she lived in a priory. I doubted that I would ever see her again. I still thought about her every day and I saw her in our son the King. It would suffice. We had had our one moment of joy and love. It was more than most men enjoyed.

One of the squires attached to the king's retinue hurried down to speak with me, "Lord, the King would have a word. He is by the main mast."

"I am coming." Henry did not like to be below deck and he spent most of his time on deck. I also slept on deck but that was because I had been used to that since I had travelled to England with my father.

Henry looked up. He was surrounded by other senior knights. Some had fought for Stephen and some for Matilda. Having spent some time with them I knew that they were all loyal. "Earl Marshal, you know Anjou as well as any, tell us of the defences there."

"Chinon is the mightiest of them. It rises from the river on a fine piece of rock. It is like Arthur's seat in Scotland. The best castles are Angers, Saumur, Tours and Blois. We need not concern ourselves with Blois. I do not think that the Count of Blois will risk war with you."

"No?"

"He will wait to see who emerges victorious. Remember, your majesty, that Brittany has a great deal of unrest there too. The people are not happy about their Duke."

"I am curious, Alfraed, how do you know?"

I smiled, "I spoke with sea captains whilst we were in London. They have much information if you ask the right questions. It was they who told me that Geoffrey holds Chinon, Mirebeau and Loudon. Your brother, William, has men besieging Chinon."

"And we could sail there."

"I believe we could, majesty. The Vienne is not as deep as the Loire but I have heard that ships sail there. These are not deep draughted vessels. We could certainly get closer that way. However, the horses would need time to recover." I had not brought horses but many of Henry's knights had.

"I think that horses will be the least of our worries. Chinon, from what you tell me, will require siege works and that takes time. Perhaps I can persuade him to surrender."

"Perhaps but can you trust him? This is not the first time he has betrayed you."

"I know."

Few others knew how Geoffrey had tried to abduct Eleanor when she had been on her way to meet and, ultimately, marry Henry.

We were aided on our journey by the winds which came from the south and west. Had they been against us then I am not sure that we would have managed to make it as quickly as we did. Ultimately, we had to stop a mile from the castle. We saw it dominating the skyline in the distance but the captain would not risk his ship. He did not want it to be grounded. We disembarked.

I went with Henry, his bodyguards, and my squire. We were closely escorted by William of Le Havre and Phillipe of Aix. They had been his bodyguards for some time. Ten of his household knights also walked with us. I left my four servants to unload our war gear. With swords drawn, we walked along the path to the camp of William Fitz Empress. When we arrived at the tent with his standard he was seated with a priest reading to him from a book. We sheathed our weapons.

Henry asked, "Reading, brother and not pressing forward with the attack?"

He jumped up, "Your majesty!" He bowed, "This is a hard castle to take and I was studying Vegetius."

Henry, like his brother, was well-read in military tactics, "The Roman writer?"

"Aye, brother. The castle is well situated and I did not want to waste men in a fruitless frontal attack."

I stepped back. Their mother would be pleased, as would their grandfather. The two brothers were thinkers. As they discussed what William had learned I took out the map I had made in London.

It was not the most detailed but it told me all I needed to know. Chinon was the northernmost castle held by Geoffrey. The other two, Loudon and Mirebeau were due south. It would take time to reduce Chinon, even with the aid of Vegetius. Rather than waiting for it to fall, I believed that we could do something else. I folded the map and waited for the brothers to finish.

"If we build two rams and some onagers then we can use the onagers to keep down the heads of the defenders at the gatehouse while the two rams can be pushed up the ramp. We have archers here, thanks to Sir Leofric, who can pluck the eye from a hawk. It might take longer but it will be less costly in terms of men."

Henry nodded. I could see that he approved. It was time for me to make a suggestion. "I think it is the best plan and, while the siege engines are being built, your majesty, if I might suggest, we take a column of men south."

"South?"

"There are two more castles held by your brother. Neither is as strong as Chinon. It is why he chose Chinon. He wishes to be safe. He thinks those two castles protect his supply lines. I believe if we visit each of the castles then we might be able to persuade their castellans to surrender. It is one thing to rebel against your lawful ruler when they are a sea away but facing you might change their mind."

William said, "And having the wolf of the north, the Empress' champion, with you cannot hurt either brother."

"How long will it take to build the machines?"

"I have the plans and the materials. It will take no more than four days."

"Then we will leave tomorrow. The Earl Marshal and I will need horses."

He nodded, "Sir Leofric is here with his conroi. He has some fine horses."

I turned to the king, "Then James and I will fetch them. I need to speak with my knight. Where is his camp?"

William Fitz Empress pointed east, "He is closer to the better grazing. His men do not have as far to go when they are needed to send arrows at the walls."

I saw my knight's standard. He had a well-organized camp. When I had fought for old King Henry I had seen some bad practice amongst Angevin knights. It had led to unnecessary deaths. Sir Leofric had learned from me.

I was recognised, as I approached the camp, by Griff of Gwent. One of the last two archers who had gone to Anjou with Sir Leofric, he was now completely white, "It is the Warlord! Now we shall take these walls."

Sir Leofric came out of his tent. His squire, Alfraed, was with him. The last I had seen Alfraed he had been a boy and now he was a man. "It is good to see you, Warlord. Has the king come too?"

"He has, Leofric." I held my arm out, "This is James son of Sir Edward."

"Your father was a great warrior. I miss him."

"Thank you, lord, one day I may be a knight and I hope to emulate him."

Griff of Gwent and Robert of Derby brought over two half barrels for us to sit upon. "How goes the siege?"

"They have learned to respect our bows. Their crossbows have hurt others but our men are too clever for them."

Griff of Gwent spat, "A devil's machine and as slow as an ox to load!"

"The King is here now and he and William Fitz Empress have plans to build siege engines."

"Good. Sitting idly by is no good for the men. Mine are well disciplined but there are others who cannot control their men and there have been fights."

I knew what he meant. Some warriors who became bored took to drinking and then what might have been a fist fight without drink turned into something deadlier.

"That may change tomorrow. The King and I are taking the mounted men to Loudon to see if we can persuade the castellan to surrender. To that end, we need half a dozen horses."

"We brought plenty. For the last six years, I have been breeding larger mounts. I won a fine stallion at a tourney to celebrate the end of the war in Normandy and I was given a good mare by the burghers of a town I relieved. From those, we have a herd of war horses. Robert, go and pick out six." As his man at arms left he asked, "Will I be needed?"

"I do not think that the King will have forgotten what a fine leader you are."

"I will have my men at arms prepare then."

The horses were magnificent. Robert led a chestnut to me. He had a blond mane and reminded me of a younger Scout. His tail was blond too and he had one white foreleg. What was most noticeable, however, was the white blaze on his head which looked, for all the

118

world like a sword. "This, lord, is Sword. You can see why we named him."

Leofric came over to the horse which nuzzled him. "He is the best of the horses."

I looked at Leofric, "He is yours."

"Let us say that he was but he deserves a greater lord than I."

"Then I shall borrow him for this campaign. Hopefully, I will not ruin him for you. When we leave then he will be returned to you."

Leofric showed the relief in his eyes and his words, "Thank you, lord."

I did not mount him. We led them back to the King's tent which had now been erected. My servants had put mine next to his and Tom had planted my banner. The King had his leopards and I had my wolf. The King said, "What a magnificent beast!"

I smiled, "Aye, he is Sir Leofric's and he has allowed me to borrow him."

There was clear disappointment on the King's face but he was gracious enough to nod. "One day I shall inspire my men to be as loyal as yours." He put his arm around me and James led my horse and his to be tethered close to our tents. "I have forty knights and forty men at arms for the morrow. Will that be enough do you think?"

"We will make it enough. It is the banners he will be counting. Have some of the men at arms carry the banners of knights who are staying here at the siege. It will double the numbers of our knights. He will fear you, lord."

"More likely he will see your wolf and wet himself. I will do as you advise. I leave William to command here."

"He is young but he makes wise decisions."

We left early the next morning. Henry knew how to make an impression. Every knight had a burnished helm and armour. The rebels would see us coming from a long way away. That was the intention. Sir Leofric and Alfraed were given the honour of being the heralds. That too was clever for the rebels would know of his association with me. They would know that the Warlord was coming!

The road took us through farmland and then into a forest. I was annoyed that the King had not ordered scouts but he had overruled me. "The enemy are within the walls of Loudon. There may be bandits and brigands inside the forests but they cannot harm us."

The King had taken a young Angevin as his squire. Guiscard D'Aubigny was just thirteen summers old and delighted to be a squire to a king. He saw great things in his future. As he rode he held his head up proudly and preened for his peers to see. He died with a crossbow bolt in his throat. James and I had been fighting more recently than any others and, having seen where the crossbowman hid we galloped towards the hidden assailant. The others looked around bewildered. I knew that the bolt had been aimed at the King. He had been lucky. Who knew how many others were hiding in the dark forest? Our sudden charge would disrupt them. The crossbowman who had tried to kill the King would be reloading. He was fast. I saw his crossbow come up and it was aimed at me. James leaned from his saddle and swept his sword across the throat of the would-be assassin. I would have preferred a prisoner but I was grateful to my squire. I heard hooves and saw riders, some ten of them fleeing north. There would be little point in pursuing them. We were mailed and they were not. We reined in and rode back to the dead crossbowman.

Sir Leofric and a dozen knights and men at arms were there. "You have not lost your touch, lord!

"And the King nearly died." I pointed to the men at arms. "From now on you will form a screen on either side of the column, understand?"

The sergeant at arms nodded, "Aye Warlord."

Sir Leofric jumped from his saddle and went to the dead crossbowman. His squire dismounted too. While Sir Leofric searched the dead man Alfraed systematically smashed the crossbow. All of my men hated the infernal machines.

"There is nothing to identify him save this, lord." He flicked a gold coin to me. It was a large one and it bore the head of the King of France.

I turned it over, "This does not prove anything."

Sir Leofric laughed, "No, lord, but it points in one direction."

Henry frowned when I told him the news. "It is bad enough having rebels but when we have assassins too then it really is too bad. I suppose we ought to have outriders."

I nodded, "I have given the command, your majesty."

We passed through a second forest without incident but I breathed a palpable sigh of relief. We did not have far to travel before we saw the castle looming up ahead of us. Loudon was not a large castle. It had a donjon, outside wall and stone towers but, unlike Chinon, it would not require a vast number of siege engines to make it fall. We halted four hundred paces from the outer ditch and Sir Leofric rode ahead.

King Henry was a little worried. Perhaps it was the sudden attack in the forest which had unsettled him. I saw him glancing nervously behind as though we had not brought enough men. I leaned over and said, quietly, "If they do not surrender we have lost nothing. We have had a ride in the woods and a little excitement. The death of your new squire was unfortunate but if they say no then we head to the next castle and try there." I could see that he was not convinced, "What else would we do? Watch men build onagers and rams?"

"You are right. I fear I am worrying about Scotland and Wales."

"My son will deal with Scotland and Wales... when this is over we can give those wild men our complete attention."

"How can you remain so calm, Warlord?"

"I do not worry about those events over which I have no influence."

Sir Leofric rode back. "They will talk. They will allow my squire and me, your majesty and the Warlord." He smiled at me, "The castellan knows you, lord. It is William son of Richard d'Avranches."

I turned to the King, "His father was one of your grandfather's inner circle of knights and advisers. What is he doing supporting a rebel?"

The walls were lined with men but there were no weapons aimed at us. We had removed our helmets before we approached. William son of Richard d'Avranches did not follow the dictates of such meetings and he spoke directly with me. "You are still alive, Warlord. I thought they were just rumours!"

I could not remember the man. He must have been a squire when I had known him but I did not want to upset him. I would use whatever means I could to capture the castle. "There are always rumours. I have learned to trust my own eyes and nothing else." He nodded in agreement. "But would your father approve of this, lord? Here is the rightful Duke of Normandy and Count of Anjou."

He shrugged, "I was told by your brother, majesty, that his father had promised his County to him."

"And like my death, that was just a rumour. If you wish, Sir William, I can bring priests with the Duke's will..."

I saw him shake his head, "No, I can see now that it was a lie. The Warlord would not support a usurper." He looked at Henry,

"But if I surrender, your majesty, what happens to me? What becomes of my people?"

Henry showed me that day the maturity that was growing in him. "You were misled. Open your gates and I promise that I will forgive you."

The constable looked directly at me. I saw the King colour but he said nothing. I nodded. The constable said, "Open the gate and admit the Duke of Normandy!"

We were feted and there was no animosity. The constable had had nothing to do with the death of the squire, that much was obvious. As we ate King Henry bluntly asked about the constable of Mirebeau. "Ah, he is a different matter. He is Charles of Alençon and…"

King Henry nodded, "We know the man. He has not been duped. In fact, he may well have instigated this whole rebellion." Looking at me he said, "He will not surrender for he knows the death sentence will be upon him."

"Then we take the knights from Loudon with us. We tell him that Loudon has fallen and imply that Chinon has too."

"We lie?"

"No, your majesty. We let our devious foe fill in the gaps between our words. Men who lie often see lies in half-truths."

"How can we do that?"

"Leave that to me, majesty. I have dealt with men like Charles of Alençon before. They do not speak truly themselves and they are always looking for mistruth in others. The men in the castle will be the ones who will decide. Their Constable will be alone."

"How do you know?"

"We fought a civil war here in Anjou, Maine and Normandy. We fought one in England. Men are sick of internal strife. When they see the rightful king, duke and count they will come to their senses. Besides, it will be as it is here. There must be men who fought for your father or your mother. This cannot sit well with them."

We had scouts and outriders before us as we headed south and east. We had almost doubled our number with the men we had brought from Loudon. This time we all halted four hundred paces from the castle. Like Loudon, it was smaller than Chinon. The difference was that this one would be defended.

"If I might suggest, majesty, we have the men deploy into a three-deep line. Let us intimidate them with our numbers. They will see and count the banners. This time I will ride with Sir Leofric and his squire. Perhaps my banner, carried by James, might make them fear my archers."

"But they are in England!"

I smiled, "They do not know that."

"You are an old fox, Alfraed, but be careful. This castle means nothing. It is Chinon which we must break."

Taking off my helmet and mittens we rode towards the battlements which were lined with armed men. This time weapons were aimed at us. Was I being arrogant and gambling with other men's lives? I did not think I was. In my mind, I was trying to save lives. We rode slowly. It was more intimidating that way and showed that we were not afraid. When a crossbow bolt slammed into the ground just a pace in front of Sword I did not slow down. We reined in three hundred paces from the walls.

I shouted, "Do none of you understand that we come to talk? I hope that the fool who let his crossbow release a bolt will be punished."

It was Charles of Alençon who spoke to me, "We did not invite you to talk! Speak and then leave. Nothing that you say can make us change our minds."

I nodded and gestured behind me, "Loudon has fallen. There are many lords who realise that they were duped by Geoffrey Fitz Empress." I took from my saddlebag one of my maps. It was rolled like a parchment. "I have here a document which is the truth about the heir to Anjou. This is proof, if proof were needed, that Geoffrey Fitz Empress was promised nothing." I let that sink in. "King Henry of England has only recently taken the throne. He has yet to decide what titles and lands will be awarded. There are many who defended Chinon who will be given lands and titles. The King is a fair man." I pointed the parchment at Charles of Alençon. I was guessing but I had a feeling he had something to do with the ambush and I tested the waters. "Your leader, Charles of Alençon, has conspired with the King of France to have the King murdered on the way here. His brother would not support that. Are you willing to support such a traitor!"

I heard the murmur of dissent. I saw men turning towards each other. I watched as Charles of Alençon tried to regain order. Suddenly he bent down and picked up a crossbow. It was already loaded and the bolt flew towards me. I know not how I did it but, jerking Sword to the left I blindly batted with the parchment. I was lucky. The bolt had had three hundred paces to travel and Charles of

Alençon was no expert. Even so, it came close to me. It tore the parchment from my hand.

From behind me came a roar of anger from our men. I held up my hand, "I am unharmed! Do not move!"

As I looked back towards the walls I saw that Charles of Alençon had disappeared. Behind me, I heard the hooves of the knights and men at arms as King Henry brought the army up to me. There was no more movement from the walls. What was happening? Was the traitor planning some other trick?

The King reined in next to me and shook his head. "You could have been killed!"

"But I was not and look! The ruse succeeded." Ahead of us the gates swung open. The banner of Charles of Alençon was lowered. We had taken the second castle. The question remained, where was the traitor?

Chapter 13

Still wary of a trick from the traitor, we donned our helmets and I sent men at arms ahead to secure the gate and to ensure that the King would be safe. The words I had overheard in London still echoed inside my head. '*The County first and then… who knows. Trust me, lord, to guide your path.*'

It was, however, safe. As we rode through the gates I saw that weapons were sheathed and heads were bare and bowed. I recognised a knight from the wars, Sir Alain of Tours. I rode up to him, "Sir Alain, where is Charles of Alençon?"

He looked up with an apologetic expression upon his face, "I am sorry, lord, he and his men fled through the rear gate. When he left, we opened the gates for you." He handed me the traitor's banner.

I turned to the King, "Do we pursue?"

He shook his head, "There will be time for him to pay for his sins." He looked down from his horse. "You, Alain of Tours, you hold the castle for me?"

He bowed, "I do, your majesty."

"Then all of you swear allegiance to me." He was learning.

After they were sworn we took half the men and headed back up the road to Chinon. We had doubled our force and it had cost us nothing. Our one casualty had been the squire and that was nothing to do with the rebellion. That had been an attempt at assassination. I had already spoken with William and Phillip, the King's bodyguards. We would have extra security around his tent while we were in Anjou. My son had told me of the assassins in the Holy Land. I did not think they had them here but the audacity of the attack in the forest had worried me.

The machines were still incomplete when we arrived back. While the new men were allocated camps I sat with the King and his brother. King Henry was keen to make an assault. He wanted the rebellion snuffed out quickly. "How much longer for the machines, brother?"

"The rams will be ready on the morrow. The onagers? The day after."

"Then we have two days."

"Use them wisely, majesty."

"Use them, Warlord? How? Prepare for battle?"

"No, speak with your brother. Your voice has worked twice and now you have even more power to persuade him." I handed him the banner of Charles of Alençon. "Tell him that we have his other two castles and that he is alone."

"He will not surrender for he will fear death to be the punishment."

William said, "Then do not threaten death, brother. Keep him close. The Warlord told me how he fled the last time. Choose men to be gaolers who you can trust."

The King smiled, "Little brother, you have grown. I will think on that. After a good sleep, I will consider. If I do ride to him I will be flanked by you two. I think you are both counters he will respect in this game."

After the King had retired I said, "Keep a good watch about yourself, William. The King of France plays a dangerous game. The King needs you here in France, especially as he will be fighting in Wales soon. Guard yourself and surround yourself with good men."

"And yet you walk around alone, lord."

I laughed, "I was important once but no longer. Your brother is kind to keep an old warrior like me around but I do not think that any will try to kill me here in camp."

He looked over my shoulder and smiled, "And your men are there to ensure that any attempt will fail."

I turned and saw, in the shadows, James, Robert of Derby and Griff of Gwent. "What are you doing?"

Robert of Derby grinned, "We were just taking a stroll in the night air, lord and thought to escort you back to your tent."

"I do not need to be escorted. Here I am safe."

Robert knew me well. I had fought alongside him many times before he had joined Sir Leofric, "Aye sir, it is us poor little sheep who need your protection!"

I shook my head, "You are incorrigible!"

He was not put out by the comment, "If I knew what that meant, lord, I would probably agree!"

126

My tent was close to that of Sir Leofric. His archers had been hunting and there were venison haunches being cooked as we arrived. Wilfred handed me a platter, "Here lord, the haunch will take some cooking but we sliced the heart and cooked it. Tasty!"

"Thank you, Wilfred."

"Osbert is fetching the wine, lord."

Unlike many lords, Sir Leofric and I were quite happy in the company of men at arms. We fought together. We ate and drank together. The most senior of Sir Leofric's company were seated around the fire. We were easy in the presence of one another. We both knew that a good man at arms was the equal of most knights and the superior of many. The heart was well cooked and just what I needed. They made good wine around Chinon. It was rich, red and heavy. It complimented the heart well. When I had first come from the east, several lifetimes ago, I would have baulked at eating heart and red wine. I had been used to finely cooked and spice delicacies in the east. The wine I had enjoyed had been white and chilled. How I had changed. The sliced heart was delicious and just what I needed.

"You are pensive, lord."

"Just thinking back, Leofric. We have had a long journey since we began in Stockton."

He nodded, "When John and I were your squires, in England, I thought that I would end my days on the Tees. I was content. Yet here I am, an Angevin now, with a wife and family. I doubt that I shall ever return to England. Is that wrong?"

"No, I was just thinking of myself, a young arrogant man who left Constantinople and was resentful to be dragged to a cold inhospitable place like Stockton. Life is a journey and none of us can know where we will travel or who we shall meet. It is better to accept what comes your way and to make the best of it."

Brian came over to me and topped up my wine.

After he had gone I said, "Brian there is a good example. He lost his eye and was disfigured. He has told me that no woman can bear to look on his face. It would have been all too easy for him to succumb to drink and feel sorry for himself but he did not. He is a man and accepts what fate has dealt him. That is how a man should be measured; not in titles and armour, not by money or power but how he deals with hardship and adversity."

Sir Leofric raised his goblet, "Amen to that, lord." He drank deeply.

Platters were brought with the first slices of the venison. A little charred they had been thinly sliced. My servants were all experienced soldiers. Venison took a lot of cooking on an open fire, thin and charred was better than thick and tough.

"I think that this will be over by the end of the month and then I will be returning to Wales with the King. Have you any men at arms and archers who might wish to travel with me?"

Sir Leofric trained both men at arms and archers for us. Griff of Gwent and Robert of Derby chose prospective candidates and assessed their ability. When they had completed training in Anjou then those who wished to go to England were sent on the *'Adela'*. Since the end of the civil war there had appeared no need to send more men. The war in Wales and William's campaign in the north now meant that we did.

Sir Leofric looked over to his two senior warriors. They both nodded. Robert of Derby said, "Aye lord. I have five or six lads who would return to the land in which they were born."

"They are not Norman? Angevin?"

Shaking his head, he said, "There were many who came here from England with lords to fight in the wars. Some lords are not like Sir Leofric. When the war ended they severed their ties with their men and went home thinking to live like princes. With no civil war, why keep expensive men at arms? With respect, Warlord, you and your knights are an exception. You have never changed." He nodded towards James, "I remember Master James' father when he was a man at arms and you knighted him. None of us could believe that. Aye, sir, Roger, James, John, Harry, Arne and Wilson have all told me that they would return home. I will speak with them."

"Thank you. And archers?"

Griff of Gwent wiped his mouth, "They are rarer than hen's teeth, lord but I have four who would do. Tom the Fletcher, Robert of Sheffield, Will Green Leg and Rhodri of Ruthin."

I looked up from my venison, "A Welshman?"

He laughed, "Aye lord but he is a northerner. They are a funny lot of there in those mountains. All mystic like; full of bards and druids those hills are. But he is a good archer. There are few men the equal of Dick but Rhodri is. He is like a barrel. Powerful arms, lord."

"Then ask them to see me when the siege is over. I would not distract them before then."

I was woken by the sound of hammering as the men building the siege engines were chivvied and chased to complete their work.

King Henry was up and about. I was pleased to see that his two bodyguards were within arm's reach of him the whole time. I had broken fast well and, with James in attendance, strode up to the two brothers.

"Well, majesty, have you decided?"

"There is nothing to be lost by speaking with my brother and if we can sow the seeds of doubt in his men's mind then that cannot hurt either. I have sent a man to ask for a truce so that we may speak."

The messenger came back agreeing that we could speak with Geoffrey. He would not leave his walls but he would speak from the barbican at the top of the ramp.

I shook my head, "Your brother has made a bad mistake for that will also allow us to see their defences. If your brother had more courage and more sense then he would meet us between the castle and our lines."

King Henry laughed, "He was not trained by the Warlord. My father and I were!"

I rode with King Henry and his brother. We had no helmets but King Henry wore his crown. The ramp which led to the gate passed a wall that was lined with embrasures and men. Without protection, it would be a death trap. There were slits through which crossbows could send their bolts at point-blank range. However, I noted that the slits had a narrow angle. There were places that the crossbows could not cover. The ramp was cunningly constructed so that it twisted. I noted that. Whoever was in the ram would need to be aware of that particular problem.

The barbican had a pair of double towers. They were not huge but the tour de Moulin which was nearby gave elevation and would be an obstacle for the men there could add to the rain of missiles on the ram. There was no moat. The castle was built on solid rock and that eliminated a problem I had envisaged. As we rounded the curve in the wall I saw that the gate had metal studs in it. It would not yield to an axe. Back at our camp, the men were fire hardening the stake in the ram. We had a couple of spares too. There were crossbowmen and men at arms on the walls of the barbican and in the towers but no stone-throwers. I looked for and found the holes through which they could pour oil, pig fat or boiling water. The tell-tale column of smoke that accompanied such devices was missing. That did not mean they would not have them but Geoffrey struck me as someone who was ill-prepared. His lieutenant Charles of

Alençon was not with him. As the King had said, Geoffrey had not been trained by me.

We reined in twenty paces short of the walls. I said nothing. I was there to intimidate Geoffrey. My silence would be seen as a threat. Henry did the talking and I studied the defences. We would only be able to use one ram. The ramp and the gate were not wide enough for two. We would have to support the ram with archers and pavises. They would have to be constructed. Fortunately, they were easy to make and there were plenty of willows by the river.

King Henry spoke first. I had instructed him to do so. It would set the tone. We were not there to plead, we were there to demand. "This is a dark day for our family, brother."

"You should have heeded my father's wish for me to be Count of Anjou." Geoffrey sounded as petulant as ever.

"Are you still deluding yourself with that? I have his will and he makes no mention of you nor of our brother William here. Instead, he asks me to decide who should be Count. I have only been king for a short time. I have yet to decide who shall rule in Anjou, Maine, Touraine and Normandy. You have been ill-advised."

"Our father told me I would be Count!" Geoffrey's voice sounded shrill and whining. I watched the knights who were close by on the fighting platform. They did not approve of his tone. He was more of a child than a leader.

"And I say again that I have yet to make a decision. Yield this castle to me and we can speak of your future."

Geoffrey laughed. "You are a fool, brother! I have three castles and I control the south!"

William raised his arm and, without looking, I knew that behind us, Richard d'Avranches had led his men with their banners so that they could be seen from the barbican.

Geoffrey's face showed his shock and then he raised his head and said, defiantly, "That is but one castle, Richard d'Avranches is not a true knight. I still hold Mirebeau!"

William reached behind him and, taking the standard of Charles of Alençon, threw it to the ground. Geoffrey was not clever enough to feign disinterest. His face fell and his mouth dropped open.

King Henry's voice was reasonable and measured when next he spoke, "Brother, this is all that you have. Those knights whom you had in your two castles have now sworn allegiance to me. We have twice the men that we had. I ask you to save your men's lives for we shall win."

I stared up at Geoffrey and almost willed him to look at me. I saw him look at the King and then his younger brother. Finally, he dragged his eyes around to stare at me. He could only hold the gaze briefly and then he shook his head, "Do your worst! I have cast the die! Your men will bleed on these walls."

King Henry nodded as though this was to be expected. He looked at me and gestured with his hand. I nudged Sword forward. I stood in the stirrups and pulled back on the reins to make him rear. It was a dramatic gesture. My horse obligingly neighed. As he landed I shouted, "I am the Earl Marshal of King Henry, I am the Warlord of the North and the Empress' Champion. Know this, all within Chinon's walls, if you resist us then you will incur my wrath. I am an old and vengeful warrior" I swept my arm along the wall. "I have fought with many of you and you know that I do not lie." I pointed at Geoffrey, "The boy who leads you has not fought. He has been led astray. If you follow him then you are doomed. I give you a fair warning. I have spoken!" I wheeled Sword around and followed King Henry and William down the ramp. We rode slowly and I was aware of every eye watching us. Charles of Alençon's standard lay before the gate. It was a reminder to Geoffrey that he had failed.

When we reached the camp William asked, "Will he surrender?"

I shrugged, "He may see that he has no choice but to fight. If I were you, majesty, I would use the onagers to begin battering the barbican. I paced out the range as we came back. Although they do not have a clear line of sight there is no obstacle before them. If we use pavises we can protect them. They may not be able to see the gatehouse but we can use a spotter close to the castle. While the rams are being built it will be like the sound of impending doom."

"You are right and it will give the men the chance to do something rather than just sitting around."

It took but a morning to make the pavises. Made from fresh willow the oblong shields were quick to make and were as tough as a shield. Each would stop an arrow or a bolt. We made enough to protect both the ram and the archers who would accompany the war machines. The archers moved forward with them. The range to the barbican was just over a hundred paces. The onagers would have to be further away. The fact that they could not see the barbican was a problem but the Tour de Moulin was a good marker. Once the pavises were in place the archers, led by Griff of Gwent began a steady rain of arrows. If they had used crossbows they would have had to lower the pavise before release. The archers had no such problem. The archers began to clear the walls. This allowed the onagers to be brought forward. We would use them in pairs. The tensioning limited their use and we had two replacements ready to be brought up when the first two onagers showed signs of wear and tear.

When the war machines snapped it sounded like the crack of lightning. It took four boulders before we were rewarded with the sound of stone hitting stone. The lonely spotter had used his hands to correct the fall of stone and, now that we were hitting he returned to us. The men working the machines nodded their satisfaction and gave a cheer. They had the range. The archers shifted their target and rained arrows at the barbican. Fresh archers relieved the first ones so that the shower continued all afternoon. As darkness fell the archers were replaced by men at arms who would guard the machines and pavises in case Geoffrey tried a sortie. I did not think that he would.

That evening we discussed the day's events. "Will he surrender, Warlord?"

I looked into the fire and after a moment or two said, "If it were you inside Chinon then I would say no. You would have machines of your own. You would sortie forth. You would not have allowed us to dominate this day as we have done. I know not your brother. What little I have seen of him has not impressed me. The lords I saw with him are good soldiers. I wonder what he has offered them in return for this treason? If Geoffrey does not surrender then his lords may."

William said, "The rams are both ready."

"Then I will order the attack to begin in the morning. I will choose a leader to go with the ram. Perhaps Sir Leofric?"

I shook my head, "There is but one choice, your majesty, me!"

"You are Earl Marshal! What if you fall?"

"Then that is meant to be. Sir Leofric is a good choice but I am a better one. If the lords with whom we fought see me then their resolve will weaken. Besides I have assaulted more castles than any." I could see that the King was not convinced. "Your majesty, trust me. I have no intention of dying. I have a son and grandchildren in England. This is calculated. My presence may save lives."

William asked, "How so?"

I turned and said, flatly, "Because every crossbow bolt will be aimed at me." Both the brothers knew that would be true.

132

I sought out Leofric. "I will need the archers and men at arms you promised me."

"Of course. May I ask why?"

"I will be going in behind the ram tomorrow. They will need to bring large shields. I think I will be attracting every missile they have in Chinon."

"Lord..."

I smiled, "The King asked for you. I would take it as a great compliment. I chose this task."

"And I would gladly have gone. Are you sure about this?"

"Do not worry, I have thought it through. Unless they have suddenly built catapults or onagers it is only the bolts that can harm me. I will rely on your archers to hit the crossbows before they hit me."

He nodded, "They will have fewer bolts aimed at them and they are more accurate."

"Exactly. Send them to me after they have eaten. I wish to make sure that all know what we are to do."

James walked back to my tent with me. "They are right, lord, it is dangerous."

"Getting out of bed in the morning can be dangerous. Meeting with Ralph of Bowness has reminded me of stories my father told me of the housecarls of King Harold. When the Normans charged at them they held their shields above the heads and before them. They were not touched. When the Breton crossbows loosed their bolts at them they did not penetrate their wall of shields."

We had reached our camp and my servants appeared with drink, food and seats. "But was not King Harold killed by an arrow?"

I smiled, almost triumphantly, "He was indeed, an arrow! An arrow which was loosed vertically to plunge down and hit him. Have you seen any archers on Chinon's walls?"

"No, lord."

"Nor have I. With shields above and before then, we should be safe. However, just to be certain I will wear my gambeson beneath a surcoat, then my mail and finally another surcoat. When I spoke with my son he told me of Seljuk Turks who fight that way. I know not how, but it is the different layers which can stop a bolt or an arrow from penetrating."

He nodded, "I understand."

"You will not have to fight on the morrow. You will hold my standard and your shield. That is all that is needed from you. If there is fighting to do then my men at arms and I will do it."

"You think we will not have to?"

"I believe that if we penetrate their gate then their resistance will end. Besides, that is all we need to do. We break into the barbican and we break their will to fight." It was dark but there were glowing patches showing where the rooms and chambers used by Geoffrey were to be found. "See those lights? They are close to the barbican. Geoffrey's quarters are close to the gate. He will capitulate but we must breach the gate."

We had finished eating when the ten men sent by Sir Leofric arrived. I stood, "You are from Sir Leofric?"

One of the men at arms, a tall blond who looked like a Viking, nodded, "Aye lord. I am Arne Arneson."

"You understand that if you serve me you will be in great danger."

Disconcertingly they all grinned and nodded. Arne said, "Aye, lord! But men say that as well as being dangerous being with you is lucky. Better a lucky leader who puts us in danger than a careful leader whom the gods do not favour."

"Gods?"

He shrugged and held Thor's Hammer and a crucifix for me to see, "A warrior needs all the help he can get, lord!"

I waved over Lame Tom, "Tom, have ale and food brought for my new men."

"Aye lord."

"Sit and I will tell you what we will attempt tomorrow."

I waited until the food and drink were served. "Make sure that no one overhears us."

"Aye lord."

My servants were all armed and formed a circle at the edge of our camp. I could see that I had their attention. "The gate we assault tomorrow is not wide and that is why we use the one ram. The ram will be manned by strong warriors who can push but they are not the ones who will break in. That will be us!"

They nodded their approval. "We will be behind the ram and we will be so close that we shall know if one of the men farts!" They laughed. "We will have an old-fashioned shield wall. Like the Roman testudo or the Saxon shield wall. The only sign that there are men within will be the wolf standard which James will hold. It will rise from the wall of shields like a harbinger of doom."

I turned to the archers. "You four will carry two pavises. Your task will be to slay any crossbow men that you see. The rest will be keeping the heads of the men on the walls down but the curve in the ramp means that they cannot see their targets. You will. I see three of you wear helmets. I want all of you with helmets and a coif too."

The one without a helmet said, "I am Will Greenleg, lord, and will get one. My other was damaged."

"Good, you shall need one. As soon as the gate is breached then we move through the ram and I want to take the barbican."

James asked, "Not the second gate?"

"No, James, for the barbican is higher than the second wall. Our archers will rain death upon them. We will hold the barbican and then the two rams can attack the wall and the second gate. Your task will be to tear down their standard and raise our own. Arne, you will lead Wilson, Harry and James of Tewkesbury up the left-hand tower and I will take the rest up the right!"

When they had all finished eating we practised making a shield wall. It was not as easy as it sounded. We had to use the different heights of the men. Eight men were small for a testudo but the Romans had had one for a contubernium and that had eight men. I was hopeful.

After we had finished I was introduced to my men at arms, Roger of Bath, James of Tewkesbury, John son of John, Harry Lightfoot and Wilson of Bristol. The other archers were: Tom the Fletcher, Robert of Sheffield and my Welshman Rhodri of Ruthin.

I was tired but I knew the value of bonding with my men and so I sat up with them as they chatted. My servants joined in the conversation. They had shared battles, skirmishes and lords. I listened more than I spoke. Rhodri of Ruthin asked me, during a lull in the conversation, "When this is over, lord, what then?"

"I am the Earl Marshal of the King. Where he goes, so go I. Eventually, I hope to return to Stockton where my son lives." I stood to address them all, "You should know that our first journey will be to Wales." I looked at Rhodri, "We go to the marches. King Maredudd ap Gruffydd has been taking English land."

"I fight for England, lord. I severed any ties I had with my homeland long ago." He sounded bitter and I determined to discover why when time allowed.

Chapter 14

We did not get much sleep. After I had prayed and James had ensured that my weapons were sharp I lay on my cot and dozed for an hour or two. It was not a sleep but I rested. Some of my new men were up before me. I was pleased to see my archers choosing the best arrows to put in their quivers. I knew that we were lucky to have a fletcher among our numbers. All archers could fletch but a good fletcher could gain a few paces from an arrow by skilful selection and positioning of the feathers. I made my morning prayers and broke my fast. I did not eat a lot and I only drank small beer. If I survived, then I would enjoy a hearty meal.

James helped me to dress. After I had donned my gambeson he placed some extra padding over my shoulders. Then he slid my old surcoat on top of it. After donning my chausses and coif, we slid my mail byrnie over the surcoat. While I had been waiting in Stockton for word of my son, Alf had made sure that there were no weak links. Finally, my surcoat was placed over my byrnie. It felt a little tight but I knew that the extra padding would be worth the discomfort. James held my helmet and I left my tent. My men were ready and dawn had broken. I heard the creak of wood as the ram was pushed into position. As soon as it was light the onagers would continue their barrage of stones. All eyes would be on the ram and my banner. When we started up the ramp then it would only be the archers who would be attacking. We dared not risk a stone sent from our own war machines hitting the ram.

King Henry and his brother appeared behind the ram. We moved out of the way so that it would be ready to push up the slope. Until it reached the bend another twenty men at arms would push it to help it gather momentum. When they retreated, we would take their place. "All is ready, Warlord?"

"We are prepared. We have made our peace with God and each man knows his task." My archers appeared with their two willow pavises. My men at arms were fiddling and adjusting leather straps on their shields and swords. It was a ritual which good warriors performed before they fought.

There was a mighty crack as a stone hit the gate. Those hits were lucky but the ones working the machine took it as a sign from God. Any hits on the gate would weaken it and make it easier for the men in the ram. There was a second creaking crack and this time the men in the ram cheered. The mixture of men at arms and knights would be nervous. Walking in the blackness of a ram, not knowing what the enemy would throw at you was hard and a real test of nerves.

My men at arms shouted encouragement to those inside the dark interior of the ram. "We will be right behind you, lads!"

"We will show these traitors what true Englishmen can do!"

"Aye and Welshmen too, boyo!"

The ram creaked up the gentle slope of the ramp. It would get harder. The twenty or so men at arms who would push it until it reached the bend fell in behind and locked bodies to push. At their side were men at arms with huge willow shields.

William commented, "The men sound confident."

"They have to believe they will succeed, lord. If they did not then they would falter at the end. However, they do not believe that all who ascend will be alive at the fall of the castle."

I saw William's face. Like his brother Geoffrey, he had minimal experience of actual battles. He could use a sword, a lance and ride a horse but he had never been in a fight to the death at the top of a fighting platform. Henry had and he understood, I think.

As the men pushed past us I said, "Form up."

Arne Arneson was the largest of the men and he stood next to me on my right side. Wilson of Bristol was large too and he stood on my left. James was behind me with Roger of Bath on one side and James of Tewkesbury on the other. John son of John and Harry Lightfoot were the rear rank. We had our shields at our sides. We would only raise them when the men helping the ram returned.

There was another crack on the gate. God was on our side. Our archers walked to our right as we moved towards the curve in the ramp. The pavises they carried protected us from bolts and arrows. I idly wondered what would happen if they built a second wall to the left of the ramp. Then we would be assaulted from both sides. I was grateful that they had not done so already. Two of the men at arms pushing the ram fell as they turned the bend. The sergeant at arms shouted, "Back!" switching the shields which had lain over their backs to their right side they began to walk backwards towards us.

The archers who were supposed to have protected them now ran, rather belatedly, to take their positions. It was not Leofric's men this day. It was a Norman lord's men. One was tardy and a bolt struck him. He fell, dead. It was fortunate that they were crossbows as they could not keep up a high rate of missiles.

Once the men at arms had passed us I said, "Shields!"

I held mine before me and peered over the top. There were no embrasures at head height. If I kept my gaze downward then, in theory, I should have been safe from a bolt. Arne and Wilson held their shields before us while James placed his above us, across the middle. That allowed the other James and John to use their shields to protect the side. James, James and John had their spare hand tucked inside the belts of Wilson, Arne and myself. It helped to keep us together. We carried no spears. This would be sword and knife work.

I set the pace by shouting, "Sword, shield, sword, shield!" The men moved their sword leg and then their shield leg. I took small steps and we moved after the ram. I was peering over the top of my shield. I wanted to move steadily. Even so, we began to catch the ram as it laboured up the slope. The ram was sturdy and heavy. I knew that, behind us, the second ram would have begun its journey. I heard the twang of bow strings as my archers picked out targets. Then bolts hit our shields. As I had expected they were aiming for us. The ram had a hide and wood roof. When they neared the wall then stones would plummet down and they would do the damage but eight men struggling up a slope were a better target for a crossbow.

I heard a strangulated cry and heard Rhodri shout, "Got you, you bastard!" It would be a battle of wits between my archers and the crossbows. The advantage my men had was that they could send six or seven arrows for every bolt. They could send an arrow at the slits and, if they were lucky, it might bounce off the wall and cause a wound. Even a glancing blow could send pieces of stone into the face of the crossbowman. A tiny splinter of stone could blind.

As we neared the rear of the ram I said, "Slow!" Timing was all. When we reached the back of the war machine I lifted my shield and placed it over my head. We now had extra protection. James moved his shield back a little and the two at the rear were better protected. My four archers were sending four or five flights at the enemy and then moving their willow shields further up. The other archers did not move. Their task was to continue to rake the walls.

I could see through the ram. The gate was just forty paces from us. Bolts were rattling off the shields of my man and archers. I heard them strike the ram but the hide covering prevented penetration.

From the front, the sergeant at arms shouted, "They have something hot for us!"

A young knight asked, "Oil or water?"

The sergeant laughed, "It makes no never mind, lord, either way, it will burn your balls off!"

I shouted, "Keep going! We have the finest archers in the land. If they are going to pour hot fire on us they have to show themselves. Trust the archers and to God!"

"Aye lads and we have the Warlord with us! That little pipsqueak will be wetting himself! We have the Wolf Banner! It has never failed yet! On lads!" The sergeant at arms had done this before.

I felt a stone ping off my helmet and then, a moment later my head was shaken as a bolt struck it. The helmet held and the leather cap I wore saved hurt. Both were glancing blows but I was grateful to Alf for making such a strong helmet. As we neared the walls the missiles striking helmets and shields increased. We were now closer to the gate and the ground was flattening out. The ram moved faster. "Keep the same pace!"

I heard a cry and saw a rock fall in front of the gate followed by a man at arms with an arrow in his chest. I also saw that the gate had two large vertical cracks and several smaller ones.

"Aim for the large crack!" When we were just ten paces from the gate a rock crashed into the roof of the ram. It was a large rock. It tore one of the hides from the roof and fell by the side of the ram. I said nothing but the first defence against fire had gone. We were leaning into the ram now. Our mailed weight made it move faster and our speed was faster than it had been. We thudded into the door. As stones clattered onto the roof the men inside the ram pulled back on their ropes.

The sergeant at arms yelled, "Now!" The ropes were released and the ram cracked into the door. There was another scream from above and this time a body fell onto the roof.

Then I heard Robert of Sheffield shout, "Ware above! Fire!" he had seen the smoke which told him that they had brought something heated to the battlements.

Despite my archers' best efforts, they had managed to pour something hot. It was boiling water. If the stone had not torn the hide then we might have escaped unscathed. As it was the four men beneath the racked roof were doused in boiling water. It penetrated their mail and burned their skin. They screamed. The sergeant shouted, "It will pass boys! Come on keep the ram going!"

It was as we helped the ram to smash a second time that I realised the mistake the defenders had made. They could not use oil now. The wood had been struck by water. Although boiling it was still water and the ram would be harder to ignite. That was no consolation to the men who still screamed in pain. Stones continued to clatter and boiling water fell a second time. This time it hit the undamaged hides. Men were spattered with boiling water but none screamed.

The Sergeant at Arms shouted, "Lord, I can see daylight!"

That gave us hope and the men pulled with renewed vigour. I heard the second ram trundling up behind us. A bolt came through the crack in the wood. It struck the sergeant in the shoulder. He made not a sound and continued to pull on the rope. Suddenly there was a crack. The gate had a hole in it.

"One more should do it!"

Another bolt came through the hole and then there was a cry and Rhodri shouted, "Another one to Wales!"

Rhodri's arrow was too late for the sergeant. This bolt had plunged through his coif and into the brave sergeant's neck. Blood sprayed us all.

"Keep going!"

The next swing was the one that broke the gate and the hearts of the defenders. It hit the bar holding the gate and it shattered.

"Push!" Drawing my sword, I stepped under the roof of the ram and swung my shield around. The weight of the ram and the men pushed us into the gateway. We had a way in but then defenders ran to the front of the ram and, using spears to thrust them into the first two men pushing the wooden beast.

"Step to the middle and let us through! Henry!"

I ran crouched along the ram. I saw more men racing to get at the men at arms inside the ram. I burst out and just ran at the nearest man at arms. I think he was taken by surprise. My shield smashed into his face and he fell down. I stamped on his face and swung my sword at the middle of the second man. Arne and Wilson were alongside me and our three swords swashed before us and bought the rest of my men time to join me. The ram continued to trundle through the gate and it allowed my archers in as well as the second, undamaged, ram.

"God be with us!" I ran towards the right-hand tower. My archers led the other archers to begin to send arrows at the warriors who raced through the second gate to get at us. Geoffrey had been ill-advised. He should have taken the loss of the barbican and defended the second gate. As it was the men he sent to rid the barbican of us fell to my archers' arrows. The men who had attacked us made a second mistake. They failed to bar the door to the barbican. As one traitor ran through it I stabbed him in the side before he could close it. I stepped over his body and hurtled after the others who were racing up the stairs. They should have turned to stop me. A defender always has the advantage on a spiral staircase. They did not. I slashed across the hamstrings of the man above me and he tumbled down. They kept running upwards. They were desperate to get to the fighting platform. These were not real warriors. They did not know how to defend. We, on the other hand, were past masters of attack.

I burst out onto the fighting platform at the same time as Arne. His tower had been similarly poorly defended. The defenders on the fighting platform had no shields. They ran at us with spears. I batted one away with my shield and then rammed my sword into his middle. I pulled it out and, after blocking a spear to my head, dropped to one knee and hacked beneath the byrnie of a knight. My sword bit into his leg. Arne was fighting like a man possessed. Backed by Wilson, the two of them carved a path towards me. As Harry and John fell upon the survivors I heard a cheer from our lines. I looked up and saw my banner fluttering from the top of the tower. James had not forgotten my command. We had done what I had said.

I turned and growled, "Surrender now and you live. Resist and you will die!"

The ten survivors from the garrison threw down their weapons. Rhodri led my archers and some of Leofric's up the stairs and they began to rain arrows onto the fighting platform below us. At the same time the second ram, filled with fresher men, was being pushed towards the second gate. The first ram, with fewer men, was following more slowly. I knew that William would be bringing the onagers up too. I could hear the rumble of their wheels. It was as I looked across to the Tour de Coudray that I saw the standard of Geoffrey Fitz Empress being lowered. It was the sign that they had surrendered. The men all around me began to cheer. The men in the rams saw the lowered standard and they left the confines of their rams and began to chant, "Warlord! Warlord! Warlord!" The rebellion was over.

I saw that my men were bloodied but stood. I nodded and raised my sword to them. "Our first foray together and it went well. Take what you will from the dead."

"Thank you, Warlord."

As my new men began to strip the mail from the knights and men at arms, as well as the purses and swords they carried, I turned to James. I pointed to the standard, "That was expediently done."

"I was glad to be doing something. It felt as though I was doing nothing just carrying the standard."

I took off my helmet. There were dents and marks from the stones and the bolts they had sent at us, "It did what it was supposed to. It drew the missiles to me and the ram was able to do its job."

"Lord, the second gate is opening."

"Thank you, Will. When you have taken all that you wish have the prisoners taken to our camp. The King will decide their fate."

One of the prisoners said, "The King said he would be clement."

I rounded on the man, "And that was before you fought us. You cannot be treacherous and then expect clemency. You chose the wrong brother!" I slipped my shield across my back and said, "Come, James, we will join the King,"

The bodies still lay on the stairs as we descended. James shouted up the stairs, "And there are bodies here too, Arne!"

"Thank you, Master James."

We had to be careful for the narrow staircase was slick with blood and gore. I heard the tramp of feet up the ramp as we left the gloom of the guardhouse and stepped into the sun. William and the King were there. The King clasped my arm, "Where would I be without you, Alfraed? None else, not even my uncle, could have done what you did."

"You have brave men." I pointed to the dead sergeant at arms. "He was braver than the rest. If he has family they should have some riches from this."

The King nodded. "Phillip, make enquiries."

"Aye lord."

"And now let us see what my brother has to say for himself."

King Henry showed that he was a true leader that day. He could have ridden up the ramp at the head of a triumphant army but he did not. He marched with the rest of us. It endeared him to those who knew him. There were others who said he was cold and uncaring. He was not. I know that I was biased but the press of men behind us as we walked up to the second gate was a testament to their loyalty and men are not loyal to a poor leader.

As we passed the two rams the men and knights who had been inside them were waiting. They cheered and banged the side of the ram. The joy of victory was on their faces. The horror of the water and the stench of death was passed. They had survived. To have only lost a few men in an attack was a wondrous thing. It was no wonder they were happy. Those in the rams would be rewarded for their efforts. The couple of knights who had volunteered could expect manors while the men at arms would have that which they wanted, coin. Geoffrey would lose his treasury. The knights who had supported him would lose manors. Some would go to Henry's men while others sold and the coin given to Henry's loyal troops. War was a gamble. The price you paid was in blood and gold.

The gates stood open and Geoffrey, flanked by the knights who had supported him, stood bareheaded and awaiting us. Behind them were the men who had defended Chinon. This was a castle with but one way in and one way out. The only way down was to scale the walls. None had done what Charles of Alençon had done and fled. They were all there to take their punishment.

William Fitz Empress showed his increasing maturity, authority and confidence. He shouted, "Bow to your rightful Count and King. Make obeisance to King Henry of England, Duke of Normandy and Count of Anjou, Maine and Touraine!"

I saw Geoffrey give a surprised look at his younger brother and then he, like all the rest, dropped to one knee.

Henry nodded his thanks to his brother, "We gave all of you the chance to surrender. Then you might have expected clemency. As it is you refused the offer and fought. If I wished it then all of you could lose a nose or a hand as a mark of the traitor." I saw him let that sink in. "Viscount," he turned to William, "have our rebellious brother taken to the Great Hall and I will join him there."

"Aye, your majesty." With his household knights around him, William led his brother towards the royal apartments.

Henry turned to Robert de Gavette, "Bring up men to man these walls."

"Aye, your majesty."

"Guillaume of Angouleme, I would have the knights separated from the men at arms. I will speak with the common soldier. Have the knights taken to the inner bailey. I will speak with them there."

"Aye, your majesty."

While the two knights began to marshal their charges, Henry took me to one side. "There are more prisoners than I thought there would be. What do we do?"

I pointed to the men at arms, "I know these men. They obeyed their lords. These are not swords for hire. These are the same men who fought for your mother and your father in the war. They thought they fought for your family still. Most are good men. They deserve a chance."

He nodded, "You are right." He turned to one of the priests who had accompanied us. "Father Michel, fetch me a bible from the chapel."

"Aye, your majesty."

When the knights had been led into the castle and Father Michel returned with the Bible, the King said, "You have all been led astray by my young brother. Kneel now and swear, on this Holy Book never to take arms against your rightful ruler."

Every man knelt. They were grateful for the chance of life. Most of them did not know Henry. They had heard that he was both cold and cruel. Now that he showed them mercy they could not wait to swear allegiance.

Leaving others to take the men at arms down to our camp we headed for the inner bailey. "And now these. Were these led astray or were they motivated by greed and the hope of power?"

As we approached them I saw that there were about sixty knights. I recognised some of the older ones. I slowed and the King slowed with me. "Some of these are good knights, lord. Perhaps they could be used."

"Used?"

"The rebellion is over. I assume you do not want to waste time and effort hunting down Charles of Alençon?"

"I would have him punished but you are right. He is not important enough now. He is that grain of sand in the bottom of my mail. It irritates but does not hurt. How can we use them?"

"Wales. We need knights to go to Wales. If we take these knights then they cannot be subverted by Louis or Theobald and we will need men to fight. Offer them the chance to redeem themselves."

He smiled, "We gain an army with little effort. You are a wise warrior, Alfraed."

"Wisdom comes with age and there are few left who have lived as long as I have."

He nodded and we continued walking towards them. They looked sorry for themselves. With heads hung low they expected the worst. All had heard, before the assault, our words, and knew that they could expect dire consequences from their actions. I have no doubt that many of the older ones would have risked fighting on had their young leader not surrendered. They were like me. You fought until you could not fight any longer. There was always hope.

After he had allowed them to feel uncomfortable in the silence he had created the young King said, "You have disappointed me. My mother, my father and my uncle led many of you to fight our enemies and unify my lands. The Warlord has fought alongside many of you. I have not taken lands from you and yet you chose to rebel against me. Do any of you deserve mercy?" It was a rhetorical question. The younger knights blanched.

"However, I believe that every knight should be given the chance to redeem himself." Faces lifted at the glimmer of hope which appeared in Henry's words. "I am taking an expedition to Wales. There Maredudd ap Gruffydd has taken English land and I intend to reclaim it. If any wishes to keep their manors then they will bring their men and accompany me to Wales." He paused to let that sink in. "The alternative is to lose your manors and be banished."

With such a choice, every knight and baron clamoured to join what they saw as a crusade against the Welsh. Just as Henry's great grandfather had persuaded his knights to come to England with the lure of land in another country, so Geoffrey's knights were easily suborned.

As we left them Henry said, "And now we grasp the nettle. My brother will not be so easy."

Entering the Great Hall, I said, "You could put him in the Tower. Your grandfather did that with his brother."

"Perhaps."

Geoffrey was seated alone in the hall. His head was bowed. Henry said, "All save the Warlord and my youngest brother leave us. I will be safe."

"Aye, your majesty."

The hall felt enormous with just four of us. "What to do, little brother."

Geoffrey looked up. Gone was the truculence and petulance of the confrontation before the battle. He looked contrite and fearful. This was the second time he had crossed his brother. He thought his life was about to end. "I was led astray, brother. Charles of Alençon told me that if I rebelled then when King Louis conquered this land I would be given the Dukedom."

I laughed, "And you believed that? Majesty, your brother should be restrained for his own good. King Louis would have made Charles the Duke!"

Henry held up his hand, "Thank you, Earl Marshal, I believe you are right but it still leaves me with the problem of what to do with you."

In a very small voice, Geoffrey said, "Am I to die?"

He looked younger than his nineteen years. He looked younger than his little brother, William. I saw now that Henry had been taken to war by me when he was young. That had hardened and matured him. Geoffrey had been indulged. His father had spoiled him.

I saw that Henry would not have him executed. He smiled, "I think not. Until I have decided what to do with you I will have you closely watched. After London, I cannot trust you or your word."

The next few days saw Henry organising his lands in Anjou. He appointed Sir Leofric as Warlord of Anjou with his young brother William as Marshal. The inclusion of Leofric in the arrangement was at William's request. He was a sensible youth and knew that he had not enough experience yet. A letter arrived from their mother exhorting Henry to show mercy towards Geoffrey. Henry looked pleased that his actions had been vindicated.

We were about to leave for home when the guards announced a deputation from Brittany. Henry had supported Count Conan when he had ruled but since his death, his uncle, Hoël, had ruled and he was a violent and unpopular man. The deputation of senior peers from Brittany sought an audience with the King. Along with William and myself, we listened to what they had to say.

"Your majesty, we are here to beg your intervention in our land. None of the royal family, save Hoël, remain and he has proved to be a leader we cannot follow. We have imprisoned him."

Henry nodded, "And what do you want of me?"

"We would have you appoint one of your family to be the Count of Nantes."

Henry's eyes flashed at me. The question was obvious. Was this some sort of trick or ruse?

I stood, "I am the Earl Marshal of England and I advise the King. This is a generous offer. However, it comes as a surprise."

The spokesman, Guy of Rennes, nodded, "It would seem so. Conan was a good Count and King Henry supported him. His uncle is a venal and corrupt man. There is none of that family left. If we appointed a Count from within our ranks there would be division and conflict. Your King is young but he seems to have a wise head." He smiled, "Besides, Brittany is a small, rocky County. We are hardly worth worrying about." He turned to Henry. "Since the time of your great grandfather, we have been vassals of Normandy. In the main, it has served us well. We will be happy with whomever you choose."

"Then if you will allow me some time to ponder these matters I will give you a decision." He waved a hand, "My servants will find you some quarters."

After they had gone I said, "This is a good day, your majesty. You secure your Dukedom and now make secure a potential threat to Anjou."

He smiled, "And the choice is obvious. William, will you be Count of Nantes?"

To the surprise of both of us, he shook his head, "No brother. I am content, for the moment with the title I hold. Viscount of Dieppe and Marshal of Anjou suit me. Besides, I have realised that I need to read more. Had I not read Vegetius we might still be trying to force the walls."

"Then who?"

William said, quietly, "There is but one choice it must be Geoffrey. Think about it brother, you kill two birds with one stone. You give our brother that which he wants, someone to rule, and you save yourself the problem of guarding him. The Bretons will not allow their Count to make war on you. They imprisoned Hoël. If Geoffrey tried anything they would stop him. They will be both his gaolers and his subjects. It is a perfect solution."

The Empress would be proud of her youngest son. He had shown wisdom beyond his years. Henry was as clever a man as I had ever met and he quickly realised the advantages. He sent for Geoffrey. I have never seen so dejected a man. He came expecting a death sentence. His shoulders sagged and his head drooped.

"Brother, I have an offer to make. It is a simple choice accept it or say no. There will be no third way."

He nodded, "I am resigned to my fate."

"Then I would have you become Count of Nantes and rule Brittany on my behalf."

I watched as Geoffrey wrestled with the words he had heard. Was it a trap? Was his brother trying to trick him? The three of us watched as his agile mind ran through all the possible outcomes. "I do not understand. I was a traitor and I rebelled, yet you reward me. Why?"

"Firstly, you are right you did rebel but you are of my blood. Secondly, the Bretons have asked me to name a new Count. I offered it to William but he suggested you."

Geoffrey looked at his younger brother and clasped both his hands, "Thank you, brother, I..."

"This offer, Geoffrey, means that you will have to rule and yet remain loyal to me and to William. If you cross that line again then you will lose your head."

Geoffrey dropped to his knees, "I swear, brother, that I am a changed man. I will be as loyal as the Warlord here."

Henry laughed as he raised his brother to his feet, "I accept your words but know this, Geoffrey. It is impossible for any man to be more loyal than the Warlord. However, if that is your ideal then I am hopeful that you are truly a changed man."

Part Three

Wales

Chapter 15

London was a hive of activity. Henry had been like a man possessed as he gathered the fleet which would take his army back to England. Leaving all of his castles well-defended he took large numbers of knights, men at arm and, to my archers' dismay, crossbowmen. The only respite he had was during the first two days when he was reunited with his queen. During that time, I had men scouting the neighbouring counties for horses. I also sent my archers to recruit more archers. I knew that, against the Welsh, we would need them. It was at about this time that a priest joined us. Thomas Becket was a clever young man. I had met him briefly at the coronation. To me, he never seemed particularly pious. He was too worldly but he was efficient. I found him a useful man for he was happy, like most clerks, with lists and details. He enjoyed the minutiae of planning. He made sure we had enough arrows, horses and spears.

I wanted to choose my own horses and I needed numbers of them. Sussex had fine grazing and I took my men at arms and James to buy some. Money was not a problem. King Henry had rewarded me well for my services in Anjou. I needed a pair of good war horses for me as well as a pair of horses for each of my men at arms, archers, James and my servants. James would also need a war horse. I bought thirty horses in all. Thomas Becket had arranged the purchase of draught animals and carts. One did not let a priest choose a horse that would be used in war! I knew enough lords now to be able to discover a reliable breeder. Ralph of the Downs was such a man. He reminded me of Aiden. He seemed to be able to talk to the horses. He had a number of war horses but two stood out for me. One was a magnificent chestnut. Ralph had named all of his horses. The chestnut was called Warrior. With just one white sock and a blond mane, he reminded me a little of Sword, save that he was bigger. Storm Bringer was black as night with a lightning blaze on his head. He reminded me of Badger. The most interesting of his horses was the palfrey he sold me.

"My lord, this one is a mare. She is the cleverest horse I have ever bred. She is not the biggest but she is strong. Even my stable boys can talk to her and she understands their words but she has other skills. She has a nose and ears which can detect friend and foe from great distances. I know not how she does it. If she stops then there is danger. If she nods her head then it is a friend. I had an old Dane who worked for me and he brought her into this world and named her. He called her Skuld. He died soon after she had finished nursing." He lowered his voice, "I know that it is not Christian, lord but I swear that Ragnar's spirit lives within her."

I walked up to the horse. Ralph was right. You could see the intelligence in her eyes. I put my nose close to hers and let her smell me. Her rough tongue licked my face.

Ralph nodded, "She is yours, lord, whether you will or not."

He had no need to persuade me. I bought all three. When it came to James' warhorse we bought one which none other would buy for it was a grey. Many knights did not like a grey. They were said to attract arrows and bolts but James knew that Snowbird was meant to be his as soon as he saw her. We rode back to London with our herd. My men at arms and archers had spent their money wisely. Some had bought mail or weapons but all had left some with the Jewish bankers who lived in London. With luck, they would survive to be old men and then the money they had earned would buy them an inn or slaves. They anticipated more riches when we headed west. I would be in the thickest of the action and that would mean closer to the richest pickings. I had surcoats made for them all. I had learned that the sight of the wolf brought fear into the hearts of our enemies. I had to have my standard repaired too. It was riven with many bolts and arrows. The sewn repairs were badges of honour.

Eventually, as the harvest was gathered in, we were ready to march. The journey to Gloucester would take six days. If the army had all been mounted we could have done it in three. Henry had sent his marcher lords a message for them to gather in Gloucester. He led a hundred knights and a hundred men at arms. With his forty crossbowmen and forty archers, he had a well-balanced force. My men were not counted amongst his. The servants and baggage added another hundred to our column which snaked along the old Roman Road, Akeman Street, towards the west.

We used the castles along the route to accommodate the senior knights. The men at arms and archers along with younger knights camped. When we were at Oxford castle Henry said, "That priest is a clever man. The Archbishop of Canterbury thinks I ought to make him Lord Chancellor."

"That would make sense, lord. Your grandfather left the country rich. Stephen spent that money. You need someone who can gather in the money you need."

He smiled, "We are in agreement. At last, I have a priest I can trust."

As we headed west I reflected that the last time I had been in the Thames Valley we had held Wallingford as an island against King Stephen. How things had changed. The knights who had fought for the Empress were now dead or living as priests. I was the last of them. The knights who rode alongside me had no idea of the battles we had fought. Henry had only been there with me and his mother briefly. It felt like another country and another life. Gloucester too was familiar. The old constable had been a stalwart ally of the Empress. I had fought here and my men had died.

It was my pensive mood that prompted a question from Henry, "What worries you, lord?"

I smiled, "Nothing, your majesty. It is the ghosts of the past who come to haunt me. It will pass." I changed the subject, "This Lord Rhys, Maredudd ap Gruffyd, what exactly has he taken from us?"

"Striguil and the manors thereabouts. He has fortified the castles in the valleys. We hold the coast but the road to the west is now in the hands of our foes. There are islands where the lords hold on; the de Clare family is one. It is the threat of attack which worries my lords here. The Severn Valley produces much of the food we eat. The whole of this land is the richest farmland in England. If the Welsh were to take it then we would be all the poorer. Striguil castle guards the way into Pembrokeshire. I fear that the lords we lost in the war with Stephen have not been replaced with men of mettle."

I thought he was being harsh but I let it pass.

There was a fine gathering of knights in Gloucester but I recognised few of them. One was Sir William of Liedeberge. He was the castellan of my estate which lay to the north of Gloucester.

I had not seen him in years. He had aged but, then again, we all had. He was pleased to see me.

"It has been many years." He frowned, "You still receive the dues I send?"

"Of course. My steward commends you on your diligence." In truth, I had no idea if he sent the dues but I was just grateful to have one knight upon whom I could rely and I would have a comfortable hall in which to sleep should I need it.

"How many men do you have?"

"Roger, my squire, fifteen men at arms and fifteen archers, lord. I have the levy too but..."

I shook my head, "It is easier with soldiers rather than eager volunteers. Have you had any trouble from the Welsh?"

"A few cattle raids; we caught and hanged them. We have had no trouble for a while. Those who live closer to Monmouth and Striguil are the ones who are plagued."

That made sense. There were few crossings of the Severn, Worcester, Tewkesbury, Upton upon Severn and Gloucester were the only ones. The bridges there were guarded well. The ones who raided my manor must have been desperate. The Wye was close by. They would have had to risk crossing through a defended town or taking a chance on a fast-flowing river.

"Who else do you know, William?"

"Walter De Clifford is the most vocal of the knights. He lost land around Striguil and he is keen to reclaim it. Richard de Clare is interesting. He is a fine knight although his father fought for King Stephen. Apparently, the King has revoked his title of earl. De Clare is not happy."

I had not known that when speaking to the King. It shed much light upon Henry's thoughts. "Which is he?"

He pointed to a tall knight. He had a red face but he had no beard. I saw him watching the King carefully. Most of the knights were all of an age with Richard de Clare. De Clifford was the oldest of them. None, save William, had fought with me.

The King mounted his horse so that he might be seen. "We are pleased that so many of you heeded our call to reclaim the lands stolen by the Welsh. Just as the Warlord's son, William, is doing in the north, we shall do here. We will take back what is ours!"

He had said the right thing. I saw Walter de Clifford shouting, "Long live King Henry!"

Everyone took up the call. Henry knew how to say the right thing. It would not always be so but, in his youth, he had that skill.

"When all my knights are gathered, we will cross the river and gather at Hereford!" This time Walther de Clifford looked less pleased. Hereford was north of Striguil.

I turned to William, "Have the Welsh taken Hereford?"

"Not yet, lord but it has been attacked many times. There is a new cathedral there now and a bridge over the Wye."

I nodded. That made sense. I could understand why Henry wanted to keep Hereford. Striguil was lost. If we could defeat the Welsh near Hereford then it would make it easier to retake Striguil. It made me wonder at his intelligence. I had not known this. King Henry was a careful leader.

He drew his sword, "We will retake the Welsh Marches!"

That was what his lords wished to hear and his name was sounded by all. He dismounted and made his way to me. He was flanked by his bodyguards. They would not risk the King's life here. "Well, Warlord?"

"You set the right tone, majesty. It bodes well."

He was followed by de Clifford and de Clare. The two bodyguards began to draw their swords. I put my hands on their sword hands, "Easy, there are friends. They are just keen to speak with the King, is that not so gentlemen?"

The elder of the two, de Clifford, nodded, "Sorry, your majesty but I was anxious to discover why you are not going to Striguil? The Welsh have not taken Hereford."

"I know and that is why we go there. It has the best crossing of the Wye and we can cross there and strike at the hinterland of Deheubarth. When we have inflicted a defeat on Lord Rhys, as he is styled, it will be much easier to take Striguil and I have sent ships from London. They will be here within the month. It means we can attack your home from two directions."

The old lord was mollified and he beamed, "I am sorry your majesty. I am anxious for my home to be back in Norman hands."

"And it will be."

He scurried off. The King looked at de Clare. I saw him frowning as he tried to remember his name, "Richard de Clare, your majesty. My lands are far to the west. My father was Earl..." He had a slightly high-pitched voice. It was not his fault but it was an annoying sound and I saw Henry's nose wrinkle. It did not suit the King.

"And you wish the title returned to you." He shook his head, "I told the Bishop you sent that you may keep the land, I am not vindictive, but the title is not yours. Your father fought my mother. Until you have atoned for that then there will be no title."

"But…"

"I have spoken."

He bowed but I saw the anger on his face. He left us alone. The King had not been as diplomatic as he could have been. De Clare would have to be watched.

"It would not cost anything to give him the title, your majesty and it would give you a strong ally."

"The de Clare family were staunch opponents of my mother and my uncle. The discussion is ended, Warlord." I was summarily dismissed and my advice was ignored.

We settled into the comfortable hall. I did not need to ride to Liedeberge. It was almost twenty miles away. William did return home. We would have to pass his manor on the way to Hereford. He had to make sure that his lands were safe before he left for Hereford.

I rose early the next morning. Phillip of Aix greeted me, "Lord, some visitors arrived just after dawn." I waited. "They are Welsh and from the Kingdom of Powys. They wish to see the King."

"Then let them."

"They may be a danger."

"How many are there?"

"Four of them."

I gave him a sideways glance. "Four? I tell you what, my squire and I will join you and William. I am certain that we can handle them. I will fetch the King. Just take their weapons from them if you are worried."

The King was poring over maps with his clerks when I found him. "Yes, Warlord?"

"You have visitors from Powys, majesty. There are four of them."

He stood and looked at the map. "That is north of here. They have not attacked us before have they?" He asked the question of the clerks. All were monks. I think that the Archbishop of Canterbury had sent them partly to gain favour with the King and partly to spy on him.

"No, your majesty. Their king is Madog ap Maredudd."

I did not know where the monks gathered their news but I remembered that Archbishop Thurston had a network of spies. Priests could be devious. I was pleased that mine was an honest man.

"Then let us see them and discover if this is another new threat." He turned to me as we descended the stairs. "It may be that this Madog ap Maredudd thinks we have designs on his land." He grinned, "We do not… yet!"

He was in a good humour. Three of the men we greeted were warriors. They were typical Welshmen from the hills. Short and squat with jet black hair they did not bother with mail. I saw that Phillip and William had disarmed them. The fourth man was a cleric. The warriors stood behind him. It would be the cleric to whom the King spoke. King Henry waved a hand and servants appeared with wine, bread and cheese. He had given strict orders that this was to be so. He was clever for it made him look as though he was hospitable. That often disarmed an enemy and allowed a friend to reveal more than they ought.

"Welcome. And what brings four travellers from the far north to visit with me here?"

The priest spoke, "I am Brother Iago. I come as the representative of the King of Powys, Madog ap Maredudd. These warriors are my escorts."

I watched their faces. They had not understood a word the priest had said. His Norman was perfect. I kept that information to myself.

"And what does your King Henry want of me?"

The priest held his hand towards a goblet, "May I?"

"Of course."

The priest drank, briefly and then jabbered something in Welsh to the three men. They each took a goblet and began to drink. The priest said, "They were suspicious. They believed you might poison them. They have an irrational fear of Normans. I know not why. They do like their wine; when they can get it, of course."

I nodded and drank my own wine, "Of course."

I saw his eyes flicker to my surcoat and the wolf. "And you would be the Warlord."

I nodded, "I am."

"We have heard of you and also of your son who wears the Welsh dragon of Gwynedd on his chest."

I frowned, "That is a gryphon, not a dragon."

He smiled, "Some warriors at the court of King Malcolm saw his banner. They said it was a dragon. I had not seen it. I would have known the difference, of course."

King Henry was curious but he was also impatient, "Dragon, gryphon… what does your king want?"

"Ah, Warlord, the young are so keen to get to the point." He placed his goblet on the table and wiped his mouth with the napkin which was there. "Your majesty, King Owain Gwynedd has raided the Duchy of Chester on many occasions. Your Earl there now stays within his walls for it is safer that way and he lives with the lost cattle and sheep. This same King of Gwynedd also makes war on King Madog. My king would have an alliance. More than that he would have you help him to drive King Madog from his mountain stronghold."

There appeared, on the surface, no reason why King Henry should listen further. A few sheep and cattle stolen from Chester was not a good reason to march into the heartland of the fiercest of warriors.

Henry said as much, "I appreciate your journey but it has been wasted. If the Earl of Chester or his wife, my cousin, asks for my help then I will send men north but, as it is, I am too busy here in the south."

"King Owain is an ally of King Maredudd."

"Again, when Maredudd has been defeated then I will look north." He began to rise; a sure sign that the meeting was over.

"Of course, your majesty, there is the matter of the gold. Unless of course you have a full treasury and do not need a mountain full of gold."

The hairs on the back of my neck began to prickle. How did this priest know that our treasury was depleted? Perhaps the network of spies crossed nations? King Henry, however, took the bait.

"Gold? In the land of Powys?"

"Sadly, for us, no. It is under the mountain which lies close to Dolgellau. The King would have you join him in a joint action. We have men who are skilled in the mountains, good archers and the like but your knights, your horsemen, are superior to all others."

It sounded like flattery but it was not for it was the truth. That said there was no reason for us to take on a battle with someone who was not even a threat, just for gold.

"You have my interest, Brother Iago. I will, of course, have to speak with my senior leaders but I shall give you an answer in the morning. Will you be my guest?"

"If you do not mind, your majesty, we will stay with the bishop. I have letters for him from the Abbot at the monastery of St. Asaph. It is one of the reasons I was chosen. I speak your language but I was coming here anyway."

I was not simply curious. I was suspicious and I bluntly asked the priest about his motives. "This strikes me as a little too convenient. Why should the abbot of a monastery on the other side of the land wish to communicate with the Bishop of Gloucester?"

"The Bishop of Gloucester is just one stage on the journey of the letter. The bishop will send it to the Archbishop of Canterbury and he will send it to Rome."

"Rome?"

"I will speak openly but you must keep my confidences to yourselves."

"Of course." Henry glared at me and I nodded.

"Ireland does not subscribe to the Church of Rome. There are priests there who wish to join our one Church. This is an attempt to encourage the Pope to intervene."

Henry beamed, "There, Warlord, that sounds perfectly reasonable to me."

It sounded reasonable to me too. Too reasonable. The priest was too slick and slippery for my liking.

"Come after matins in the morning and I will give you my answer."

This was a web and I did not like it. However, I knew I had lost the argument when the two of us were alone for Henry chastised me. "Warlord, this is not like you. The priest is no threat to us and this alliance suits us. We have the opportunity to enrich the treasury at little cost to ourselves. I am not a fool and I know that someday we may have to fight Powys and Gwynedd. This is the perfect opportunity to let them both bleed while we look on. I can scout out the land of Powys. I have heard that they have fine farmland to the east of their country."

I could not believe my ears, "But what about the marches? Striguil, Hereford?"

He smiled, "That is simple. I will take my Angevin knights to Powys and you will command the knights and men of the borders. I will send my fleet to Anglesey and soon wrap up this little campaign. My cousin, Henry Fitz Roy will command the fleet. I am certain that you will be able to defeat King Maredudd. Even if you cannot then we will not be long on this northern raid and I can come and help you finish him off."

"Your majesty…"

He waved his hand peremptorily, "I will speak with my map makers and see what they say."

As quickly as that the young King had his head turned with promises of gold and I was left to recapture English lands with half the men we had brought.

Chapter 16

King Henry was a clever leader. Had he taken me with him to raid Gwynedd then his Marcher Lords might have become angry. However, they saw me as the knight who had defeated Stephen and curbed the Scots. As Henry marched north the men of the marches cheered them. I still wondered about Brother Iago but I could not work out how he would benefit. I did not have long to speculate for if we were to make headway before the onset of winter then we had to move towards Hereford. I let the lords organize their own trains and I led the smaller army to Hereford. It was thirty miles and I pushed to be there in one day. As many of the lords had large numbers of men who were marching rather than riding it was hard going but we made the border town on the Wye before dark.

I was pleased that Walther de Hereford, the son of my old friend Miles of Gloucester was Sherriff of Hereford and Gloucester. His presence gave me hope. I spoke with him privately before my other lords arrived and I learned much about the land in which we would be fighting.

"Do you wish me and my men to fight alongside you, Warlord?"

I shook my head, "No for I fear that the King's foray north has left the back door to Gloucester open. I would have you watch our backs and keep the land hereabouts safe. I am taking William of Liedeberge with me. This move by Powys may be a trick to lure us away from the heartland of the Severn."

"You are wise, Warlord. I will be vigilant."

I held a council of war in the sheriff's hall. Walther de Hereford stayed silent and watched the other lords for me. Lord Mortimer, Braose, Fitz Alan, Chaworth and Giffard sat around the table along with de Clare and de Clifford. The Sherriff sat at my right.

"My aim is quite simple. I will strike south towards Striguil." I saw de Clifford bang the table in joy. "We will head for Llancloudy first. I do not know the country. My men are all from Anjou." I swept my hand around the room. "I will be reliant on your scouts to find the enemy and then I will bring them to battle." I took a drink from the cider they had provided. "I do not need to tell you, lords, that the Welsh are good at ambushes. If we are ambushed then God help the knight who commands the scouts! He had better hope for a speedy death from the Welsh!"

De Clare raised his arm, "Lord, my men live the furthest west. We are surrounded by enemies. I have good scouts although they are not knights nor even men at arms."

I shook my head, "That matters not. My chief scout in Stockton used to be a slave. It is not their title which concerns me, it is their ability."

"Then we will not let you down."

"Good." I stood for I wanted to make sure that they could all both see and hear me. "Other than William of Liedeberge none of you have fought with me before. We fight one way; my way. All of the archers will be mounted. They will all be under the command of Rhodri of Ruthin. He is my man. He will be captain of archers. When the scouts find the Welsh then the archers will ride and pin them. The men at arms will attack the rear of the Welsh and the knights will charge their front."

Roger de Braose asked, "And what of the men on foot?"

"They will protect us should the Welsh be foolish enough to attack us. Other than that, they guard the prisoners we shall take, build and then watch the camp."

"That is all?"

"That is all. We move quickly, my lords. We do not wait for the men on foot. The Welsh are slippery by all accounts. We keep our spears in their backs and drive them to Striguil."

"Will they not augment the garrison there?"

I nodded. De Clifford was not a stupid man. "And they will not have enough food for them. The men who finally get to Striguil will have been beaten time and time again. They will enter your castle and tell tales of the invincible Normans who have chased them for forty miles through their land. They will be our ally! We retake Monmouth first and drive towards the coast. The King has taken the fleet which might have aided us and so we will use our best weapon; our speedy horses."

I allowed them to talk about that and to discuss it. There were some raised voices. I ignored them and gradually the room quietened as they saw that the plan might work.

"So, my lords, any questions?"

"What do we do with the prisoners we take?"

"We sell them, of course. If any of their archers wish to defect then I will offer them employment."

"You will take on Welshmen?"

"I have a number already. They are fine bowmen. If there are no further questions you have until noon tomorrow to get horses for your archers. We leave after noon."

I was annoyed that the King had taken off more than half the army north to fight a war he had no need to fight but part of me was pleased. This meant that I could make the decisions without recourse to Henry. I wanted this campaign over and over quickly. With Anjou safe then a swift campaign here in the marches would mean I could go home and visit my son and his family sooner. Queen Eleanor had been given the power to make decisions in Henry's absence but she too had urged her husband to return to London as soon as he could.

As I went around my lords to ensure that they had understood my orders I reflected that making an ally of Powys might not be a bad thing, Owain Gwynedd was a more dangerous foe. That much became obvious as I went around the lords I was to lead. Richard de Clare summed it up best. He had fought them both.

"The Welsh do not have many knights. Had the civil war not raged...."

"A war in which your father fought on the wrong side."

He nodded, "A mistake, I can see that now, lord. If we had not fought the civil war then we would have met the Welsh with our knights and they would have been scythed like wheat. The men of Gwynedd, on the other hand, have their mountains into which they can retreat. Their only weakness is the valley of the Clwyd. If that can be taken and held then there is a chance they can be contained. Horses cannot operate in those mountains."

I liked de Clare and I agreed with his appraisal of the situation in the north. I had fought there with old King Henry. We had won but we had caught the Welsh unawares and we had used the Clwyd.

"I would not worry about the title of earl."

"That is easy for you to say, lord, you are Earl Marshal."

"True and I was offered the title of Duke but I turned it down."

I had surprised him, "You turned down a Dukedom?"

"It is a title. Does it change who I am? Would it mean I have to behave differently? This suits me. You seem a well-respected knight. You have your lands and your castles. The King could have taken those from you. Do not let this fester within you." I shrugged,

"Advice from an old man who came to this land with almost nothing."

"Your reputation is well deserved. You need not worry. The Welsh are my enemy too. I am no traitor but I would have that which is mine by birth. The King fought for his titles did he not?"

"He did but do not travel that road. It is riven with traps which could end with you losing your head. The success of this campaign lies in your scouts. A successful outcome will make the King look more favourably upon your request."

I left my lords and found Rhodri and my men. My Welshman shifted from foot to foot. A sign that he was unsettled, "Lord, this honour you do me, to lead the archers, do I deserve it?"

"Rhodri, Sir Leofric told me of your skill as a leader. I have seen it too. Only four of you are my archers but I know you and I trust you. You may have to bang together the heads of some of the archers you command but you can do this."

"Lord," he nodded.

"I need you and the archers to neutralize the Welsh archers. You will have the advantage that you are mounted. When we find the enemy then drive their archers from the field and chase them. When their archers flee their army will follow. Their archers will tire and we both know that tired men do not pull a bow as well as a man who has ridden. When they are gone then you attack the flanks of their army."

"I will do as you command, lord."

My last visit was to my six men at arms. They were with our horses and my servants. Along with James, they were packing the sumpters with our spare weapons and equipment. "We eight will be the tip of the spear which is driven into the enemy's rear. You wear my wolf and that will afford you authority. I will use you to pass orders to my knights." They looked surprised. "If we have to, then the eight of us will strike at the enemy. Stay close to me."

"Aye lord."

"Tom, keep the spare horses and the sumpters close to the rear of the army and ahead of the rest of the baggage. You are not like the other servants, you are warriors. I have but one squire. If Warrior falls then fetch up Storm Bringer."

Tom knew his business, "Fear not, lord, we may not wear mail but it is good that we are with the army again. We have purpose!"

My retinue, being the smallest was ready first. It spurred the others. I waved to de Clare and he sent his six scouts off along the road to Llancloudy. When I determined that the rest were ready I

162

signalled my men forward. Rhodri led the fifty archers. My lords had secured horses for all of them. Not all were the best of beasts but they were mounted. While we rode along the road we would go in a single column. I had decided on the order. That was to save petty squabbles over rank and precedent. I had de Clare behind me and de Clifford at the rear. I intended to save de Clifford and his men for the attack on his castle. I hoped that the other nine conroi would be able to contain the enemy until then. De Clifford had the largest number of men. They would be my reserve.

It was not a Roman road and it twisted and turned. We had a buffer before us. We had scouts and we had archers. We had not travelled six miles when we saw the efficacy of our scouts. We found the bodies of four Welshmen. Arne Arneson spat as we passed them, "Welsh scouts, lord."

"Aye and that means that they know we are coming. It was as I expected. The question now is where will they meet us? Will it be an ambush or open battle?"

I had already begun to doubt myself. There was another crossing of the Wye at Ross. The bridge there was a wooden one but it did cross the river. I had mentioned it to Henry before we headed for Hereford but he had wished to launch his attack from a larger town. What if there were men at Ross on Wye? We were nearing a road that led to the other crossing. "Roger of Bath, go with Wilson of Bristol and ride to Ross on Wye. See if there are Welsh there. Meet us on the road further south. You can travel across the fields and through the greenways."

"Aye lord."

I felt better once they disappeared. It was a fine afternoon and the autumn colours made the valley look beautiful. It was a beauty that could be dangerous for the autumnal colours made it easier for the enemy archers to hide. The woods on the valley sides were no longer green. There were patches of green, brown and even yellow. Maredudd and his men would fight us; the question was where?

It was late afternoon when we found out where. One of de Clare's scouts came hurrying back. "Lord, we have found the Welsh."

I held up my hand and the column halted. "Where?"

"They are four miles away at Monmouth. It is a good place they have chosen. They occupy the land between the Monnow river and the River Wye. They have men in the castle."

"Stone castle?"

"Wooden walls, lord but a stone keep."

163

"Numbers?"

"It is hard to estimate, lord, for they are hidden in the trees but we counted ten banners on the walls and four at their camp."

"Where are Rhodri and my archers?"

"He led them across the river. He told me to tell you that he will try to get in a position on their flank, on the other side of the Severn."

"Good. We will camp close to their lines. Keep me informed."

"Aye Warlord."

I waved the column forward and then signalled for de Clare to join me. "They are at the castle of Monmouth. What do you know of it?"

"It belonged to the Fitz Osbern family. The lord, Roger was slain by the Welsh and his family fled. They have estates in Buckinghamshire. It has a good keep but they have not yet got around to making the outer wall of stone. There are two good ditches. The town is well defended by rivers. They flank the town and there is but one bridge across each river."

I nodded, "My archers are on the east bank of the Severn. They will attack on the flanks on the morrow."

He gave me a surprised look. "You will attack without seeing their defences?"

"I know what they will have done. They will have a ditch and a barrier. Their archers will be hidden and they will attempt to slay us as we charge."

"But…"

"First, I will go to speak with them. I will offer them the opportunity to withdraw. They will refuse. I will return to our lines and signal Rhodri to attack their flank. We will attack on foot."

"On foot! We are knights; we are horsemen."

"And we will save our horses. I need you to help me persuade the others for they, too, will be fearful to fight on foot. It will work. We need to fix their gaze to allow our archers to attack their rear. We save our horses for the chase to Striguil; for there will be a chase."

"I will support you, Warlord. I cannot fault what you have done so far but this is not how I would have attacked."

I ruffled my beard, "That is how you get grey hairs and do not die young. You use your head." I waved over Harry Lightfoot. I saw de Clare listening to my instructions. "Fetch Osbert and his horse."

"Aye lord."

When my servant arrived I said, "I would have you ride to Rhodri. He is across the river. You will have to swim your horse. Can you do that?"

He grinned, "Aye lord. I do not need five fingers to swim!"

"When you find him tell him to cross the river south of the town and hide him and his men close to the enemy. When he hears the trumpet sound three times, in the morning, then he is to attack."

"Aye lord." He smiled, "Thank you, lord. You have given us the chance to be warriors and useful once more. I will not fail you."

De Clare said, as my servant galloped off, "You use servants?"

"Osbert was a warrior. He wears no mail but he needs none. If he meets an enemy then, believe me, the enemy will die."

My men at arms returned having found Ross on Wye without enemies. That gave me peace of mind.

We saw the enemy lines when we were eight hundred paces from them. The ground was flat. There were some abandoned huts there. The English settlers who had lived there had fled when the Welsh had returned. I had the foot make the camp while my horsemen formed a solid line four hundred paces from the Welsh. I heard their horns as they rushed to their lines. I wanted them watching me and not the south. My archers would be moving around their flank. I had no intention of attacking but they did not know that. They could not see my men digging a ditch and erecting stakes to build an armed camp. We had a line of horsemen as a barrier. We used the huts as corners to our improvised fort. I would not be caught napping in my sleep by Welsh assassins.

As I did with my knights on the Tees so I did with my Marcher lords. I explained in detail how we would fight.

"Each of you will form a wedge with your conroi. We will make a large hedgehog with me in the centre. We keep a tight formation. Some of you will have larger wedges. Mine will be the smallest and we will be in the centre. I will have my men at arms and those of William of Liedeberge in the centre."

I paused to allow that to sink in. De Clare had spoken with me and understood my thinking. "And that means our stronger flanks will push around theirs."

"Exactly. By trying to get at me they will outflank themselves."

There were nods when they understood the strategy. Raymond de Mortimer asked, "And the foot?"

"They will form a double line behind our wedges. The horses and baggage will be guarded by the servants and pages."

"What if they are attacked? We will lose our horses."

De Clare laughed, "Perhaps we should emulate the Warlord. He has old soldiers for servants."

"I do not think that we will be in any danger of losing our horses. Firstly, we are not attacking the way that they expect. They will expect a charge of heavy horses. That will make them confused. Secondly, Rhodri and the archers will be sending fifty arrows every few moments into their unprotected backs. I hope to decimate their archers."

De Clifford was not the cleverest of knights. "Let me understand this, Warlord. We mount our horses, in the morning, as though we are going to make a charge. Then you and I will go with De Clare and we will try to negotiate their surrender."

"That is right."

"Then, when they reject our terms, we come back, dismount, form wedges and attack."

"That is the plan."

He shook his head, "I can see that you are from the east. That is far too complicated for an old warrior such as me." My lords laughed.

"Once we have breached their line then I want you, de Braose, to take the foot and your conroi. You will surround the castle."

"Do I assault it?"

I shook my head. "From what I have seen there is only one way in. They cannot have enough supplies inside. When the wind is in the right direction you will burn the Welsh bodies so that the smoke and the smell goes towards the castle. It will be a warning of what might happen if we fire their wall. Once we have reached Striguil I will return."

"You wage a different sort of war, Warlord."

"I have been fighting these many years. I have learned what wins battles."

The other knights all laughed. It was a small step but these knights, some of whom had fought for Stephen the usurper were now coming together. England was healing and it was the Welsh who would suffer as a result. That night I walked the horse lines with Arne Arneson and James. I had some apples I had bought in Hereford. They grew good apples in this part of the world. I gave our horses an apple each. I had bought a bushel and I still had some as a reward for after battle. I spoke with as many men as I could. Some of the men at arms touched the hem of my surcoat or my scabbard for good luck. Warriors are always superstitious. I was known to be a lucky leader. They believed that luck might rub off. I did not mind. When that was done we returned to our camp and James put my mail in a sack of sand. It was a good way to clean it. Once the sand was removed he oiled it. That would stop rust. The weather was changing and the nights and early mornings were damp. Then he began to burnish my helmet. It was not all for show: a shiny helmet and an oiled byrnie were better at deflecting blows. They could do nothing about a direct strike but, in the heat of battle, some edges slid off mail and helmets. It was those small margins that might be the difference between life and death.

His final action was to put a good edge to my sword and two daggers. The sword had the blue pommel stone from Harold Godwinson's sword. To the Normans that would mean nothing but my father had put enough store in its magic for him to have hidden it in his home in Constantinople. I knew that, following its fitting, I was more confident with my sword and I believed it had power that aided my own. It might have been nonsense but warriors have an affinity with their weapons. A warrior who is unconcerned about the weapon he uses will lose. My men at arms also began sharpening their weapons. It contrasted with some of the other camps where the men were gambling, drinking and telling tall tales. William of Liedeberge and his men were with us.

"You will be behind me next to Arne. James will have my banner behind the two of you and your standard will be in the rank behind. It will confuse the enemy. Our men at arms fight together. Mine had done this recently. It will give your men confidence."

"I have rarely attacked on foot."

"In many ways, it is easier than on a horse. Some horses can misplace a hoof or become afeard at nothing. The difference is the way you use your spear. It will appear heavier for you will not have the head of a horse or a saddle on which to rest it. Trust me, William, this plan is better than a frontal charge by heavy horse!"

That night after I had given my final orders I prayed to God to protect my son and his new family and I asked him to give us victory. I slept in the open, covered with just my cloak. It would be enough.

I woke before dawn. I was at that age when nature made me rise whether I would or not. I was the first of my men to rise although Roger of Bath and Lame Tom were watching our camp. My breath formed in front of my face. It was cold. I made water and then walked over to them. There was not even a hint of grey in the eastern skies of England.

"How goes the night?"

"Quiet, lord. John son of John said he heard some movement in their lines just before I took over but I have heard nothing. We have had an early hard frost. It will help us to march. God is with us."

Lame Tom said, "I'll fetch some beer and the last of the bread and cheese." He scratched his chin. "There may be a few good apples left too." He grinned, "First to rise feasts the best!"

I stretched and looked towards the castle which rose in the southwest. "With luck, Roger, we will not have to take that beast. It is no Chinon but I am not sure these marcher lords have assaulted a castle."

He chuckled, "They are keen enough, lord."

There was a movement behind me and James appeared, "You should have woken me, lord!"

"There is time. I do not sleep as much as I once did."

Lame Tom brought us beer. He handed the tankards to us. "Come, Master James, you can help fetch the food."

They headed back into the hut where we had stored our mail and food. "We use the same formation as at Chinon, lord?"

"Aye. Save that we will have the men of Liedeberge with us. I will be alone at the front and this time we use spears."

"Rhodri said that his countrymen are fierce archers. They kept the Romans from this land and defeated the lords hereabouts many times."

"They are good and we know how useful an archer can be. The difference is in their armour. The Welsh can send an arrow a long way and they are strong but they wear leather caps and no armour." My archers had a leather vest that was studded with iron. It did not restrict their pull but gave them protection. In addition, each one had a helmet, a shield and a sword. "We will need to suffer the arrows while we attack but they have built a fence. That means they have to send their arrows into the air. They cannot send them horizontally." He looked puzzled. "Our shields can be held above us. Their arrows can penetrate mail but not a good shield." I laughed.

"Does something amuse you, lord?"

"I was just thinking that crossbows would be useful alongside their bows but the Welsh do not use them."

He laughed, "Aye lord, that is funny."

Lame Tom and James brought the food and we watched the first grey line appear to our left. "Better rouse them, Roger, and have the horses fed and watered."

"Aye lord."

When we had finished the food, James and I retired to the hut so that we could dress. By the time I was ready, dawn had broken and our camp had come to life. I walked back to survey their lines. I saw that they had increased the height of their hedge by cutting brushwood and piling it up. It worked in our favour. They thought we would be on horses and wished to stop us leaping the defences. Their archers would not have a clear sight of us. As we had discovered at Chinon, sending arrows blindly over a defence used many arrows but had little effect. I heard swords being sharpened in our camp and men complaining that there were too many others waiting in the queue in front of them. It was another reason why my men had sharpened theirs the previous night.

James brought over Warrior. I nuzzled his muzzle. "Hopefully you will not have to endure arrows today. With any luck, we shall just have a chase to Striguil!" He whinnied. I hung my helmet from the cantle. James had also fetched Snowbird. Had I used Storm Bringer then it might have had a dramatic effect. A black horse and white horse looked good next to each other. I would bear that in mind the next time we went to war. James had groomed them well. Their tails and their manes were immaculate. The coats of the two horses shone. We both wore new surcoats. As the campaign wore on we would become shabbier but that day we had to look our best. My men led their horses out. It was all for effect. They had polished their helmets and armour. They, too, shone.

I decided it was time and I mounted, "James, fetch de Clare and de Clifford."

"Aye lord."

The two lords must have been awaiting my summons. They were soon back. I said, "Arne Arneson, be so good as to ask Raymond de Mortimer to follow us to the starting position."

"Aye lord."

It was like a game of chess with real men. I was marshalling my men into position to make the Welsh react. I wanted to push them in one direction and then switch. I spurred Warrior and, bare headed and with open palms, we rode to a point four hundred paces from their defences. We were beyond the range of their bows. We waited.

I made conversation. "King Henry will need a lord for this manor when we retake the castle. Is there a landless lord in the marches?"

De Clare said, "No lord. There are knights whose homes have been taken. They would rather we retook their homes."

"Then King Henry has a gift to give."

"What of the Fitz Osbern family?"

"You said the males were all dead?"

"Aye, and they have gone to the lady's estates."

"Then they have lost Monmouth."

"Lord, there is movement." I looked and saw that the Welsh were having to remove part of their defences. As it happened it was directly opposite us. Four riders came through. I saw that their horses did not step down a long way. I noted that fact. It was a shallow ditch. As convention dictated they would have the same number to discuss terms.

"Which one is the King?"

De Clare said, "The one riding the red coloured horse. The one next to him is Llewellyn ap Cynan. He is the one who captured de Clifford's castle."

The King was a young man. I took him to be mid-twenties. He had a red beard but it was not well-trimmed. He looked squat for the horse was not big and yet he barely rose above the horse's head. He had a mail byrnie and a sword but I could not see a shield. That meant he was no warrior. Llewellyn ap Cynan was a warrior. He was older and he had both a shield and a war hammer. Taller than his King, he rode a jet-black horse. All of their horses were smaller than Warrior. I would be looking down on them when we spoke.

They reined in. We had arrived first and it was incumbent upon me to begin the discussion. "I am Alfraed of Stockton Earl Marshal to King Henry of England, Duke of Normandy and Count of Anjou, Maine and Touraine," I spoke in Norman.

The Welsh King looked at his men and then answered. His Norman was good but his high-pitched voice displayed his nervousness, "I am King Maredudd ap Gruffyd. Why have you come here to disturb our peace?"

"I have no intention of disturbing any peace, your majesty. I am here, on King Henry's behalf, to reclaim the lands that have been taken from our lord." I pointed to the castle. "This is the first and then there is Striguil. There are others but these two are the closest. When you evacuate them and make reparations for the harm you have done then we will have peace again."

Llewellyn ap Cynan showed that he was the real power behind the throne. He snarled, "You Normans took this land from us! You are now in Wales! You will have no reparation from us! All that you will have is the edge of our swords and the barbs of our arrows."

I nodded and, ignoring the Welsh lord, spoke directly to the King. "When I was a young man, like yourself, majesty, I went with the Earl of Gloucester into Gwynedd. The King then, I forget his name, made a similar boast. After the battle, his knights and lords were held to ransom and we took over three thousand head of cattle as reparation. Before you answer or someone answers for you think about the consequences of that answer."

Once again Llewellyn ap Cynan answered. He shouted and he raged, "We outnumber you! I see a handful of knights a few men at arms and a rag time collection of poorly armed peasants! You do not even have any archers! All of you will die! Your bodies will lie for the carrion when we have done with you!"

I looked at the King, "Your majesty?"

I saw that he was unsure. All of his lord's words made sense and yet I appeared so confident. I was the Warlord of the North and I knew that he had heard of me. He would have heard of the raid the Earl of Gloucester and I had made in the north. I later learned that he was quite intelligent. He should have asked the question, where are their archers, but he did not. Instead, he sided with his lord. "Leave our land or die! I have spoken. Bring your horses and we will feast on their bones!"

Llewellyn ap Cynan laughed, "Well spoke, majesty!" The fact that he spoke Norman told me that the words were for our benefit as well as the King's confidence.

I turned and we rode back to our lines. What they had not realised was that my line had moved two hundred paces closer to the Welsh. We would not have as far to walk. When we reached our men, we dismounted. The whole of my line did. Servants, pages and peasants led the horses away from the front line. Arne handed me a spear and I turned to face the Welsh line. I saw that they had barely managed to replace the bushes and hurdles they had used to make their defensive barrier.

"James, sound the horn!"

The horn sounded three times. I waited until our giant hedgehog was ready and I shouted, "Forward for King Henry and England!"

My men cheered. We marched to battle.

Chapter 17

We did not run but we stepped forward at a good pace. The ground was flat and still hard after the night's frost. It would be harder once we neared their ditch but we had caught them unawares. I saw the men behind the barrier pointing at us. A few desultory arrows rose into the sky. I pulled my shield up. I heard a couple clatter, ineffectually, on the shields of the men behind me. That was a sign of their nerves. They should have released together. We were close enough for me to hear the angry voices of sergeants ordering their men into some sort of order.

I fixed my eye on the hurdles and bushes they had replaced to allow the King and his party through. They had not been fixed in place. I could see just twenty paces behind the barrier the King and his handful of knights on their horses. Their banners made a target I would use. I held my spear halfway down. It was easier that way. When I drew close I would hold it closer to the end. Then it would be much heavier. I heard an order sound. It was the command to release arrows. This time, when they fell, it sounded like hail in a thunderstorm. I also heard cries. It could have been warriors whose shields were not in the right position or it could be the peasants and unarmoured men who followed us. Casualties were to be expected.

The ditch was just twenty paces from us. I saw that they had just taken a couple of spadefuls of earth and used that to make a mound in which they had planted hurdles and bushes. It was insubstantial. As we neared it I heard a collective wail from ahead. I did not need to ask what it was. I knew. King Maredudd ap Gruffyd had just discovered that I did have archers. Arrows still fell and my men still died but there were fewer of them as the Welsh archers had to respond to the threat from behind. Rhodri had obeyed my commands and sprung my trap.

Stepping into the ditch was the hard part. For a brief moment, I did not have the protection of other shields and then I was through.

The hurdle and bush defence was two paces from the ditch. Lowering my shield to my front I shifted the grip on my spear and waited for a moment. I felt Arne and Sir William press their shields into my back and I shouted, "Forward!"

Ironically their defence, intended for horses, worked in our favour. They could not strike us. I realised that the one part of my plan which would not be as I had outlined it would be the fact that I would not be the one behind the flanks. As the three of us pushed, the hastily repaired fence fell away. It was not men at arms who awaited us but archers. They had neither armour nor shields. I rammed my spear at a surprised looking archer. I twisted and pulled. He fell writhing to the ground. The weakened fence was brushed aside by my conroi.

I spied Llewellyn ap Cynan as he lowered his spear and led his men to charge us. "Halt!"

I braced my spear against my foot and supported it with my shield hand. Llewellyn ap Cynan came directly for me. I saw him pull back his arm as his horse trampled over archers who could not get out of the way in time. He thought we would break. I was willing to let his horse crash into me but I knew it would not come to that. Had we been one single line then the beast might have vaulted over us but we were a hedgehog of spears. As Llewellyn ap Cynan rammed his spear at me his horse baulked. The spear struck air. I took my chance and thrust my spear with two hands at his thigh. The spear head tore through the mail, into his leg and into his saddle. The tip must have pricked the horse because it jinked and jerked to the side as it tried to flee the pain. Llewellyn ap Cynan was a good rider. He kept his saddle and dropped his spear. Two other knights had tried the same technique. One lay dead and the other was beneath his mortally wounded horse.

Our very success slowed us down for we had dead men and horses before us. We clambered over them and I saw that our wedges were almost intact. King Maredudd showed his true mettle. He shouted orders. I could not hear what they were but a double line of spearmen backed by knights began to form before us. It was brave. His archers had lost the battle with mine. He was buying them time to flee the field. He knew that, in a long campaign, he would need archers.

We marched towards the spearmen. Some were mailed some were not. The twenty knights and squires who were behind were. The King was giving his support to the sixty or so spearmen who waited for us. Sadly, for them, they would not all be receiving our attack at the same moment. There would be ten points of attack. Each point would be a lord. They were better armed and trained than the spearmen. I readjusted my spear again. We marched across the body littered field. A double line of spears awaited us. Four or five spears would strike at me. I pulled my shield up a little more. With my full-face helmet, the only vulnerable spots were the eye slits and Alf had made what appeared to be eyebrows. They were cunningly created for they would catch a spear as it came at me. It still meant I could lose an eye but it was unlikely that I would be killed.

It was six spears that thrust at me. It was too many for they got in each other's way. One hit me just above the eye slit, one on the top of the helmet and the other four hit my shield. My left arm and shoulder would ache the next day. I thrust blindly upwards as Sir William and Arne used their spears to strike too. I heard a grunt and felt something soft. I punched with my shield and leaned into the Welsh. I was close enough to see a bearded Welshman facing me. He began to curse me. My spear was in him and the press of men around him prevented him from pulling away. I pushed harder and twisted. I saw a tendril of blood seep from his lip. He adopted a frozen expression and then the life went from his eyes. As he fell, I felt my spear going with him and so I released it.

Holding my shield before me I drew my sword. This was a better weapon for a shield wall battle. I reached up with my sword hand and pulled forward the shield held by the spearman to my right. It came towards me and Arne rammed his spear through his surprised mouth. His spear came out of the back and into the next man. We had broken through their two lines. I saw the King debating what to do. One of the knights to his right took the decision for him. He grabbed the reins of his horse and led the King away. It was probably the right thing to do but it cost many Welshmen their lives. The sight of the King and his knights fleeing was the signal for a rout.

I heard de Clare shout, "Horses!" He must have had a better view than I did but it was the correct decision. The chase to Striguil was on.

Even though they were routing the battle was still not over. The castle was still held and individual pockets of foolish Welshmen fought on. I saw that de Braose had obeyed my orders. He was shouting to the peasants to follow his men.

I saw a dozen of them come towards me, "Obey your orders. Follow Lord Braose!"

A couple looked at me as though I was speaking a foreign language. Harry Lightfoot growled, "Over there, you dozy turnip picker!" He pointed with his sword as he kicked one in the rump. They turned and headed to the castle. Harry grinned, "Sorry lord but you have to use the right words."

Lame Tom had ridden Warrior and led another four horses. He was a master with animals. My other servants led the rest. I mounted Warrior while Tom held a spear. A knight who chased needed a spear. Men on foot would lie on the ground out of the reach of swords. We had to make the Welsh fear us. That meant being ruthless. I surveyed the battle. I saw that we had lost a few men at arms but the casualties we had suffered appeared to be peasants. De Braose had reached the walls of the castle and they were now slammed shut. De Giffard had taken prisoner those who had surrendered.

I turned to Sir William, "Take your men and head down the Striguil road. Keep your men together but do not let the Welsh rally."

"Aye lord." He smiled, "A great victory. I had almost forgotten the taste."

"James, stay here and organize the men. I will go and speak with de Giffard and de Braose." Turning Warrior, I galloped over the field. There were wounded men and there were dying men. The wounded looked up fearfully as I galloped past. I halted close to de Giffard. "Keep the knights for ransom."

"And the men at arms and peasants?"

"Let the wounded go. Put the rest to work. Have them take down our camp and fetch it to Striguil."

"Aye Warlord. Your plan worked."

He sounded surprised. "If it had not I had another. This is just the beginning, de Giffard. The King has charged us with reclaiming that which was lost. Lord Braose, collect the enemy dead and burn them where the smell and the smoke will reach the castle. It will make them more likely to surrender. When it is surrendered then garrison it and follow us!"

"Aye lord."

Whipping Warrior's head around I rode back to my men. De Clare had his horses and he fell in behind us as we headed down the road to Striguil. In the distance, I saw Sir William's men and they were being followed by de Clifford. We had at least three conroi of men. That was more than enough to deal with the stragglers we might meet. As we reached the town I saw Rhodri and our archers. They were leading their horses.

I reined in and waved de Clare forward, "Keep your swords in their backs."

"Aye lord."

"You did well, Rhodri."

He nodded, "Some of the archers from the other lords were not as disciplined as they ought to have been, lord. We lost more men than we should but it went well enough. We need more arrows, lord."

He sounded apologetic, "Go back to the camp and rest. Have food before you join us. This is a day for men on horses. Follow with de Giffard. He will be bringing the camp with him. Your mounted archers will ensure that he has no trouble."

I waved James and my men forward. We passed a few dead men who had been caught by my horsemen. Only their knights had been mounted. The more sensible of the peasants and men at arms had left the road and headed away from the thunder of pursuing horse. That was part of my plan. If they fled east and west they could not go south and reinforce Striguil. I wanted as few warriors in Striguil as possible.

The delay in speaking with Rhodri meant that we were alone on the road. As we approached the hamlet of Trelleck I slowed down. I had spoken with de Clifford about his lands and knew that the road forked at Trelleck. Both forks ended up at Striguil and the sea. Which one did we take?

We reined in at the hamlet. I saw a couple of dead men. The awkward angle of their bodies suggested that they had been fleeing horsemen. I looked south. The road to the east led alongside the Wye while the other took a longer loop west. There were woods ahead of us.

Arne said, "It looks to me as though both lead where we want to go, lord." He pointed to the churned-up ground. The hard frost had melted and hooves had galloped along the verges of the two roads south. "I would say that our men have taken both roads."

I nodded, "Then we will take the Wye road."

We turned our horses and headed south along the river road. Sometimes we think we make decisions but we do not. They are meant to be. So it proved, that late autumn morning as we rode cautiously down the tree-lined road. We did not gallop. We had lost too much time already and I did not want to thrash our horses to death. Ahead of me were three larger conroi of men. They would follow the King to Striguil. As I followed Harry Lightfoot and Arne Arneson I began to calculate what forces might be waiting for us in Striguil. The Welsh had fought with no more than forty or fifty knights and horsemen. We had accounted for at least twenty. The garrison would not be a large one. King Maredudd would be holding Striguil with less than fifty men. He might see reason. I had seen, during the battle, that he was intelligent. It had been Llewellyn ap Cynan who had been reckless. The King might accept the loss of two recaptured castles in the hope that he could build up an army and then retake them.

Our cautious gait was what saved us. A rabbit darted from the woods to the east and that made Arne stop. He was an experienced warrior. Animals do not race in front of trotting horses unless they are startled. When men are around they freeze and remain still. He and Harry had their shields up and their gaze to the left as a wounded Llewellyn ap Cynan and ten horsemen galloped out of the woods. They had been hidden inside the trees and now they burst towards us.

He screamed as he charged directly at me with his sword held before him, "I will end your life, Norman! I will have honour before my King!"

Pulling our shields up, we all wheeled our horses around to face the threat. We had rearmed with spears and the Welsh knights and men at arms had shattered theirs in the battle. As they came towards us I could see that their horses were already lathered. They had ridden them hard. It was the difference between us. They had surprise on their side and they had speed. We had fresher horses and longer weapons.

I spurred Warrior and pulled back my arm. I could see that Llewellyn ap Cynan had a bloody leg from my spear thrust. He had had a bandage applied but that was red. He was weaker. His anger gave him the strength. His face was a mask of hatred. Warrior's sudden burst brought us together quickly. As I pulled his head to the left I thrust with my spear over Warrior's head. The Welsh lord's sword slashed and scythed towards where my head might have been. My spear rammed over the cantle of his saddle and into his side. With his weakened leg, he tumbled from the back of his horse. I dropped my spear and drew my sword as a second knight saw his chance and rode at me.

"My brother will be avenged, Norman! Prepare to die!"

He must have thought that he could not miss me. My right hand was weaponless and he was but four paces from me. Warrior was well trained. The breeder had done well with him. As I pulled up the shield I used my knees and body weight to shift him around to the right. I used us both as a barrier. The Welshman's horse tried to turn away from the obstacle before him. The rider jerked him back around for he wished to use his sword. He was parallel with me as he brought his sword to smash into my shield. He was young and he was powerful. The blow shivered my arm. I drew my own sword and, as I stood in the stirrups, swung it at him. His shield was on the wrong side and he had to flick his sword up to block the blow. Our swords rang together.

I wheeled Warrior to the left. The Welshman's back was exposed. We were in the woods now and isolated. This was a battle between two knights. He spurred his horse and wheeled it around a tree. It was a clever move and took him away from me. I was patient. He was angry and wished vengeance. I did not need to chase him. He saw an old man and he thought he would defeat me. The white hairs in my beard belied my strength and skill.

He charged again. His horse was, like his brother's, lathered. I held Warrior and prepared my sword. His horse could not gallop and so I waited for his arrival. He came at my sword side and so I pricked Warrior's sides. He jumped forward and we swung our swords together. He was aiming at my head. I was aiming at his sword guard. Mine was a stronger sword. As they clashed and cracked together sparks flew. I drove his sword towards him and the blade smacked into his nasal. As his head went back I used my quick hands to pull my arm back and swing at his middle. His sword was in the wrong position and he could not block the blow. My sword sliced through the mail links and ripped into his gambeson. I pulled Warrior's head around and saw that my sword was bloody.

I am not certain that he felt the cut to his middle. His nose was bleeding and I guessed that his eyes were streaming from the sword blow. He turned his horse to continue the fight. "Yield, you are wounded!"

"It is nothing. I do not yield. I fight on!" He tried to spur his horse again but the horse was weary.

"Then you are doomed to die!" I stood in my saddle and swung my sword horizontally. His vision was impaired and his sword blocked nothing. My edge took his head. It tumbled from his shoulders. After a heartbeat, his body slid from the saddle.

"Lord!"

I turned and saw James, besmirched with blood, and Roger of Bath riding through the trees towards me. "I am safe. And the rest?"

"We slew five and the rest fled when they saw their lord dead."

"Roger of Bath, take this warrior and put his body on his horse. He was a foolish knight but a brave one."

We loaded the bodies of the knights onto their horses. John son of John and Wilson of Bristol had wounds but they were not serious. We rode down the last few miles to Striguil. This was a substantial castle and my heart sank as we emerged from the woods and saw it rising above the river and estuary. I wondered how de Clifford could have lost it. The only place to attack was from the landward side and, like Chinon, it had a high position and strong walls.

Despite the fact that it was de Clifford's castle, Richard de Clare had taken charge. His men had begun to build a line of defences between the town and the castle. That was the right thing to do. It meant we could use the houses for food and shelter whilst denying the castle any aid. I dismounted and walked over to William of Liedeberge, "How many managed to get inside?"

"No more than forty, lord. We caught up with those on lame horses. We slew some and the rest are there, prisoners." I looked over and saw six disconsolate knights and four squires.

"Have the fishing boats drawn up on the beach and guarded. I want none escaping that way."

"Aye, lord."

De Clare came over with Walther de Clifford. "We almost have victory, lord. They have many banners within the castle but I see few men at arms and archers. We passed the bodies of their dead bowmen when we crossed the field. Our men won that battle."

I turned to de Clifford, "Tell me, Lord Clifford, how many archers did you have in your castle when it was taken?"

He shifted uncomfortably, "I only had ten. I prefer crossbows."

I stared at him. "Then perhaps that is why you lost such a fine castle and why we now have to fight to win it back for you. When we reclaim it, I will watch to make sure that you are better defended."

He reddened, "I am an earl and I do not answer to you!"

"The King has made me his second in command. He will not be happy that you were so careless in your defence. If I choose to give the castle to another then the King will support me." I was not certain that he would but de Clifford did not know that.

He became less belligerent. "I am sorry, lord. I will do better."

179

"Tell me of the defences."

"There is a sally port at the other end of the castle. I have sent men there to watch it already," he added quickly.

"Good."

"There is a ditch and drawbridge. It is good stone and the keep is hard to take."

"Yet the Welsh managed it." This time he did not argue. "Come the two of you. We will ride around the side of the castle." The Wye bordered one side leaving just the steep slope and the high walls for us to assault. My heart sank as we rode around the walls. A direct assault was out of the question, we would have to besiege them. With winter coming that might not take long but I was anxious to take as much back from the Welsh before winter set in.

By the time we returned to the main gate the rest of our army had arrived. They were in an exuberant mood. We had trounced an army far bigger than our own. Admittedly the men we fought had not been the best equipped of foes but there had been enough booty to satisfy the lords. With de Braose camped outside Monmouth it would only be a matter of time before that castle fell.

I stayed on my horse, I would dismount and allow him to rest when I had spoken to my men. We were four hundred paces from the gate at Striguil. It was not just the lords who gathered around but the men at arms too. The archers would be the last to arrive for they would be escorting the baggage train. I spoke loudly. I spoke so that my words would be carried to the gate. I did not know if King Maredudd would be there but I suspected that he would. My words were intended for both audiences.

"Warriors of England, we have had a great victory this day. This is just the beginning. We have the King of this land bound within his stolen castle. We will not shift until he is gone."

They cheered.

"We will put a ring of steel around this castle and, beginning tomorrow, we will ride abroad to seek the food, animals and slaves which the Welsh think are safe. They are not. We will be rich men and well fed, I'll be bound."

The cheer was even louder.

"Lords, choose your own camps but I want a close watch around this camp and the river. None sail to the castle without my leave."

As they moved away I turned to James, "Have the horses and bodies of the knights we slew brought up. Tell my men at arms bring them."

"What do you plan, lord?" He looked apologetically at me, "I ask only that I may learn. I know there is a strategy in your head but I cannot fathom it."

I smiled and waved him closer. He was a clever youth but his father had not taught him the games of strategy when he was young. It sharpened the mind and allowed a warrior to think of new ways of winning. "I will offer the bodies back to the King. It saves us having to bury them and it will be seen as a noble gesture. It also shows that his most vocal knight is dead. If the King refuses to accept the bodies then his knights will think less of him. He is young and lacks confidence. When you add the men camped around him it will eat into his confidence. Burying the knights will be a reminder that he lost the battle. My archers will arrive and I intend to array them around the gate. I will then speak with the King. By then I hope that his resolve will be weakened. Tonight, we will feast on the animals which my men have taken. The smell of their own beasts being cooked will add to their hunger pangs."

"Thank you, lord, I am learning."

There were seven horses with their dead riders covered by their cloaks. I turned, "Take off your helmets and keep your hands from your weapons."

We rode towards the castle. I heard trumpets sound and men rushed to the gatehouse. Crossbows and bows were levelled at us. I stopped by the drawbridge. It had been raised and this ditch was substantial. It had been built by Fitz Osbern and not de Clifford. I waited.

King Maredudd appeared. He was not wearing his helmet and I saw this his face had been cut. "Earl Marshal, I did not think that a warrior with your reputation would come to gloat."

"I do not, your majesty. We fought these knights on the way here. It is Llewellyn ap Cynan, his brother and five other knights. They fought well and I did not think to despoil their bodies. I have returned them to you."

"I apologise, Earl Marshal, for thinking badly of you. Leave them there and withdraw to your lines." He gave an apologetic smile, "You understand."

"Of course." I turned to my men and said, "Lay the bodies on the ground and then return to our camp." As they did so I looked up at the young King. "The horses we will keep. They are not as good as our own but then you may need them for food before this siege is over and I would that it ended sooner rather than later." I turned and followed my men and the horses back to our camp.

The King was cautious and we were five hundred paces away before the gate opened and men rushed to take in the bodies. Their interment would add to the demoralising effect of my visit.

The archers and the baggage arrived just after dark. We had already prepared a defensive camp for them. With a ditch and stakes, we would guard our horses and baggage. We had just begun the campaign.

That night I sat with my knights. "Beginning tomorrow we will send out two conroi each day. I want them to go in different directions. Tomorrow it will be de Clifford and William of Liedeberge. Your task, my lords, is to make sure there are no warriors close by. You will evict any Welsh people that you find and bring them here. You will confiscate any goods or animals. The next day we send out two more lords. If we find serious opposition then we stop but I do not think we will. I do not intend to waste our time here. The rest of us will probe for weaknesses. We will use our archers but I want every knight and man at arms to be close behind our archers. I want everyone behind their shield. We are threatening to attack. When de Braose comes from Monmouth we will pretend to make a ram. That should do the trick."

De Clifford knew the land close by and I left him to brief the other knights. Since our little confrontation, he had gone out of his way to be both pleasant and helpful. Until he had his castle back I suspect it would continue. I sought out Rhodri, "How many archers did we lose?"

"Too many, lord, but the ones we have left have learned to obey me." I noticed that his knuckles were scraped. He had had to impose his authority.

"Are we well supplied with arrows?"

"Aye lord. The Welsh have good arrows and good bows. We took the arrows from the dead archers and found a great quantity in their camp at Monmouth. With the ones we already have we are well endowed."

"I want your archer with me tomorrow. We will use the pavises again. I want you to pick off men from the walls. I do not want a shower of arrows. I want them to see our skill."

"It will take a long time to clear their walls, lord."

"I wish it to be as a drip of water which, over time, makes a hole. I want none of our archers to suffer but I want their crossbowmen and archers to pay with their lives. They have fewer of them now."

"Aye lord." He added, "We took coin from the dead archers and those on the battlefield."

"That is good. It is yours to keep. Thank you for telling me."

I was awoken in the middle of the night by Arne Arneson, "Lord, the watch found two men trying to escape from the castle. They used a rope to climb down towards the river. One tried to flee and was killed the other fell and broke his leg. We have him."

I went with my man at arms. The prisoner would be lame for the rest of his life. A priest was tending to him but I could see both bones jutting from his leg, just above the ankle. He was a young man. I guessed him to be a squire. Rhodri was close by. I knew that he would have been summoned by Arne in case the man did not speak Norman. His clothes identified him as a gentleman rather than a man at arms.

"Your companion is dead."

He nodded and spoke through gritted teeth as the priest applied a splint, "I know, lord. He was my cousin, Iago."

"Your leg is broken and you will be in pain for some time. Would you like some wine to ease the pain?"

He glared at me, "And to loosen my tongue. I am not a fool. You will learn nothing from me."

"And we need to know nothing. The two of you were going for help. The King asked for volunteers and you and your cousin agreed to go." I took a guess. "We brought back your father's body today."

His face showed his surprise at the accuracy of my words, "It was my uncle and brother but how did you know?"

"A guess, nothing more. What is your name that I may tell the King tomorrow? They should know that you are alive."

I saw him chew his lip as though debating if the information constituted a treasonous act.

I made it easy for him, "I will just tell him that Iago is dead but his cousin has a broken leg. Take care of him, priest. He is brave."

"It is Gruffyd, Gruffyd ap Llewelyn."

"Thank you."

As I walked back to my bed Arne said, "You could have pressed him, lord. His leg was injured. He would have told us all. Where are the men he sought?"

"Do you really need to torture a brave young man? Besides, Arne, it is obvious, is it not?" From the blank expressions on their faces, it was obvious that it was not. "They went to the river. Upstream is England. Downstream is the fishing port and boats. They would sail around the coast to the heartland of King Maredudd. There are Norman castles along the coast but inland it is still held by the Welsh. That is why the boats are drawn up on the beach and guarded. My plan is still viable."

The next day I sent James, alone and bareheaded to tell the King the news of his foiled plan. When he returned I asked, "How did he react?"

"His shoulders slumped and he thanked you for your kindness."

"Then we begin our attack today."

After speaking with Sir William and Walther de Clifford I went to gather the men to attack the castle. As the two conroi headed off I wondered what the defenders would make of that. Mailed and mounted on Skuld I rode, with James and my banner, to a little beyond bow range. I had no doubt that Maredudd had archers who could reach me but not many of them. I gambled on the fact that I could avoid a single arrow. My shield was ready in any case.

Rhodri brought my archers with the freshly made shields. I saw him cast a professional eye along their defences. "They have just five crossbows." He pointed to the slits in the walls. "They will be hard to shift. It takes a lucky arrow to hit through a crossbow slit."

"If there are only five then we can ignore them, for the moment."

"He has twenty-five archers on these walls." He rubbed his chin. "They must be all of the ones he has left. The other wall is by the river and there is no threat there. There are eight at the gatehouse."

"Then clear those first."

"Aye lord."

He was careful and he and his men first placed the huge shields in position. Bolts and arrows thudded into them but they were carried by archers and they knew how to minimise a target. The narrow frontage actually helped us. Next, he and the archers moved forward. They used their bucklers to protect themselves as they ran the forty paces to their willow shields. Arrows struck shields but none were hurt. I raised my sword. My knights had been waiting and they rushed forward. I heard trumpets from the battlements and men ran to their positions. My knights and men at arms presented a double line behind the archers.

"When you are ready, Captain of Archers."

"Aye, Earl Marshal." He took his own bow with the perfect arrow he had selected. Every archer did this. The first arrow was always their best. It would be sent when their strength was undiminished by the drawing of the bow. It helped them to gauge the range.

"Draw!"

There was a collective creak as the arrows were drawn back. Unlike a normal battle, Rhodri had identified his targets. He had been down his line and assigned specific targets to specific pairs of archers. Two arrows aimed at one target had the best chance of success. Of course, after the first two flights, it would not be as easy for they would know we were targeting their archers.

"Release!"

Not all the arrows went at the same time. There was an elongated thrum sound as the arrows headed to their target. Arrows and bolts thudded into the willow shields. Two of Rhodri's archers fell clutching their shoulders. The Welsh showed that they had skill.

I peered at the walls. I knew where the archers were. I saw those on the gatehouse all fall. I am not certain that they were all dead but a wounded archer could not draw a bow. It was enough. Three archers on the battlements also fell.

"Draw!"

"Release!"

The second flight cleared the archers from the gatehouse and another two fell from the battlements. The Welsh had, by now, realised what we were doing and men at arms raced to shield their remaining archers.

"Second targets!"

"Draw!"

"Release!"

We caught them out again. Men at arms and knights fell as they tried to protect archers and were, in turn, hit. They took cover and the only missiles which headed our way were crossbow bolts. It took time to load the infernal machine and the five bolts seemed to keep time for us. Rhodri and his archers sent five arrows at the walls for every bolt that hit their shields. Some of Rhodri's men, the more powerful ones, were now sending arrows into the town.

After a large number of flights Rhodri nodded. His men were tiring. Half of them suddenly picked up the willow shields and moved them forty paces closer. The archers all ran to take shelter behind them again. It was so sudden that not even the crossbows managed to send a bolt in their direction. Instead of releasing more arrows, the archers took shelter as the men at arms and knights moved closer too. The Welsh wasted bolts and arrows as the wall of shields closed with the castle. At noon, I had beer and food brought to the archers and men at arms. We had plenty of both. In the afternoon Rhodri and his men, now rested, each sent another twenty flights of arrows in to the castle. It was hard to see the effect but Rhodri and his men were convinced that they had hit defenders.

We ended the attack when we spied the return of our two raiding parties. They had cattle and slaves with them. Leaving some men at arms to guard the willow shields we retreated back to our camp.

That evening I discovered that there were no castles close by which were held by the Welsh. Their strongholds were in the mountains to the north of Caerdyf. Eventually, knights would come to the aid of their King but that would take time. We ate well that night. I was about to turn in when a rider galloped into our camp. He threw himself from his saddle, "Earl Marshal, Lord de Braose has captured Monmouth. We set fire to their walls and they surrendered. We have fifty prisoners including six knights."

"Tell your lord well done from me. Have him send the prisoners here. I want them to arrive before dawn."

"Aye lord." I knew that my command would not go down well but I needed the sound of men marching into our camp while it was dark. King Maredudd would have no idea who it was and that would add to his worry. I intended to display the prisoners and then ask him to surrender again.

I was awoken by the sound of horses and complaining men marching. I rose and James rushed to my side. "Time to dress, James. Today we may end the first part of the campaign."

"But how, lord?" He handed me some small beer.

"If we can punish Maredudd and hold the men who would fight for him then we can retake the remainder of the Marches. When King Henry defeats the men of the north then we can consolidate this land and, finally, head north to the valley and claim back our Scottish lands."

"And this just from the sound of marching feet?"

"I have been in a castle which was under siege, Oxford. Each morning we awoke thinking that we would be assaulted and wondering how we would resist it. Nature came to our aid that time. I know what Maredudd is thinking. This is his first siege. He has seen my men bring back captives and animals. He is trapped inside a castle and can do nothing. They do not have enough food to withstand a long siege. He will give up the castle for it is not part of his kingdom. It was stolen. We will not solve the problem of Deheubarth but we will set his ambitions back a little."

My archers and men at arms were in position just after dawn. I had the captives from Monmouth paraded so that their King could see that he had lost his castle. With de Clifford and James, I rode, bare headed, towards the castle. I sat and looked at the gatehouse. Angry eyes stared back at me. There were warriors there who wished to end my life. I kept a stoic face. King Maredudd was having his own dilemma and debate.

I shouted, "I wish to speak with the King."

Eventually, King Maredudd appeared. He looked to have aged. I felt sorry for him. Had he not listened to Llewelyn ap Cynan he might have had more men and not been in this position.

The King's voice was defeated even if his men still stood ready to fight. "Yes, Earl Marshal?"

I said, flatly, "Monmouth has fallen. My knights are, even now, scouring the land for any remaining Welsh warriors. You have few archers left. If I assault now then my men will be so angry that I cannot answer for their actions. There would be a great slaughter."

He held up a hand, "I will come down and speak with you. It is not seemly to speak of these matters in the hearing of all and sundry."

"Of course."

He disappeared and, dismounting, I turned to de Clifford, "Say not a word. I will negotiate!"

He was contrite. He had seen the sharp edge of my tongue already, "Aye Earl Marshal."

I waited patiently. Eventually, I heard the bar of the gate as it was lowered. King Maredudd emerged. He gave me a wan smile as he drew close. "I should have heeded the old warriors who advised me not to risk a battle with the Warlord of the North." He shook his head. "What are your terms?"

"Leave this castle and return to your own lands. If you wish your men at arms, archers and knights returned then you will pay ransom for each one. There will be reparations for Monmouth and Striguil. They amount to one thousand gold pieces for each castle."

He looked surprised, "That is all?"

"That is all that I wish from you but I will be taking my men west to restore all of the castles and manors taken by your lords during the civil war. I will return them to their former owners. I would advise you to inform the men in those castles of that. I will punish them if they do not surrender when I arrive."

"And my men? The ones you captured?"

"They leave with you."

The King looked at his advisers. They nodded, "I agree to the terms."

I smiled, "It might be best if you had a cleric draw up a document."

"You are a careful man. Would that I had someone at my side like you."

I shook my head. "You need none, your majesty. You are a true King. I salute you." I took out my sword, raised it and saluted him.

"Thank you, Earl Marshal. That means more than you can know."

Chapter 18

De Clifford could not believe that we had succeeded with so little loss. I admonished him as though he was a child. "Now, lord, you must work to hold on to your land. You have more power here than lords in England. Use it!"

I sent my other lords out to continue our search for our foes. The King and his people began to make their way west. I did not allow de Clifford to enter the castle until the King and his men had left. It was courtesy. The King was the last to leave the castle. He leaned down from his horse. "I will send the reparations here, Earl Marshal, to you."

"Thank you, your majesty."

"Tell your King that this is not over. This land is mine. I am young but I will learn. We will battle again."

"I know, your majesty but you should know that if you fight me then you may well lose."

He laughed, "Even the Warlord cannot be in two places at once. Your heart lies to the north. I can be patient."

He left.

I watched him go and wondered if our paths would meet again. Then I went back into the castle. I had much to do. I used my authority to have my men housed in the castle and our horses in the stables. I then sat with Sir William Liedeberge and Richard de Clare. We had maps and I was keen to make the Welsh Marches secure once more. That meant scouring the lords who still clung on to Norman land.

Sir William wondered at that, "But the King has withdrawn. Surely that means his men obey his command and withdraw too."

I shook my head, "The King withdrew from Striguil. He said nothing about his other castles." I looked at de Clare. "You hold on to your estates. Who lies between us and your lands?"

"Apfael ap Iago holds a swathe of castles to the west of here. None are as strong as this one. They are made of wood but they form a barrier to Pembroke and the west."

"Then when de Mortimer and de Chaworth return from their raids we will rid ourselves of that barrier." A sudden gust of wind flurried through the castle. "We do not have long for it will be winter soon."

"And the castles of ap Iago are in high land that suffers snow. If we have not rid ourselves by All Saints then it will be too late."

"Then we have less than four weeks." I looked at the line of castles marked on the map. "Whose land is this?"

"De Mortimer and de Chaworth."

"Then they shall have the task of assault."

Two days later we were ready to ride. I left de Clifford to his castle. De Braose returned to his castle at Monmouth. I retained their archers. We were smaller in number now but we would not be facing a large army. According to de Mortimer, ap Iago had just six knights. The bulk of his army were little better than brigands. The garrison at Caerleon had joined the King when he had left. We moved swiftly for we had to head into the mountains and the journey would be harder than the one thus far.

De Mortimer rode with me. "So tell me of this castle of Tidfelly."

"It guards the valley. My father built it to watch the farms in the valley bottom. It is made of wood, lord."

"And how did it fall?"

His head drooped, "The civil war, lord. We were summoned by the Earl of Gloucester. We sought to support the Empress and her son." He shook his head. "As soon as we left the Welsh swarmed into the valley. They slew the settlers and took over the castle."

I nodded. In many ways that helped. There were no innocent victims here. We did not need to enter the valley cautiously. We could sweep in and drive the Welsh from their recently acquired castles. Thus far I had not seen any attempt to replace wooden walls with stone. The valleys all headed north to south. Tidfelly was the larger of the line of castles. I chose it because it was the larger. If we took that one then, being in the centre, it weakened the whole line.

The weather had changed almost as soon as we headed west. Skies darkened and rain fell. Winds blew and it was a most uncomfortable journey. It also made us ride closer together, wrapped in our cloaks. The exception were the archers of de

Mortimer. There were four of them and they acted as scouts. They knew the land well. Rhodri accompanied them. He had grown well into the role of captain of archers.

The valley road kept to the bottom of the valley. It passed through cultivated and tilled farmland. The valley sides were rock and tree-filled. I kept a wary eye on them as we headed north. If I was ap Iago then I might have launched an ambush. Ap Iago did not have many knights but he did have men who could use a bow and hide in the rocks and the trees. We had been riding for a few hours and I had called a halt when a movement in the tree line, three hundred paces from us, caught my eye. I wondered why the scouts had not spotted it. I had older eyes.

I dismounted and pretended to tighten my girth. "James, fetch Tom the Fletcher and my archers."

"Lord."

De Mortimer looked up, "Is there something wrong, lord?"

"There may be. Do not appear alarmed. Just warn your men that there are watchers in the woods."

Tom arrived with my other archers and James. "Lord?"

"There are men watching us from the woods. Back track down the valley and then approach them. If there are too many for you then alert us and I will bring the rest of the column to your aid."

He glanced up at the trees and then back at me. "If they are there then they are well hidden, lord. That means they may be brigands or bandits."

"Aye, they may be. Let us see who they are first."

He nodded. Turning to the other archers he said, "Let us see if we can find the cloak my lord lost."

He said it loudly. He was clever. The Welsh, for I was sure that they were locals, might not hear all of the words but they might be less suspicious of the small number who headed back down the valley road. As we mounted and continued north I wondered if the men were scouts for ap Iago. The castle was just ten miles ahead of us. Had it not been such a dank and dismal day then we might have been able to see it. As it was we were surrounded by misty rain. I knew that we would have to complete our campaign sooner than I had expected. I hoped that Henry was on his way south. From what we had been told by King Madog the combination of King Henry's men and the men of Powys would easily overcome Owain Gruffydd.

James and de Mortimer rode with me. "It may be nothing, lord."

"De Mortimer, you ignore such things at your peril. My archers, in Stockton, are the masters of such ambushes. I have known them to destroy whole columns of knights. They know how to use cover and their arrows are deadly. We are fortunate here that the trees are more than a hundred paces from us and they are on our left."

"How does that help, lord?"

I turned to James. "We are carrying our shields on our left arms. It is what we do in hostile territory. If the woods were on our right then we could be ambushed more easily. Dick and his archers have taught me the art of ambush."

The valley turned a little east and a slight break in the cloud and the rain, albeit brief, showed us the castle. It was a dark shadow rising above the valley but we could see where it was. It seemed to me to be less than five miles from us. Then the rain returned like a curtain and the castle was hidden once more. We halted.

"I am not certain that we will reach the castle before dark. De Mortimer, you know this valley better than any, find us somewhere to camp. Dry would be good."

"Aye lord. There are some farms just a mile away. One belonged to Sir Richard Ferrers. It had a hall."

I remembered Sir Richard. He had died in the debacle at Winchester when the Earl of Gloucester had been captured. I was about to tell him to secure it when Arne Arneson shouted, "Lord, Tom the Fletcher and the archers!"

I looked up at the treeline. My archers were escorting seven Welsh bowmen down the rock covered slopes. The bowmen were barefoot each wearing an animal skin cloak but they were bowmen. They had the familiar Welsh bow. With rougher wood, it was unmistakable. The bowmen were short and squat with barrel chests. Tom the Fletcher and my men rode easily alongside them. There was no danger here.

They stopped when they were ten paces from us, "Lord, these men wish to serve you." I held Tom's eye. He nodded, "I have spoken with them. Their English is not the best but Rhodri has given me enough words of Welsh for me to talk with them. I believe they are honest."

I had learned, over the years, how to read men. Tom the Fletcher was honest and I trusted his judgement but I needed confirmation. "James, signal Rhodri to return."

My squire sounded three blasts on his horn. Our scouts reappeared from the mist ahead of us.

"Lord?"

"Tom has found these archers. They were in the woods to the west of us." Rhodri flashed an irritated glance at one of de Mortimer's archers. That must have been his job. "They say they would serve us. I need you to question them and discover the truth."

"Aye lord." He dismounted and approached them. I knew perhaps two or three words of Welsh but I could not understand a single word of the interchange. "De Mortimer, go and find us shelter. We cannot reach the castle this day."

"Aye lord."

He and his men rode down the valley and were soon swallowed up in the drizzle.

Rhodri turned, "I think they speak truly, lord. They are from a valley to the north. Lord Apfael ap Iago went to their village a year since. It was remote and in the mountains. They had no lord and kept themselves to themselves. When ap Iago arrived, he needed women. He and his men took their women from them. When the men objected he had six slain. These are all that remain from the village. They became bandits, living in the woods. Some of their women escaped but ap Iago hunted them for sport. These men have been hunting the men of ap Iago. Two days since they caught a rider. They tortured him and discovered that we were coming. That is why they waited here. Ap Iago knows of our intentions. He has been reinforced by six knights and their men from the neighbouring valleys. He has emptied the other two castles. They are set to trap us."

I looked up at the skies. We had been cursing the weather but it had saved us. Had it been better weather then we would have been seen.

Rhodri held out a medallion, "They took this from the dead rider. It is the sign of the Welsh king."

King Maredudd had wasted no time in organising his defences. That meant we had a short time in which to win back these valleys. The advantage we had was that all of our enemies were gathered together.

"Which is their leader?"

Tom pointed, "Tomas ap Tomas."

An older warrior stepped forward and bowed. He spoke to me. I understood his words. "We have heard that you are the lord of the wolves. You have come to defeat this evil man. We would serve you, lord."

"Then join us to help defeat ap Iago and when we have done so you can decide if you wish to follow my banner." He nodded. "You will serve under my captain of archers, Rhodri. He is a Welshman like you."

"Aye lord."

"How many horsemen does he have?"

"There are fifty since the other knights arrived. He had but twenty before they arrived. He had more but we know how to trap horsemen."

I turned to de Clare, "Let us head down the valley and hope that de Mortimer has found us somewhere safe to shelter. It seems that we were the hunter but now we are the hunted."

Heading down the track which de Mortimer had taken, Richard said, "And we have just four conroi of men. We only have five knights. He has more horse than we do."

"But we have something he does not; information. We know that he expects us. He will believe that we travel in the dark. Never underestimate the importance of that. Surprise on a battlefield kills as many men as a sword."

One of de Mortimer's men met us, "We have the hall, lord. It was defended but they are dead now."

I saw, when we neared it, that it was a Norman hall. Although made of wood there was a stable under the hall and but one entrance, up a staircase, to the main hall. We would be able to defend it. I saw that there were six bodies covered with cloaks. They were men at arms.

De Mortimer was bareheaded. He approached me, "I know that you would have wished prisoners, lord but they fought hard. I lost two men." He pointed to the river. "Now I am pleased that we did so." He led me down to the river. I saw the bodies of five men and girls. They were emaciated and naked. "How could men do this to women?"

"I know not but I have seen it too many times. The men who follow this ap Iago seem to me to be like their master. They prey on others." I turned and waved Rhodri down towards me. He and the scouts had returned.

"Lord."

"You had better fetch Tomas ap Tomas. He is with Tom the Fletcher. I believe these may be their women."

Rhodri's mouth tightened, "Bastards! Sorry, lord. My men and I will help them. It is no wonder he chose to follow you."

I watched with a sinking heart as my suspicions were confirmed. Two of the younger men threw themselves to the ground and began to weep as they cradled the bodies in their arms. Tomas turned to speak with Rhodri. He nodded and came to me, "It is their women, lord. One is the daughter of Tomas. They ask permission to bury them."

"Of course, and I will ask Father Matthew to speak over them."

We had a young priest with us. I hoped he could offer comfort. That night we ate in sombre silence. What I had hoped would be a short campaign had suddenly taken on a sinister significance. I sat with my knights and planned our battle.

Chapter 19

The rain stopped during the night but the effects were clear to see. Mud had washed down onto the already poorly made road surface. The river was high and those warriors who had not bothered to protect their armour now had rusty blemishes appearing. The shelter and the grain had, however, benefitted our horses. After making sure that my knights and Rhodri knew what they were doing we headed back to the road which led to the castle.

As soon as we reached the spot we had left the previous evening then we could see the castle. It stood on a rocky outcrop above the widest part of the valley. I could see why de Mortimer's father had built it there. His castellan could survey the rich farmland from the wooden walls. Unlike de Clifford this castle had not been lost due to incompetence but duty. I would ensure that it became Mortimer land once more. Rhodri and the archers left their horses with the baggage train and headed up through the woods. They had Tomas ap Tomas and his vengeful men to lead them. Ap Iago could not know of this one advantage. He would see a column of four knights and thirty odd men at arms heading towards him. I had no doubt that he had already made his plans. I did not want him to change them.

The road dropped down towards the farmland of the valley bottom. Our banners made the farmers and their families take to their heels and run towards the castle. The fact that they were admitted so readily confirmed that Apfael ap Iago knew we were coming. His banner fluttered above the gate. We rode steadily. I wanted him to think that we suspected nothing. It gave me the chance to examine the battlefield. There were trees six hundred paces to our left. They followed the line of the edge of the cultivated land. The fields were dotted with sheep and a few cattle. The trees thinned out closer to the rocks which marked the tops of the hills. The trees had been cleared to within three hundred paces of the castle. To our left and right were fields where animals grazed but a hundred paces closer to the river were fields with crops of winter barley, oats and cabbage. What I could not see were the horsemen who were waiting for us.

We knew that they would not let us ravage the valley and take their animals. That was their food for the winter. They had been reinforced by horsemen. We had taken two castles and both were stronger than this one. King Maredudd was a quick learner. Even as he had been heading back to his home in the west he was preparing a trap for me. He would meet us, horsemen, to horsemen and use his Welsh archers to decimate us.

There were stone walls on both sides of the road. They were dry stone ones and were there to keep the sheep and cattle penned. They could also hide archers and peasants. It was why I had stopped so far from the castle. I waved my arm and men at arms dismounted and began to dismantle holes in the dry-stone walls to make gaps for us to enter. I had no intention of advancing on a narrow front. It had an immediate effect. I heard a horn sound from the castle. The gates opened and horsemen poured out. The reason became obvious as soon as Arne led my men at arms into the fields. "Lord, there are archers in the fields ahead!"

Even as he shouted a ragged flurry of arrows fell. He and his men pulled up their shields. Despite their speed, one horse was struck and threw Roger of Bath to the ground before heading away from the danger. Roger quickly rose and covered himself with his shield before racing back to the baggage train. Already our servants had begun to pull the carts and the horses into a defensive position. We had spare horses and Roger would soon be remounted.

"Form line!" Our plans had been made the previous night. De Clare and Sir William took their men to the field on my right. I stayed on the road with my men at arms while de Mortimer, de Chaworth and their men were in the field closest to the woods. De Mortimer was the bait. His banner would be known and he would be seen as isolated an easier target.

A second horn sounded and the archers moved back towards the castle and the protection of the horsemen. Having been seen they could be picked off by vengeful horsemen. Crudely armed Welsh also emerged from their places of concealment. They had been given clear orders for they formed themselves in two lines before the archers. The ones in the second rank held spears to protect the swordsmen in the front rank.

I counted the banners as they emerged from the castle. There were fourteen knights. Behind them were another twenty horsed and mailed men. The mail was, largely, the old-fashioned type of plates sewn onto a jerkin. They had pot helmets, spears and a variety of shields. Their horses were not large ones as ours were. They were stocky horses. They would gallop all day and were perfect for the rock-filled fields over which we would fight.

James handed me my spear. My helmet hung from my cantle. "Will they charge us, lord?"

"No. First, they will advance their archers and try to weaken us. You know what to sound when I give the command?"

"Aye lord, I have not forgotten since you reminded me this morning. Two blasts."

"It is not that I do not trust you, James but I cannot afford to repeat the order."

"I know, lord. Let us hope it works."

"If it does not then I will have to adapt will I not? I have not fought this Apfael ap Iago. Who knows, he may outwit me."

James laughed, "That I cannot see, lord but we are outnumbered. We need more men."

"We always need more men but King Henry took the bulk of the army north. We will fight with what we have and trust to God."

Once the enemy horses were in place, I heard commands given. The line of men armed with spears and swords moved forward to within two hundred paces for us. The archers followed and I saw that ap Iago positioned his horsemen to the right of them. It was clever. He would have the slope to aid his charge and his archers would be able to rain death on us while they charged. The bulk of his men were facing de Mortimer, de Chaworth and myself. I glanced over to de Clare and Sir William. As I donned my helmet I nodded. They both returned my nod. My plans remained unchanged.

As soon as the archers were within range they began to release arrows at us. I whipped my shield up. My men were expecting the arrows and our shields covered not only us but our horses' heads. They struck my shield. When one bounced off I looked at it on the muddy grass. It was a hunting arrow! They could still kill and would certainly hurt a horse but they were not the mail piercing arrows my men used. I heard a whinny and a cry from my left as a horse was struck and one of de Mortimer's men took an arrow in the leg.

"Now, James!"

The horn sounded and my men turned their horses as though we were going to fall back. I slipped my shield around my back. Sir William and Sir Richard led their men away and then after twenty paces turned them around and headed back towards the Welsh. We kept riding. The Welsh thought we fled and they poured after us. The ones closer to Sir William and Sir Richard were in for a rude shock.

A Welsh horn sounded and their horsemen began to gallop to cut off de Mortimer. As soon as they did so I yelled, "Wheel right!" Expecting the order, the other two knight's men and mine turned to charge the Welsh horse. It would have appeared suicidal but what ap Iago could not have foreseen was Rhodri leading my archers from the woods. Leaving my men on the right to roll up the archers and spearmen our three conroi would attack, uphill against the Welsh knights. It would be doomed to failure if Rhodri and his men could not decimate them before they reached us.

The Welsh showed their lack of experience and discipline. They hurtled down towards us as individuals. My three bands of men formed one line with just our three banners in the second rank. We were, however, boot to boot. We also had bigger horses. I aimed Warrior at ap Iago and his banner. I could see what my foe could not. The horsemen at the rear of their lines were falling. Rhodri had half of his men sending arrows while the other half moved closer. It kept up a constant shower of arrows.

The Welsh were closing rapidly with us now. Their line was even more ragged. Warrior was stronger than the other horses and I was just a head ahead of the others. Ap Iago saw that and he veered towards me. I saw the head of his spear as it wavered up and down. He would not be in a position to make a clean strike. I had mine resting across my cantle and my horse's neck. I would not underestimate the Welshman. I pulled my shield up to protect my left side.

Judgement of time and space was vital in such situations. My speed was not as great as his and I had the luxury of being able to turn. He did not. We were approaching shield to shield. I pulled warrior to the left. Ap Iago's wavering spear was aimed at Roger of Bath who was next to me. I thrust forward. Warrior's gait meant that I did not hit where I aimed, his middle. Instead, my spear went up towards his shoulder. I caught his spear and then the head penetrated the links in his mail. His speed and attempted turn drove the spear head into his flesh. Throwing his arms back he tumbled over the back of this horse.

His mob of men at arms were following in an untidy line. One thrust his spear at me when I passed his horse's head. It clattered into my shield and I barely kept my saddle. I shifted my position and then wheeled to the right. Ahead I could see Rhodri and my archers as they continued to send arrows into the mounted men. They were aiming and releasing selectively. It meant that we were in no danger and I needed to lead my men around and destroy these horsemen. De Clare and Sir William would be turning the enemy line of archers and spears but we needed to destroy the knights.

The shield of a man at arms appeared before Warrior's head as I turned. I thrust with my spear. The man at arms had been standing in his stirrups as he tried to spear one of de Mortimer's men. Unbalanced he tumbled from his saddle. It was now a disorganized mass of men and horses. Our men were more disciplined and we did not have the problem of archers sending arrows into backs.

A knight spurred his horse towards me. He was going slower than ap Iago had been and his spear was held steadily. The ground was now churned up and slippery from the recent rains and the hooves which had dug it up. It was harder to retain grip. I did not risk a sudden movement with Warrior. That could have ended in disaster. Instead, I concentrated on making a clean strike. We both thrust at the same time. Victory is often the result of very narrow margins. I wore mail mitts. His spear head slid over the back of my right hand. Without the mitt, I would have had my hand scored and hurt. As it was I was able to raise my hand as the haft slid over it and, knocking the spear away had a better angle for my own strike which found the gap between cantle and shield. My spear head entered his right side. His movement tore the spear from my hand. I released the spear. We were almost stopped and I punched my shield at his left shoulder. Wounded, he fell from his horse and it allowed me to draw my own sword and look for my next enemy.

I did not have to look far. A knight whirled his horse around and rode at me. A man at arms followed. I spurred Warrior to meet them. They had the advantage over me. Both still retained their spears and I had a sword. I aimed Warrior at the gap between them. It meant I would have the knight's spear on my shield side. I counted on the man at arms being the inferior of the two. I had my sword levelled. Both spears were aimed at me. Suddenly the man at arms pitched over the back of his horse as he was struck by an arrow. In that instant, I began to turn Warrior as the knight's spear struck my shield. The turn had angled my shield and the spear did not hit it head-on. It glanced off the side. My turn brought me around the rear of the knight. Swinging my sword, I hacked into the knight's mail. My sword came away bloody. He hurled his spear to the ground and drew his own sword. I swung again but the act of drawing his sword meant he blocked my blow but his sword was not true. It rang dully.

"Yield for you are wounded!"

"Norman! I fight for my land. If I have to die for it then so be it."

I stood in my stirrups and brought my sword down. He brought his sword and shield up to block the blow. I raised my sword and struck a second time. He did not think to strike out at me. He was defending himself. I punched at the side of his head and his shoulder with my shield. To help his balance he spread his arms. It was an invitation I could not refuse, I hacked at his chest with my sword. Not yet dulled by too many strokes it bit through to flesh. He rolled backwards over his saddle.

I had time to look around. The Welsh knights and men at arms were in disarray. I was impressed that they had not fled. My archers, however, had closed to less than fifty paces. They could not miss. I turned and saw that James and my men at arms protected my rear. Even as I watched, Arne slew a man at arms. De Mortimer, de Chaworth and their men could handle the rest. Sir William and Richard de Clare had made the Welsh archers and spears form a defensive circle. Without archers, it would be hard to break. I raised my sword, "Arne, bring our men!"

"Aye, lord!"

"Rhodri! Archers. With me!"

"Aye lord."

We galloped across the body littered field. Riderless horses grazed next to dead, dying and wounded horsemen. I saw ap Iago lying at an awkward angle. My strike had not killed him; it had been the fall. The Welsh had been pushed back towards their castle. They knew they could not win alone against horsemen but they could hold their own. I saw that the Welsh archers had scored hits. Wounded men at arms were lying on the field. Two horses thrashed as they slowly bled to death close to the spearmen. Sir Richard and Sir William had done what I had asked. They had contained the Welsh foot. I now needed to destroy it.

I reined in and shouted, "Surrender! I will offer terms! Your lord is dead and your horsemen are defeated. You cannot win!"

One Welsh voice answered me, "We bowed once to the Norman standard. We will die as free men."

"Sir Richard, Sir William, form your men into a line."

Riding with our shields to protect us, we rode across the front of the Welsh line. Arrows descended from the sky but we were able to block them with our shields. I reined in next to the other two knights. The Welsh were running out of arrows. They were husbanding them for our attack. It had taken Rhodri and his men time to return for their horses and then gallop the nine hundred paces to our position. I saw that some archers had fallen but we still had enough. Tomas ap Tomas and his small band still supported de Mortimer and de Chaworth.

"Have you enough arrows?"

Rhodri slapped his saddle, "Unlike those poor bastards we carried spares on our horses. Do you want us to end this, lord?"

"Let me speak with them again."

"Aye lord. Lads, use the horses as shields! We have lost too many men today."

I took off my helmet, "Men of Tidfelly, I give you one more chance. I will unleash my archers unless you surrender now."

In answer three of the spear men turned, dropped their breeks and bared their backsides.

Arne growled, "Well that is as clear a message as you can get. They have answered you, lord. They would die."

It was sad but it was true. Without turning I said, "Rhodri!"

"Draw! Release!" The arrows soared. As soon as the bow strings had thrummed the Welsh answered. Their hunting arrows hit saddles, they hit earth. Three struck horses which then bolted but none hit archers. From the back of my horse, I saw Rhodri's arrows plunge into flesh and gaps appeared. A second and third flight eliminated their archers. Some of their spearmen and swordsmen fell.

The fourth flight began to thin the ranks of the spears and the swords. They could still have surrendered but they did not. They turned and they ran. Part of me did not want to slaughter them but I knew that if they made their castle then we would have to besiege them and I wanted this campaign over. "After them!"

My men needed no urging. Sir William and Sir Richard had lost men and they were in a vengeful mood. My men and I had charged too many times. I would not risk my horses and so we watched as the Welsh were hunted like driven deer. Spears thrust and stabbed. Swords rose and fell. I thought that two or three might have reached the gates which stayed open until the last handful were cut down. The gates slammed shut but no arrows were sent towards our men.

They had emptied the castle of its garrison. The castle had the local watch.

We had won.

There were survivors. Some of the knights and men at arms yielded. There were wounded who were tended to by my priest but the dead filled the fields before Tidfelly. I rode to the gate. I took off my helmet and I went with de Mortimer, de Chaworth, James and Rhodri.

"I am the Earl Marshal of England and I demand the surrender of the castle."

A woman answered me, "I am Nesta, wife of Apfael Iago. When my husband tells me to surrender then I will!"

It was a brave statement and to be expected. I put my hand out and James handed me the seal of ap Iago. "Here is his seal, taken from his body. Your husband is dead."

She stared defiantly at me. She glanced at the two ancient warriors who flanked her. Then she turned, "Do your worst. Others have tried to take this castle and failed."

"Lady, I admire your courage but we have archers here who can make fire arrows. Your castle and your buildings are made of wood. I can make a bridge over your ditch and we have men with axes who can hew your gate to kindling."

"Then do not talk! Just do it!"

"The consequences for you and those within would be dire, lady. Would you want your people enslaved and taken to England? Would you want your men to lose their arrow fingers? Yield and all shall live. If there is a ransom for you then you would go free. Your King asked you to hold here. He will redeem you. My Lord Mortimer will rule this valley and he is just."

I saw the internal debate and then, after her soul had been searched, she nodded and said, "Open the gates and let the barbarians enter!"

Arne sniffed, "Cheek!"

The bridge was lowered. It had been crudely made. My horse clattered across. I had seen few weapons on the fighting platform and I saw even fewer as we entered the lower bailey. Apfael ap Iago had obviously taken every warrior he had to fight me. He must have been confident that he could defeat us. He had been wrong! I reined in as the Lady Nesta descended the stairs. I saw that she was not young. She glared at me as though she was a Gorgon and could turn me to stone.

I dismounted and said, "You made the right decision, my lady. Men who take a castle often forget that they are men. They can behave like animals in the field. I have seen it and it is not pretty."

"Why could you Normans not leave us alone? This is our land!"

"It was your land and King Henry Rhodri lost it. Now lead me to the hall. I have much to do and little time in which to do it." I did not like being so brusque but I had no choice. I turned to Arne, "Have our dead brought within the castle and find the body of Lord Iago. Fetch him too."

"The others?"

"Leave them until the morrow. It is getting late and I would have the hurts of our men seen to. I intend to return to Hereford and Gloucester as soon as Lord Mortimer can be left to rule this valley."

The castle had not been finished well. The wall and gate to the inner bailey had not been finished off. I waved de Mortimer forward.

"It is little wonder that this castle as taken. Why were the defences unfinished?"

He shook his head, "I know, lord. My father had finer estates closer to the sea. The hunting is poor and the climate damp."

"If you do not wish to live here then appoint a lord who will make it strong. The other two castles have been emptied. We can take those too but you need three lords from your retinue. Do you have them?" He hesitated. It was a sure sign that he did not. "If you do not then I will suggest to the King that he gives your land to another lord."

He stopped and turned, "You cannot do that, lord! We are Marcher lords. We have the right to rule!"

"And when you asked King Henry for help you abdicated those rights. You now rule under King Henry." I held his gaze and he nodded. "We will speak later."

I had much to do. I first sought the treasury. Apfael ap Iago had collected taxes. They were the King's. Once that was secured I sent Sir William to ride to the valley to the east and take the castle that was there. De Chaworth went with him. Richard de Clare would take possession of the one to the west. He would stay there and garrison it with some men before heading to his own lands further west. Now that ap Iago had been defeated then we had retaken the most vital of the marcher lands. We still held the coast and de Clare's family had not lost a single castle.

Nesta ap Iago had retired to her rooms. Her cooperation was over. I found one of the wounded men at arms and gave him a message for King Maredudd. "I want the King to send ransom for Nesta ap Iago to Gloucester. Five hundred pieces of silver."

He nodded. Grateful that he would not be held as a prisoner, "Aye lord."

We gave him a horse and he left. De Mortimer asked, "Will he not just run?"

"He is a man at arms and he will seek a lord. Where else can he go? This way he finds a sponsor in King Maredudd. He will do as I asked. I will take the Lady Nesta with me to Gloucester. I fear that she would be the piece of grit that hides in your mail. Better that you do not have her carping on at you. Besides, it will make the others less likely to cause trouble."

It was late in the night by the time I had finished. There had been much to do. I had spoken to de Mortimer of the piece of grit and I had one. Mine was in my head. There was something irritating me and gnawing at me but I did not know what it was. The result was that I slept little and was awake if I ever slept before most of the castle was up. I ate first and was ready to begin work. We cleared the battlefield of the dead. I had those who lived in the valley dig the graves and they were buried by priests. I wanted no one digging up our dead! I divided the captured horses, mail and weapons with de Mortimer. He would need that for his men. He had sent to his other estates by the coast for men and knights. He had heeded my word.

Late in the morning riders arrived from Sir William and Richard de Clare. They had taken their castles without opposition. They awaited relief so that they could go home as I had promised. It took three days for the column of knights from Caerdyf to reach us. There were eight knights with the column. I was relieved. Two were older knights and de Mortimer could use those to rule this valley. We had seen, as we rode up that it had little to offer in terms of farming but who knew what lay beneath those mountains? The important thing was that de Mortimer now had control of the people in the valleys. That would make the richer land closer to the coast safer.

I left with my archers and men at arms. The Lady Nesta had servants and baggage. We would not be travelling as swiftly as we would have liked. Tomas ap Tomas and his men came with us. Rhodri gave them horses and we equipped them with equipment from the dead Welsh. The leather and metal jerkins from the men at arms were perfect and we chose the better swords, shields and helmets to equip them as the rest of my archers. They looked like real warriors as we headed south rather than the ragtag brigands we had first encountered.

I flanked Lady Nesta. James rode on the other side of her. She gave me a sideways look, "I am surprised at your taking these traitors, lord. You strike me as a careful man. They have betrayed once. They might do so again."

I kept looking ahead, "Then you clearly do not know their story, lady. They betrayed no one. If anyone was guilty of betrayal it was your husband."

"How dare you speak ill of the dead!"

I turned and stared at her, "These men you call traitors lived high up in your valley. Your husband came to take their women. You knew your husband better than I did. You know if he did that for his men or his own carnal lust." She flushed and I knew that my arrow had struck home. "Clearly you lived apart from your people or you would have known what was going on."

"I am a lady. It is not my duty to have to deal with such matters."

I shook my head. The Empress, the Countess of Chester, Queen Eleanor, these were ladies who knew their duty and did it. They would not have sat idly by while their husband abused their people. "When you were granted the title with it came responsibilities. Think on that, lady."

We rode hard for, whilst it was not wet, it was cold. A wind came from the northeast. That was normally a dry wind but a cold one. We made the castle of de Clifford before dark. We were weary but we were afforded a fine welcome. Sir William had reached there before me and he told me of his journey.

"There were few men in the castle and they soon surrendered. We found but one chest of taxes. Perhaps the others were hidden, I know not."

"Then keep that chest for your share. You have served King Henry well. I give you Liedeberge for your own. I do not release you from your oath of fealty to me and I command you to ensure that your manor and the valley in which you live is well protected."

"Aye lord. I am ever your man. I owe what I have to you and to you alone."

"No, William, you are a brave knight and all that I did was to help you along the way."

I felt safer the next day, as we headed towards Hereford. We passed Monmouth and I was pleased to see that the defences were being improved, despite the weather. After speaking with the castellan there we continued along the Wye towards Hereford. William and his men did not follow along with us for they needed three of their horses shoeing. They would follow when they had been shoed. Despite the fact that we were in friendly territory I still kept my archers in a screen ahead of us. We had a lady and treasure with us. I was vindicated for my caution when Robert of Sheffield came galloping in.

"Lord, there are men being attacked. They bear the banner of Hereford."

I turned, "Wilfred and Brian! Take the ladies and guard them with the baggage!"

My two servants galloped up, "Aye, lord. Come, ladies." Without waiting they took the reins of their horses and led the women back to the baggage.

"Who attacks them? Bandits and brigands?" There were many forests close by.

"No lord. I think they are the remnants of the Welsh who were here. Many had mail."

That made sense. We had moved across the land so quickly that we had not had time to ensure that all the insurgents and warriors were accounted for. Had the King been with us then we would have had more men and might have policed the land more effectively. There was little to be gained from dwelling on what might have been. I drew my sword and swung my shield around, "Come let us go to the aid of the men of Hereford."

Walther de Hereford was the High Sherriff and he was the son of Miles of Gloucester, an old friend and a loyal supporter of the Empress. I had asked him to scour the land of the enemy. This was my responsibility. If his men were being attacked then it was incumbent upon me to do something about it.

Rhodri rode ahead of us with Robert of Sheffield. We heard the sound of battle as we closed with the trees. Rhodri slowed down and turned to look at me. We had eleven archers and there were just eight of us who had swords and shields. Rhodri knew, as well as I did that we would have to use cunning rather than brute force. We were attacking men who knew the land better than we did.

"Rhodri, split the men and outflank the enemy. Use your arrows wisely."

"Aye lord. And, lord?"

"Yes, Rhodri?"

"Be careful, I look forward to seeing this valley of the Tees."

"Do not fear. I do not feel death at my shoulder yet." As my archers were sent left and right by Rhodri I turned, "Arne, next to me. James, ride at the rear with Harry Lightfoot. Perhaps they may think there are more of us than there are!"

"Aye lord."

Spurring Warrior, I headed down the road towards the sound of battle. I saw the Sherriff's standard. There was a rough shield wall and the beleaguered men of Hereford were being attacked by the remnants of the Welsh we had defeated at Monmouth and Striguil. The horses of the men of Hereford were tethered behind them. The men had their backs to the trees but were assailed on three sides by Welshmen. There were over forty men attacking the fifteen men I saw still standing. Even as I watched the squire holding the standard was hacked down by a man at arms with an axe.

"Charge! For King Henry!"

Roger of Bath and James of Tewkesbury rode next to Arne and me. We were not boot to boot. We had no need. We were not fighting horsemen. Had we had time I would have had spears brought up but we would have to use swords.

My shout brought some respite for the defenders. The Welsh turned as we approached I leaned forward and swept my sword at the Welsh archer who had turned his weapon towards me. My sword split his elm bow in two before hacking across his chest. He was cut so deeply that I could see his ribs. I reined in Warrior and then, standing in my stirrups made him rear. His mighty hooves clattered into two men as Rhodri and his archers began to send arrows into them.

We did not have enough men to be chivalrous. We were fighting deserters who would do anything to win. They wanted our horses and our mail. I brought my sword down and split the skull and spine of an archer who was aiming at one of the men of Hereford. Arne and my men at arms were laying about them as though their lives depended upon it. I heard a shout from behind me, "My lord!"

As I turned Warrior's head I saw a man at arms with an axe. He was about to hack into the hindquarters of my horse. I watched as James rammed the pointed end of my standard into his back. James was a strong squire and the broad head erupted through the mail at the front. Waving my sword in acknowledgement I spurred Warrior and sliced into the side of a man at arms who had leapt onto the back of Harry Lightfoot's horse and was attempting to cut Harry's throat. With blood spraying from deep inside him, the Welshman tumbled to the ground. Rhodri had led his archers closer. At ten paces distance, every arrow caused a mortal wound. We had no time for prisoners for within a few sword strokes and flights of arrows it was all over.

I shouted, "Arne, see to the wounded and despatch the enemy who are beyond help."

I dismounted and went to the twelve men at arms who remained around the fallen standard of Hereford. I saw the body of Walther of Hereford. He had been hacked and sliced. His death had not been a swift one. His squire lay dead but his fingers still grasped the standard. I recognised one of the men at arms. I had fought alongside him and Miles of Gloucester at Wallingford.

"Richard, what happened?"

"The Sherriff heard of a band of brigands who had murdered some folk who lived close to the village of Ross. We came to bring them to book. We were ambushed and discovered that they were not brigands but warriors from the Welsh army you defeated. We slew many but they outnumbered us." He shook his head, "We should have mounted our horses and run. Our lord refused to flee. The Sherriff was, truly, his father's son. He believed in doing what was right."

"Come, we will head back to Hereford. Put your dead on the horses. Have your men take the mail and the weapons from the dead. We can send men out to burn them. I will not waste time on carrion. We have a lady to escort to Hereford."

Sir William and his men caught up with us just as we had loaded the last body onto the saddle. "I am sorry, lord! I was tardy."

"No Sir William. It was the hand of God."

We reached Hereford with heavy hearts. Walther de Hereford had neither wife nor child. He was the last of Miles of Gloucester's line. I was even more grateful than ever that I had at least one grandson. The death of the Sherriff upset my plans to return to Gloucester. Until Henry returned from the north I was in command and I needed to do just that. Hereford was a border town and we needed a strong Sherriff. While arrangements were made for the burial of the Hereford dead I sat with the Bishop of Hereford. Gilbert Foliot was a good man but he had fallen foul of the King by swearing fealty to King Stephen. I understood why he had done so. He was not a warrior and he had done nothing to oppose either the Empress or Henry.

"We need a strong knight, lord. As the Sherriff discovered we are too close to Wales."

"Are there any lords close by?"

He smiled, "I would have thought that you would have known that, Earl Marshal. You were the one who led them to recover our lands."

I smiled. He was a monk and not a politician but I liked his honesty, "You are right, Bishop. I can think of only one choice yet others may say I am showing favouritism. I would appoint William of Liedeberge."

Shaking his head, he said, "It would only be your enemies, Earl Marshal, and they would say that of any appointment. As for me, I think that he is perfect, save that he has no bride. He is well known to be a pious and honourable knight. He served the Sherriff well. I would concur with your decision."

"I will sleep on it and we will speak again on the morrow."

He put a hand on mine, "You have taken much responsibility upon your shoulders. I hope that the King appreciates what you have done. Walther de Hereford always spoke highly of you. He said that there were times during the war when you were the only one to oppose King Stephen." He shrugged, "I know I offended the King by swearing an oath of loyalty but you must remember, lord, that we were directed to do so by Pope Eugene and Archbishop Henry."

"Thank you, Bishop, but my lot is to serve the Empress and her son. I do not mind the responsibility."

That evening I ate with the Bishop and Sir William. I confess that I had not thought of Sir William's marital state but now that it was in my head I could not rid myself of the questions which accompanied that. I decided to take an oblique approach.

"You have much gold now, William. Have you plans for it?"

He smiled, "Now that you have given me the manor of Liedeberge for my own I can." He smiled. "The hall was adequate for myself and my squire. My needs are not great. With the war, it did not seem right to make plans but now that the war is over and the border safe I can think of making my home bigger for I would have a family."

The Bishop wagged an admonishing finger, "First, you need a wife, lord! I would not have you as some young men do and spread your seed where you will! God says that a man ought to marry."

"And I have every intention of marrying, Bishop. I could not think of marriage until now but there is a lady."

The Bishop leaned forward, "Who?"

"Margaret D'Oyly, the niece of Brian Fitz Court. I got to know her during the siege of Wallingford. We have an understanding.

Since her uncle died and her aunt entered a nunnery she has been acting as a lady in waiting to Sibyl de Neufmarché, the Countess of Hereford."

I smiled, "Then all is well." I looked at the Bishop who nodded.

Sir William looked confused, "My lord, what is going on? What do I not know?"

"Nothing untoward, William. We will speak with you in the morning after the Bishop has held services."

I slept well. We had come through a difficult time. I had wondered if we had taken too much on by retaking Wales. I saw now that God had a plan and I had played a small part in it. I was happy to leave Hereford in the hands of Sir William. It was good that he was marrying a lady who had fallen on hard times. When I awoke, I was refreshed.

Sir William was eager to return to his manor and I saw him shifting uneasily from foot to foot as he awaited us. "Lord?"

"Come Sir William. I need the Bishop."

"I am anxious to return home. Winter is coming and I need my men to begin work on the hall."

"Your coin is burning a hole in your purse. I understand."

The Bishop entered. "I am sorry, Earl Marshal. I had many requests after I had finished the service."

"It is no matter. Let us get to it directly. Sir William Beauchamp of Liedeberge, would you accept the position of High Sherriff of Hereford. I need someone who is as loyal as Sir Walther and who can defend this land."

He looked stunned. "But, I have no connections, Earl Marshal. I am just a lowly knight with a small manor."

"You retain your manor but the castle here is yours and you will be expected to defend it. The Bishop will be here to advise you for when I have spoken with the King I intend to head home for Christmas."

"Then I accept, lord and gladly!"

The Bishop warned, "But you must be married first!"

"Of course."

After he was sworn in he hurried to the home of the Countess of Hereford. As Margaret D'Oyly was the ward of the Countess, then her permission had to be obtained. It delayed my departure by half a day. Leaving Hereford in safe hands and leaving Nesta, wife of ap Iago there too, I headed for Gloucester. I would send riders to King Henry and ask permission to ride home. I had done all that had been asked of me.

Gloucester had an air of prosperity once more. As we rode through the gates I saw many people coming for the market. The civil war and then the Welsh raids had made people wary of travel. Now that I had made the border safe then the people of the Severn Valley could engage in commerce once more.

As Earl Marshal, I was accommodated in the Sherriff's castle. There was no Sherriff and Sir William Beauchamp would have to be Sherriff for both Hereford and Gloucester until the King could appoint another. Thus, I had the Sherriff's quarters which were well apportioned. I dealt with the day to day problems that had arisen since my departure and then I told James and Arne to prepare to leave for home. I was just penning a letter to the King when there was a knock on the door. I looked up and saw that it was Richard le Breton, a young knight who had been in the service of William Fitz Empress. He had come to England and was serving as one of Henry's knights. His face was spattered in blood.

"What is wrong, Sir Richard?"

"The King has been routed at Ewloe in Flintshire. He barely escaped with his life. He sent me for you, lord! He needs his Earl Marshal at his side!"

I was fated not to return home for Christmas. Gathering my men and all that could be spared from Gloucester's garrison I headed north. My work was not yet done.

Chapter 20

We headed north. Using our spare horses, we made all speed for Chester. Richard le Breton told us of the disastrous ambush which had resulted in the King almost losing his life. I had many questions to ask but the young knight was not the one to answer them. I would have to ask the King.

I turned to Rhodri, "You came from this area did you not?"

"Aye, lord." He said no more.

I waved the others further back. "Come, I need to know your story."

He sighed, "I am sorry, lord, I should have told you but each time I utter the words it brings back the pain."

"For that, I am sorry. But...."

He nodded, "I had a small farm. I was in the retinue of a knight from Twthill. Cynan ap Madog was his name. He was close to the prince. Prince Owain is now King. I had a pretty young wife." He hesitated and I saw him suck in air as though he was having difficulty breathing. "I was sent, with other archers to scour the forests along the Clwyd of bandits. When I returned home, six days later, my wife was dead. She had refused the advances of the lord. He had had her executed for laying hands on him. He thought to appease me with coin. That night I slipped into his chambers and slit his throat. I have not been back since. I am Welsh, lord but I will never fight for that lord."

"Thank you for telling me and you have answered my other questions. When we reach King Henry I intend to use you to our advantage. Your knowledge can be a weapon we use against this Welsh king who supported the murderer of your wife."

He gave a thin smile. "Then I may be able to sleep at night!"

The King was at Chester. I found him and his commanders seated around a table before the fire. They were drinking and feeling sorry for themselves. Matilda, the Countess had kept the castle as a refuge for the King. After his rout, he and his army had fled to the ancient castle. Owain Gwynedd would not be able to reduce it.

The King was shaken. I could see that his confidence had been dented. However, his face brightened when we swept into the hall. "I am pleased you have come, Alfraed! We had our noses bloodied."

I threw off my cloak and sat with him before the fire, "Tell me all, majesty."

"I was heading for the castle at Twthill when we were stopped by the Welsh who waited for us at Rhuddlan. I sent my men to outflank the Welsh but they were ambushed. The ambush was then reversed and we were outflanked. Had not Roger of Hereford rescued me then I would have perished."

Coming north Sir Richard le Breton told me that the King had sent his fleet to attack Anglesey.

"And the fleet?"

Henry shook his head, "They disobeyed my orders, Alfraed! They pillaged. The locals boarded the ships and there was great slaughter."

"Then the commander must be punished!"

"Too late, it was my cousin Henry Fitz Roy. He died in the attack."

This was a disaster of immense proportions. It was almost as bad as the Earl of Gloucester's defeat at Winchester. I had to be positive. I wracked my mind for a solution. "All is not lost, your majesty. We strike now and we strike quickly. The Welsh king will think that you will view this as the end of your ambitions. We will show him that it is not. We attack now."

King Madog ap Maredudd, King of Powys, said, "Are you mad, Earl Marshal? We have been knocked about. Those Welsh archers cut us to ribbons!"

I turned on him, "I managed to defeat King Maredudd and his Welsh archers. What happened to your archers, your majesty? Did they run too?"

King Henry said, "Is that any way to speak to a king?"

"Aye, your majesty, when it was that King's invitation which led to the defeat in the first place. If you had not come north then this would not have happened. We have retaken the Welsh marches."

I had raised my voice but my words must have struck home for the King of Powys subsided. "We have fifty or sixty archers who remain."

"Then they will do. Give the order, your majesty."

He looked uncertain. "This land is not like Normandy or Anjou where we fought. This land fights back. It is a savage land and does not suit heavy horses."

I said slowly, "I beg you, give the order, your majesty."

He looked at me. My eyes pleaded with my son. If he withdrew then the Welsh would see it as a weakness. The border would be as it had been in the Welsh marches. We could not allow that sort of anarchy. He nodded, "But only if you command."

"Of course." I turned to the commanders. I want every knight, squire, man at arms and archer ready to march. We leave within the hour. The archers fight under my captain of archers." The Countess had expensive candles marked out in hours and I went to the nearest one and held my dagger next to the mark.

King Madog ap Maredudd asked, "And where do we go?"

"I will tell you when we are on the road. If you were ambushed then there may be treachery. I know not whom we can trust. I keep our destination in my head. Now go, your majesties and prepare."

Maud came over and squeezed my arm, "I can see you have not changed, Alfraed! The King looked like a shadow of his former self when he was brought here. Your arrival has worked already. What can I do for you?"

"Have you any maps?"

She nodded, "Of course. Ranulf had many. I will get them for you."

I turned as she left and said, "James, fetch Rhodri. I need my archers."

When Maud returned I examined the maps. I spied hope. I saw what had made Henry do as he had done. He had been tricked into the attack by the Welsh King. The Clwyd valley was where I had fought alongside the Earl of Gloucester. It would suit heavy horses. Henry had made the mistake of fighting on ground which suited the Welsh. He had tried to ambush in woods. I would not make that mistake. I quickly worked out how to trick the Welsh king.

Rhodri arrived. "You know this land better than any. You know the back ways and the hidden ways. I need you to take our archers and ride towards Rhuddlan. I want you to find and kill the scouts of the Gwynedd army. I wish their king to be blind. When that is done I wish you to find their camp and make a nuisance of yourself."

"Nuisance, lord?"

I smiled, "I would use my reputation to help us trick the enemy. Everyone knows of my archers. They have heard how I use night

215

attacks to weaken their resolve. I want you to shower arrows into their camp, drive off horses. I want them to believe that we will attack them at Twthill again. Make them believe that you are many times the number we actually have."

He nodded and grinned, "And of course, you will not attack at Twthill, lord."

"Precisely. Take an old surcoat and tear it. Let it fall close to their camp when you flee for I want none lost. Make them believe it is my men who come. You stay close by until they move towards the sea."

"I know not how you will conjure that, lord, but I know that you will. We leave immediately."

Once he had gone then I felt better. By the time I reached the main gate the army was ready. I saw that they had two hundred of the fyrd there too. "The fyrd stay here and guard the castle." I pointed to the men at arms on the walls. "I want every warrior mounted. You men find horses! We ride!"

The Earl of Hereford asked, "And the baggage train?"

"We take none. Let your squires lead your warhorses and put a spear on the saddle. We move quickly!"

I could see that my approach had made many of the knights uncomfortable. I did not care. King Henry smiled, "I will not leave you behind again, Earl Marshal. I have no idea what is in your head and I know you as well as any man. I am confident that the Welsh will have even less idea."

With my men at arms acting as scouts I did not head for the road to Buckley and Mold which led to the Clwyd Valley, instead, I led them across the bridge and along the south bank of the Dee. No one questioned me and that suited my purposes. I was in no mood for questions. It was late afternoon and we had over thirty miles to go. We halted at the tiny port of Mostyn. It was just to water the horses at the fortified manor house there.

King Henry asked me, "When do we camp?"

"We do not. We ride through the night. We will be at the coast by dawn."

"I do not understand."

I led the young king to one side. "It is more than four days since your defeat, your majesty." I saw him wince at my use of the word defeat but it had been a defeat and there was no point in trying to make light of it. "King Owain will be wondering what we are doing next. He will have spies and he will know that you have sent for me. His scouts will be seeking us. He would ambush you again. That is why we have come here for he will not expect it. My archers are making the King believe that our army, led by me, is attacking down the Clwyd. There are only eleven of them but they will make it appear as though it is Dick with all of my archers. They will use their horses to move from place to place and attack the Welsh. I want him to look up the valley. When dawn breaks he will see us across his line of retreat to Anglesey. The ground between Hulle and Rhuddlan is flat. It suits heavy horse."

"Why could you not confide in the others?"

"Because I do not trust them. You were ambushed. You are a good leader and a clever general. You were betrayed and I will discover who it was."

By the time we reached Prestetone, it was coming close to dawn. Hulle was at the mouth of the Clwyd. We would rest there and then, when dawn broke fully, we would head towards Rhuddlan. I knew that my archers would already be occupying the Welsh.

I was weary by the time dawn broke. I was getting too old for night rides. The knights all switched to war horses and we prepared to move towards Rhuddlan. The castle of Twthill lay further up the valley from the town. Our appearance would threaten the King's most valuable town in the area. If Rhuddlan fell then he would be trapped.

The land was flatter and we rode up the valley in a column of knights and men at arms ten wide. We could break into a double line very quickly. The twenty mounted archers we had brought along with the forty Welsh archers were on our flanks. They were all dismounted. The Welsh ponies had been left in Hulle. I had personally given them their orders. They were to use the higher ground on our left flank and make sure that no archers came close to us. Our right flank was protected by the river.

I spied the royal standard flying from Twthill above the town of Rhuddlan. Our appearance caused great consternation. The burghers of Rhuddlan ran towards the tiny castle. I heard horns and so I gave orders to move into a double line of horsemen. We all had spears. The Welsh would outnumber us but they would be men wearing little armour and with few horses. I surveyed the ground. There was little in the way of obstacles before us. We kept moving as we deployed. I saw the first of the Welsh knights gallop towards us. There were only fifty or so and were not a threat. They formed a line a Roman mile away. We moved steadily. I did not mind how many men they gathered. We could not be outflanked. This would be a straight fight between Normans and Welsh. I knew who would win.

More men flooded down the valley. Less than a quarter were mounted. I saw a figure I took to be the King marshalling his men. He was using his spears and his archers to guard his flanks. His block of horses was just seventy horsemen. He had them in a single line. We kept moving as more of the Welsh joined their lines. As our archers raced forward and began to rain arrows on their archers a duel ensued. We kept moving.

When we were three hundred paces from them I stopped and waited until my men moved closely together. I had the knights from Powys on the two flanks. They would have to endure the arrows. I knew they would lose men but I wanted our best knights in the centre, led by me. That way we could break the Welsh horses quickly. I saw that the King and his standards were not in the line. That was a mistake.

I raised my spear and every spear and standard was raised at the same time, "For King Henry, the rightful lord of this land!"

As I lowered my spear I spurred Warrior and we moved up the valley. The key to a good charge was to build up the speed steadily. If the enemy counter charged you then it could cause problems. However, if this enemy did countercharge us we would simply ride through them. We outnumbered them. It soon became apparent that they would not charge us. At least not until the last moment. Our hooves thundered. They made the ground vibrate. My spear rested on my cantle. I heard cries and shouts from the flanks as Welsh knights were felled by arrows but the one hundred knights and men at arms in the centre were untouched. When we were sixty paces from the enemy I spurred Warrior again. We began to gallop and I looked for the knight I would strike.

When we were twenty paces from them the Welsh moved. They charged. The order had not been given but their nerve had broken. They could not endure to stand and be charged. It was too little and too late. My spear smashed across a shield and into the side of the knight to my left. I had switched target as the one I had intended to strike had been tardy in his movement. My spear ripped and tore through mail and into the knight's arm. His shield dropped and Harry Lightfoot's spear took him in the throat. To my right, Arne Arneson had spurred his horse and his spear skewered the knight who had seen his chance to end the life of the Earl Marshal.

We were through their line. It had been too thin. King Henry and his oathsworn knights had also broken through. We began to ascend the slope towards Twthill castle. I had no intention of storming the walls but so long as the Welsh did not retire behind them then I would attack. The King, his son and his household knights were taken by surprise at the ease with which we had broken through. His household knights galloped down the hill towards us. They were a ragged line. As I rammed my spear into the chest of the first knight I glanced to my right and saw King Henry's spear pierce the throat of another. The knight I had speared grabbed my shaft and, as he fell to the ground tore it from my grasp. It fell to the ground and, spurring my horse drew my sword as I headed towards the King. Warrior was a powerful horse and he was close to the King in a few strides.

Holding my sword at his chest I said, "Yield and surrender to King Henry or die!"

His two sons, Dafydd ap Owain and Cynan ap Owain belatedly drew their swords and moved towards me. Arne Arneson used the haft of his spear to knock Dafydd to the ground while Roger of Bath used his sword to smash aside that of Cynan.

"Do you wish your sons to die?"

The King shook his head and threw down his sword. "I surrender! We will have terms!" His herald sounded the horn and all along the Welsh line men threw down their weapons. We had won.

Epilogue

I was present in Rhuddlan for the meeting of the two kings but I said nothing. I was there more as a threat. His two bruised sons glowered at me during the negotiations but each time I made a move, however innocent, they flinched. I was not named the wolf of the north for nothing. My archers had arrived soon after the battle had ended. One of Tomas ap Tomas' men had been killed. He had been too slow to move. Rhodri told me that my plan had worked better than any of us could have hoped. Once the scouts had been slain they had closed with the three main camps. After slaying the sentries with daggers, they had launched arrows into the camp. Pandemonium had ensued. It had kept the Welsh eyes fixed in the wrong direction.

King Owain's voice was filled with resignation. "We will grant you the lands of Tegeingl and Rhuddlan and then we will have peace. All of our men will be returned, with the arms."

"I agree and our ships and men on Anglesey will also be returned to us."

"There will be no reparations."

King Henry nodded, "No reparations but know this, King Owain, our ambitions are not ended with this battle."

"Next time we will be better prepared, King Henry."

As the two kings stood I saw King Henry lean forward. I was close enough to hear him say, "I have the Warlord on my side. Who fights for you?"

The Welsh king was silenced and King Henry put his arm about my shoulder, "Come Earl Marshal. Once again you have come to my aid. What would I do without you?"

I smiled, "Hopefully, your majesty, you will never have to."

Perhaps the Fates or the Norns were listening. Or maybe we were so close to the mountain the druids had worshipped, Wyddfa, that my words were seen as a challenge. Whatever the cause life was never easy again.

The End

Glossary

Akolouthos – the leader of the Guard
Aldeneby - Alston (Cumbria)
Al-Andalus- Spain
Angevin- the people of Anjou, mainly the ruling family
Arthuret -Longtown in Cumbria (This is the Brythionic name)
Battle- a formation in war (a modern battalion)
Booth Castle – Bewcastle north of Hadrian's Wall
Bachelor knight- an unattached knight
Banneret- a single knight
Butts- targets for archers
Cadge- the frame upon which hunting birds are carried (by a
codger- hence the phrase old codger being the old man who carries
the frame)
Caerdyf- Cardiff
Captain- a leader of archers
Chausses - mail leggings. (They were separate- imagine lady's
stockings!)
Coningestun- Coniston
Conroi- A group of knights fighting together. The smallest unit of
the period
Corebricg – Corbridge
Cuneceastra- Chester-Le-Street
Demesne- estate
Destrier- war horse
Doxy- prostitute
Fissebourne- Fishburn County Durham
Fess- a horizontal line in heraldry
Galloglass- Irish mercenaries
Gambeson- a padded tunic worn underneath mail. When worn by an
archer they came to the waist. It was more of a quilted jacket but I
have used the term freely
Gonfanon- A standard used in medieval times (Also known as a
Gonfalon in Italy)
Hartness- the manor which became Hartlepool
Hautwesel- Haltwhistle
Hulle- Rhyl (North Wales)

Liedeberge- Ledbury
Lusitania- Portugal
Mansio- staging houses along Roman Roads
Maredudd ap Bleddyn- King of Powys
Martinmas- 11th November
Mêlée- a medieval fight between knights
Moravians- the men of Moray
Mormaer- A Scottish lord and leader
Mummer- an actor from a medieval tableau
Musselmen- Muslims
Nithing- A man without honour (Saxon)
Nomismata- a gold coin equivalent to an aureus
Outremer- the kingdoms of the Holy Land
Owain ap Gruffudd- Son of Gruffudd ap Cynan and King of
Gwynedd from 1137
Palfrey- a riding horse
Poitevin- the language of Aquitaine
Prestetone- Prestatyn- North Wales
Pyx- a box containing a holy relic (Shakespeare's Pax from Henry
V)
Refuge- a safe area for squires and captives (tournaments)
Sauve qui peut – Every man for himself (French)
Serengford- Shellingford Oxfordshire
Sergeant-a leader of a company of men at arms
Striguil- Chepstow (Gwent)
Surcoat- a tunic worn over mail or armour
Sumpter- packhorse
Theophany- the feast which is on the 6th of January
Ventail – a piece of mail which covered the neck and the lower face
Al-Andalus- Spain
Wulfestun- Wolviston (Durham)

Historical Notes

Alfraed is not a real person. He is based upon a number of people, most notably William Marshal. The title of Earl marshal was a real one. Earl Marshal (alternatively Marschal, Marischal or Marshall) is a hereditary royal officeholder and chivalric title under the sovereign of the United Kingdom used in England. He is the eighth of the Great Officers of State in the United Kingdom, ranking beneath the Lord High Constable and above the Lord High Admiral. The Earl Marshal has among his responsibilities the organisation of major ceremonial state occasions like the monarch's coronation in Westminster Abbey and state funerals. He is also a leading officer of arms and oversees the College of Arms.

Books used in the research:

- The Varangian Guard- 988-1453 Raffael D'Amato
- Saxon Viking and Norman- Terence Wise
- The Walls of Constantinople AD 324-1453-Stephen Turnbull
- Byzantine Armies- 886-1118- Ian Heath
- The Age of Charlemagne-David Nicolle
- The Normans- David Nicolle
- Norman Knight AD 950-1204- Christopher Gravett
- The Norman Conquest of the North- William A Kappelle
- The Knight in History- Francis Gies
- The Norman Achievement- Richard F Cassady
- Knights- Constance Brittain Bouchard
- Knight Templar 1120-1312 -Helen Nicholson
- Feudal England: Historical Studies on the Eleventh and Twelfth Centuries- J. H. Round
- Armies of the Crusades- Helen Nicholson
- Knight of Outremer 1187- 1344 - David Nicholle
- Crusader Castles in the Holy Land- David Nicholle
- The Crusades- David Nicholle
- The Times Atlas of World History
- Old Series Ordnance Survey Maps #93 Middlesbrough
- Old Series Ordnance Survey Maps #81 Alnwick and Morpeth

For those who like authentic maps, the last two maps are part of a series now available. They are the first Government produced maps of the British Isles. Great Britain, apart from the larger conurbations, was the same as it had been 800 years earlier.

I also discovered a good website http://orbis.stanford.edu/. This allows a reader to plot any two places in the Roman world and if you input the mode of transport you wish to use and the time of year it will calculate how long it would take you to travel the route. I have used it for all of my books up to the eighteenth century as the transportation system was roughly the same. The Romans would have been quicker!

Griff Hosker
July 2017

Other books by Griff Hosker

If you enjoyed reading this book, then why not read another one by the author?

Ancient History

The Sword of Cartimandua Series
(Germania and Britannia 50 A.D. – 128 A.D.)
Ulpius Felix- Roman Warrior (prequel)
The Sword of Cartimandua
The Horse Warriors
Invasion Caledonia
Roman Retreat
Revolt of the Red Witch
Druid's Gold
Trajan's Hunters
The Last Frontier
Hero of Rome
Roman Hawk
Roman Treachery
Roman Wall
Roman Courage

The Wolf Warrior series
(Britain in the late 6th Century)
Saxon Dawn
Saxon Revenge
Saxon England
Saxon Blood
Saxon Slayer
Saxon Slaughter
Saxon Bane
Saxon Fall: Rise of the Warlord
Saxon Throne
Saxon Sword

Medieval History

The Dragon Heart Series
Viking Slave
Viking Warrior
Viking Jarl
Viking Kingdom
Viking Wolf
Viking War
Viking Sword
Viking Wrath
Viking Raid
Viking Legend
Viking Vengeance
Viking Dragon
Viking Treasure
Viking Enemy
Viking Witch
Viking Blood
Viking Weregeld
Viking Storm
Viking Warband
Viking Shadow
Viking Legacy
Viking Clan
Viking Bravery

The Norman Genesis Series
Hrolf the Viking
Horseman
The Battle for a Home
Revenge of the Franks
The Land of the Northmen
Ragnvald Hrolfsson
Brothers in Blood
Lord of Rouen
Drekar in the Seine
Duke of Normandy
The Duke and the King

Danelaw

The Welsh Marches
(England and Denmark in the 11th Century)
Dragon Sword
Oathsword

New World Series
Blood on the Blade
Across the Seas
The Savage Wilderness
The Bear and the Wolf
Erik The Navigator

The Vengeance Trail

The Reconquista Chronicles
Castilian Knight
El Campeador
The Lord of Valencia

The Aelfraed Series
(Britain and Byzantium 1050 A.D. - 1085 A.D.)
Housecarl
Outlaw
Varangian

**The Anarchy Series England
1120-1180**
English Knight
Knight of the Empress
Northern Knight
Baron of the North
Earl
King Henry's Champion
The King is Dead
Warlord of the North
Enemy at the Gate
The Fallen Crown
Warlord's War
Kingmaker
Henry II
Crusader
The Welsh Marches
Irish War
227

The Welsh Marches

Poisonous Plots
The Princes' Revolt
Earl Marshal
The Perfect Knight

Border Knight
1182-1300
Sword for Hire
Return of the Knight
Baron's War
Magna Carta
Welsh Wars
Henry III
The Bloody Border
Baron's Crusade
Sentinel of the North
War in the West
Debt of Honour
The Blood of the Warlord (Feb 2022)

Sir John Hawkwood Series
France and Italy 1339- 1387
Crécy: The Age of the Archer
Man At Arms
The White Company

Lord Edward's Archer
Lord Edward's Archer
King in Waiting
An Archer's Crusade
Targets of Treachery
The Great Cause (April 2022)

Struggle for a Crown
1360- 1485
Blood on the Crown
To Murder a King
The Throne
King Henry IV
The Road to Agincourt
St Crispin's Day
The Battle For France

228

The Welsh Marches
The Last Knight
Queen's Knight

Tales from the Sword I
(Short stories from the Medieval period)

Tudor Warrior series
England and Scotland in the late 14th and early 15th century
Tudor Warrior

Conquistador
England and America in the 16th Century
Conquistador

Modern History

The Napoleonic Horseman Series
Chasseur à Cheval
Napoleon's Guard
British Light Dragoon
Soldier Spy
1808: The Road to Coruña
Talavera
The Lines of Torres Vedras
Bloody Badajoz
The Road to France
Waterloo

The Lucky Jack American Civil War series
Rebel Raiders
Confederate Rangers
The Road to Gettysburg

The British Ace Series
1914
1915 Fokker Scourge
1916 Angels over the Somme
1917 Eagles Fall
1918 We will remember them
From Arctic Snow to Desert Sand
Wings over Persia

The Welsh Marches

Combined Operations series
1940-1945
Commando
Raider
Behind Enemy Lines
Dieppe
Toehold in Europe
Sword Beach
Breakout
The Battle for Antwerp
King Tiger
Beyond the Rhine
Korea
Korean Winter

Tales from the Sword II
(Short stories from the Modern period)

Other Books
Great Granny's Ghost (Aimed at 9-14-year-old young people)

For more information on all of the books then please visit the author's website at www.griffhosker.com where there is a link to contact him or visit his Facebook page: GriffHosker at Sword Books

Printed in Great Britain
by Amazon

21941958R00131